I0618911

LaTonya Trilogy Relaunch 2019
McDaniel Publishing House

Cover Art: DropDeadDesigns.com

 I dedicate this novel to all of the many people I've met over the years and those I meet today. You inspire me to be a great writer. As I listen to the voices, I am honored to channel their stories and share their experiences for they are strong.

We are no longer silent.

From the Tippy Ellis Dictionary
©2012

The word Holla Me Bad™ is a word used to signify that one is a bad ass. Once you recognize you can't help but to holla. I wear this crown. You think you're badder than me? By all means meet me at the gate and let's turn it up. Do you have the courage? Or just talking smack? I ain't wacked but you might be when we're through. Despite it all, I'm still the angel you once knew. I'm alive and well, no end.

The word **Girlishcious®** used in this trilogy and as it is spelled is a registered trademark and originally used in the Tippy Ellis Story. It is also an official definition in the online Urban Dictionary.

1

It's Over Yo!

At the Portland County Jail

Darius stops by see his mother, who's been begging for him to come. Darius hasn't seen her since the police arrested her for Jerome's murder. He hired an attorney who asked the judge to provide her with drug treatment right away. She's getting help.

Darius knows he has to face his mother sooner than later. Although it won't matter much, he needs to find out why the most important woman in his life would have his brother killed.

On his way over to the jail, Darius flashes back to the early days with his mother. He remembers her crying a lot. Because of her MS, it was tough for her to keep a job. Employers found out and made excuses to fire her. And got away with it. Oregon is an At-Will state where employers can do no wrong.

For them money was scarce, until she finally received disability Medicaid. But it was only $600 a month. They did manage to get services like Section 8 housing, food and medical assistance.

Much to Darius's chagrin, his mother kept no-good boyfriends around, hoping to get extra money. They were drug dealers or married like his father and didn't stay around long.

His mother often left him with these men when they came to visit and when she ran an errand, like going to buy them more booze. They were cool except for Darrell and Kevin.

When Jill met Darrel, he told her some cockamamie story about him going AWOL from the military for refusing to attack a community of women and children. He loved women and children and wished them no harm. Jill believed him.

Darius was tough for a 10-year-old and had the ability to defend himself thanks to Jerome. His mom ran to the store and left him with big, black, mean Darrell, who was already drunk but wanted more whiskey – his favorite.

One day while Darius was watching television, Darrell grabbed him up by the back of his shirt and socked him in his head. Good thing Darrell was drunk, because Darius was able to break free. He turned and kicked Darrel in his groin and ran out. Darius refused to go home until his mother stopped seeing Darrell.

Darius stayed gone for 3 days until his mother came to her senses. Meanwhile, Jerome snuck him into his house through the back stairs room window. Jerome was grateful his parents respected his privacy but there were times Darius had to hide under the bed.

Then there was Kevin. When Darius got out of juvie his mother had moved in with Kevin, who was 15 years younger than her. The broke-ass negro had been taking her money. One night he begged for money, Jill said no and he slapped her. Darius picked up a lamp and hit Kevin over the head. Kevin fell down, bloody and unconscious. Jill packed Darius up, sent him to Oxnard to live with her brother.

Before Darius goes into see his mother, he receives a text message: AJ out. He smiles. It means AJ is definitely out of the picture for good. Darius found out that AJ had invited Tippy to opening night at the Boss Amanishakhete Resurrection tour in L.A. next weekend. Said he'd fly her and TiAnna down. Tippy said she'd think about it, which angered Darius. He thought Tippy would never speak to AJ again after what happened at the industry party.

Darius was the one who invited Uriella to the event after paying her a $1,000 to confront Tippy and tell her she was AJ's wife. Darius had no idea she planned to change the script. He called Uriella later and told her she had 24 hours to fix the shit. This meant keeping AJ away from Tippy for good or else it be her ass.

Inside the jail's visiting room, Darius sees a depressed woman, who's worn with puffy eyes, her face flushed. She'd been crying but she's also been battling the fact she has to stay clean. There was a time Darius would feel bad for his mother, but he couldn't bring himself to care right now. Darius knows he'll always love his mother, but will never forgive her.

"I'm glad you came Dari."

"Yeah I'm sure."

"So how you been Dari?"

"How've I been? For real mama?"

"I'm always gonna worry about you Dari."

"Huh. You need to worry 'bout yourself. I'm not facin' a murder rap. But I didn't come here for dat. I only agreed to visit you if you'd tell me what I wanna know."

"Does it matter really Dari? I'm the one they got. I'm okay wit' whatever."

"It does matter yo. It does matter. Who else was in dis?"

"There's no…"

"Bullshit! If you don't tell me, I swear I'll walk and you won't see me again mama! So, tell me yo! Wha'chu you do wit' the $20,000 I gave you a few months back?"

Jill drops her head, presses her hands to her face, looks up.

"Darrell arranged it. He talked me into it. He was with me at the house one day when Jerome came by shortly after his mama died. Darrell was in the back room and heard Jerome tell me you'd be his beneficiary. Darrell wasn't satisfied with the cash Jerome would drop off for you every month."

"Darrell! Are you fuckin' kidding? When did you start hangin' wit dat piece a shit again! What fuckin' cash you talkin' 'bout!"

Jill stays quiet then says, "Dari your brother would drop off $500 every month for me to send to you while you were living with your uncle along with a letter. He wanted to send it himself but I lied to him. I tol 'im your uncle was very strict and wouldn't give him mail from anyone else but me. You know you was havin' some trouble anyway. I, I want you to know, I saved those letters. You can find 'em in my top drawer."

"Aw wow. You kept my letters from me – from my brother? Then you kept da money to feed yo nigga and yo crack habit? Is his dick that damn good yo? Yeah, I see. The motherfucka dat tried to beat up yo own son, you never left him huh? Kept seeing him on the side somewhere? Using the other crazy ass nigga's as yo cova. All doze times you left me at da house wit' or without yo other niggas you must've been wit' him huh? Well mama looks like the dawg played yo motherfuckin' ass! I hope it was worth it yo!"

Darius slams his fist down on the table, gets up and says, "Have a nice life mama."

"Dari please wait. You have to forgive me. Pleeeese."

Outside the jail, Darius places a 9-1-1 call to his guardians. "Let me know when you find him. I'll handle this one myself yo."

2
In Together

8:30 p.m.
In Miami with Damon

Who's struggling with what to do about Chili, who now calls herself Stephanie. She's dangerous no doubt – a ho and a con. Somehow, he has to warn his friend but for now he'll let Chili think they have an un-da-standin'.

"Naw baby. It wa'ent who I thought. Good thing. Say I'll holla at you when I'm done at the jail."

Early evening
In Portland's Council Crest

I'm telling TiAnna about being arrested. "My daddy didn't talk to me all the way home. I know I'm grounded. At least we can hold up here together until he cools down. I'm gonna have to let 'im know you're here at some point. If he says something crazy like you can't stay – which he won't – I'll leave with you. Unc Rae-Rae will help us – you okay T?"

My BFF looks really sad. She's looking down at the floor where…

"My rug?"

"Sorry Tip. I a… I didn't know my bottle of strawberry soda spilled. I was sitting on the floor doing my yoga, my eyes closed and everything. I accidently kicked it over. I thought I had put the cap on it so I didn't see it until I opened my eyes and there's this huge red stain. Darius took it and says he'd have it cleaned."

"Girl no biggey. I can get another 1. I'm glad you're still doing yoga. So what do ya think about Darius?"

"He a'ight."

"He's available you know. Maybe once you are feelin' bet…"

"Tip! Stop acting like nothin' happened! There's no way in hell I'm interested in laying down with any dude! Not now and maybe never!"

"Sorry. I don't know what I am thinkin' T."

"Well you not thinkin.' And besides he's into you, yo. You're all he talks about yo."

Me and TiAnna laugh at how she's mocking Darius. Then I do it, but I'm not givin' it justice like she and Darius.

"T, paleeze. I don't think so yo."

"What do you mean Tip? He looks good, got swag. You need someone with hip in their step. You use to Jeremy's boring ass. Still haven't heard from him?"

"No. And at this point I don't care to. There's nothin' he can say to make me forgive him for dissing me. Had me worried, but he's doing fine. I've been readin' about him online."

"Hmmm. You never know Tip. You didn't hear from me either. But I had a good excuse, yeah?"

"I know you don't like me to do this, but I'm gonna do it anyway. I love you BFF." I roll over and give TiAnna a big hug.

"Dang Tip. Do you have to hug me so tight and mushy cheek kiss me too?"

"Yeah and I'm not going to let go so deal."

"Okay Buddha. Ha."

"Back at ya yogi. Namaste."

Atlanta

"How come you didn't tell me this before, mama?" says Luanne.

"I didn't think it was necessary Lu. I had no business givin' my child away to begin wit'. I felt really bad so I go back to the convent, but it was too late. Then I see you. This older black couple was getting ready to take you in and leave you. I stopped them and we talked. Made a deal. I figured it was the right thing, timing an all. They also told me a sad story about their 14-year-old daughter. She was raped by their 21-year-old landscaper who got away."

Cheri pauses to take in a deep breath. "When they said that, I know 'em, but they don't know me. Joshua worked for 'em. He's the one who raped their daughter. She bore his child. You my brother Joshua's child, who's really my adopted brother."

Later on
In Council Crest

Ooo snap! Daddy's knocking.

"What do you want daddy?"

"Tippy open the door. I know TiAnna's in there with you. Your uncle is here."

"Uncle Rae-Rae?" I say, opening the door, forgetting TiAnna's standing right behind me.

I grab him and give him a hug. I hold on to him for a few moments. My uncle is here finally.

"Okay girls," says my daddy stepping around Unc Rae-Rae to get in the room.

"Hey TiAnna," says Rae Ellis. He reaches out to give her a hug. She refuses the gesture by stepping back. Understanding, Rae bows his head instead.

"Now daddy, as you can see T's okay. She's staying here by the way."

"Oh so now you the head of the house?" says Robert Ellis, lifting his brows.

"Naw daddy, just saying. I know you have a lot of compassion for my BFF and you want what's best. You helped Unc Rae-Rae find her. I love you both very much for it."

Rae's attention is still on TiAnna. He asks, "How are you feeling? You weren't supposed to be discharged for another couple of months. Everybody's worried."

Now I didn't know T left rehab on her own. But it don't matter. I'm still fighting for her to stay with me. She'll be better off here.

"Yeah but aaa… um… I can leave," says TiAnna. "I don't wanna cause any trouble."

"Oh no you're not! What's with all the interrogation anyway," I say looking at my uncle.

It takes an awful lot for me to get annoyed with him. He's always been good to me, so I've never had to go-off on him like I do daddy.

"Mind your manners," my uncle says sternly. "We all want what's best for TiAnna."

"Mr. sensible, eh?" Daddy says, sarcastically.

Rae ignores the comment.

"We do all want what's best. Maybe Tippy's right. This is probably the best for her. She's close to Tippy. They can help each other," says Daddy.

"So brotha. What we going do to make sure TiAnna has the support she needs?" asks Rae looking at his brother while tilting his head toward him.

Robert Ellis scratches his forehead staring at his brother and says, "Well we, meaning me and my daughter, will give TiAnna the support she needs. TiAnna," daddy says redirecting his attention, "You still need help. I will find you a day treatment facility and set you up with the best professionals. I'll contact Dr. Ryan who works with Tippy to see if she can take on another client."

"Oh daddy, I like the idea. Maybe me and TiAnna can do some group shrink stuff," I say. "We can be nutso's together." I'm trying to be funny. TiAnna cracks a smile then walks over to daddy.

"Thank you, sir. I won't be any trouble."

"You've never given me any problems, TiAnna. Maybe you can help keep your friend in line."

Daddy looks at me like I'm some big troublemaker. But who gives a shit as long as TiAnna stays.

"Well cool den," says Rae. "No doubt you'll fix it where she can be homeschooled until she's ready to go back…"

"Excuse me," TiAnna says interrupting him. "Do I get a vote?"

Oh snap. Good looking out for yourself T, I say to myself.

"My apologies young lady," my uncle says trying to be all proper.

I remember when Unc Rae-Rae tried that around mama. He'd be funnin' actually, mocking mama being so proper. She'd laugh. He always made mama laugh even when she was sad.

"The floor is yourn," he says now sounding country like gramma Ellis.

"I'd like to go back to school please. With Tippy. I'd go stir crazy if I stay in."

"Why don't we cross the bridge a little later," says daddy. "Finish your program you were working on in Georgia. Then we'll send you back to school. Meanwhile I'll get you a tutor, so you can catch up. Deal?"

TiAnna hesitates looking over at me. *I'm nodding and, in my head, saying please girl don't look this gift horse in the mouth. Take the deal or it'll be no deal. I know my daddy.*

"Okay sir," says TiAnna extending her hand to shake his.

Over dinner Unc Rae-Rae tells us he plans to be in town through Thanksgiving weekend. Both daddy and Rae don't connect with their extended family since gramma Ellis died. They're lucky they have each other but they barely get along. Then of course they have me.

Daddy says Luanne's coming back for a few days to spend time with the kids. He tells Unc Rae-Rae she may be moving back to Atlanta for good. Her mama's really sick and she's no match for a kidney – somethin' about being AB negative a rare blood type.

They're still talking when me and TiAnna leave the dinner table and the twin brats head to the family room with ice cream to watch TV. On the way upstairs, TiAnna says her mama has the same rare blood type. AB negative.

3
Soon Forget

November 20, 2012

The DA decides not to pursue Tippy on assault charges, despite Uriella already asking for the charges to be dropped. She finds out before she leaves on tour with her husband DaMenace. But she keeps this bit of news to herself.

Although she forces AJ to stay married, he wants no part of her sexually. Uriella figures she'd bide her time – he'd come around. She remembers how good sex was between the two of them. Once they got started, they could go all night.

Uriella walks to the other side of the bed where AJ's sitting. He's reviewing his schedule. She sits down next to him and begins to massage his shoulders. AJ jumps up, crosses to the other side of the room and leans against the wall.

"We ain't fuckin' Uri. You force me to stay with you, dis is da kinda marriage you gonna get. You can bet dat."

Thanksgiving morning

All of us — daddy, Unc Rae-Rae, Darius, TiAnna, Brittany, Jayden and daddy's wifey— gather in the kitchen for the annual "cooking Thanksgiving dinner together" tradition. Looking over at Luanne she seems to be preoccupied. I wonder what's up with her. She excuses herself and heads upstairs.

Luanne is thinking about Joshua. She and the woman she knows as her mother are both worried but cannot call the cops. Joshua's a wanted man. Instead she reviews the security tape in hopes of finding an answer.

Since the murder of Loretta Ellis, Robert Ellis keeps security cameras installed on the inside and outside perimeters of all of the houses they've lived in. Although the Druid Hills estate had a security gate, the police suspected Loretta Ellis knew her killer. To get beyond the gates, someone had to let you in. Staff also had the day off, which the killer must've known.

Luanne rewinds the tape back to the day of Joshua's visit.

"Hm. Something on the tape during the time he was here."

Luanne sees Joshua enter the house, turn off the alarm, then go into the kitchen. He grabs a beer out of the fridge and downs it. Then he leaves the kitchen and heads upstairs.

Upstairs his cellphone rings. "Must've been about time I called," Luanne whispers. Joshua hangs up, looks to the right and walks toward Tippy's room. Luanne knows she told Joshua where her room was. No reason for him to head that direction unless…

Joshua goes inside Tippy's room. Luanne panics. But then she remembers Tippy isn't home — she hopes — it's a school day. Now that she knows her so-called father is a predator, she's glad she changed her mind about him meeting Robert and the kids. She felt it too risky for Robert to know about Joshua.

"Dis real strange. Where you at Joshua. Why you take so long."

Luanne fast forwards the tape and sees Darius. He's walking up the stairs behind TiAnna, heading to Tippy's room.

"Wha? Why you der. Oh Lard."

Luanne fast forwards the tape. Two guys come into the house with trash bags and a large blanket, heading to Tippy's room. Several minutes later they come out carrying a long rolled up blanket with Darius right behind them with the trash bag.

"Owe hell. Dis some shit. Joshua wha da fuck yo do!"

Peeping from the doorway behind Darius is TiAnna, smiling.

"Joshua you was up to yo tricks again. TiAnna was s'pose ta be yo victim but sumbod got yo ass. You dead I know. By who, I don't know. If Darius saw you, he'da killed you fo being in Tippy's room."

Luanne takes the tape out of the CD player, replaces it with a clean tape and puts the other in her purse. Luanne has no plans to turn anyone in, but will use the tape as leverage if she needs it. She knows Darius wants Tippy and her $100 million really bad and is afraid he will do anything to get it. Even if it means selling her out.

"I ain't got no love loss for you Joshua. You're dead and will stay dead as long as Darius keeps his en' of the ba'gain. I have the upper han' Mr. Darius."

Our way of fellowship

Each year, we cook Thanksgiving dinner together as a family. Before we eat, we visit a homeless shelter and help serve dinner. This tradition actually started with daddy.

When he and Unc Rae-Rae were kids, Thanksgiving was their favorite holiday. Gramma Ellis would bring home a huge Thanksgiving food basket – a holiday bonus – from one of the rich white people she worked for. The three of them would cook dinner and then to show thanks, they'd walk down to the church and help serve dinner to the homeless. Gramma Ellis wanted them to know how fortunate they were. Many people were doing worse than them.

Daddy is the one really, who cooks the bulk of the meal. He can cook a mean turkey, ham, greens, dressing, all the stuff, which make a Thanksgiving meal great. I do the desserts – daddy taught me. Brittany and Jayden usually sit around and lick the bowls or nibble on edibles. Luanne, well, I'm glad she's not here. She can't boil water.

Mama hated me learning domestic stuff but daddy won the argument. "Our daughter ain't too good to learn how to wipe her own ass and feed herself," says daddy.

This year we have Unc Rae-Rae, TiAnna and Darius helping. Over on the island in the middle of the kitchen, Darius and Unc Rae-Rae are chopping veggies for the dressing. I see Unc Rae-Rae every now and then look at Darius and frown. Hm?

Raymond Ellis is recalling the conversation he had with Darius yesterday. *I wonder what the real reason this yella-ass yo-ing nigga called.*

Despite his prodding, Darius refused to divulge who told him about Tippy. But he wasn't fool enough to admit to it, even though Darius tried to bate him, promising him he wouldn't tell Tippy he's her father.

"My concern is Tippy," says Darius. "She blanked out on me for a while yo. But she's safe wit' me."

"Uh-huh. I bet. You should know I'm not impressed and don't trust you as far as I can see you. Just so you know, Tippy has got lot's a friends she don't even know about. You fuck wit' her. You answer to me! Take that to the bank Broussard!"

"I gotchu yo. Loud and clear."

"Uh-huh, trying to get in good with the family," TiAnna whispers, nudging me. You know Darius wants you bad girl. No man offers to help cook unless he's gay. I'd be shocked as hell if Darius is though. If Tommy Crumbs was here, we could ask him."

We both laugh when we think of Tommy Crumbs. Wonder what he's up to these days?

Around 4, we head downtown to a homeless shelter with families. It's sad to see so many homeless people. I'm glad daddy adopted this group because it also has a school for the kids.

I think daddy has a really good heart deep down, which is why I find it hard to believe the things he does. Like setting up my Unc Rae-Rae and secretly stealing my trust fund, which I can't believe is a $100 million dollars! Or was.

On the drive home Unc Rae-Rae and daddy talk politics.

Daddy says "It's a damn shame we live in a society where the rich are extremely selfish. Those damn Republicans spend billions to get the black man out of office. Their money could have ended hunger."

"That's the Grand Ol Party for you. They don't give a damn about real people," Unc Rae-Rae says.

"We can at least agree on that brotha," Daddy says, glancing at Unc Rae-Rae seated up front with him on the passenger's side.

We are riding in the family van, which comfortably seats all 7 of us. It has a TV in the back for Brittany and Jayden. When we prepare to leave downtown, I feel guilty. Here we are warm and cozy while those families will be making the cold streets their home tonight.

4
Getting Along

7:00 p.m.
In Council Crest

We're using the formal dining room, for the first time. Daddy's seated at the head of the table, I'm to his right and Luanne to his left. Her face is flushed and she looks sad. She's been like that since yesterday. On her left is Brittany, then Jayden. My Unc Rae-Rae is seated at the opposite end of the table, across from daddy; then TiAnna and Darius next to me.

This is the happiest I've been in a while. We've finished eating dinner and without drama. I'm so full I won't need to eat for months.

Darius is on his 2nd helping of pie and hasn't been as talkative. I know he's missing his mama. He opted out of having Thanksgiving with her over at the jail. OMG. I can only imagine how he must feel finding out his mother had his brother killed. If it were me, I couldn't handle it. Especially if it really was daddy who killed mama. Ooo. I'm glad daddy is no longer a suspect and I know he didn't do it.

"Mm, mm, mm. Girl this is the best pie I've ever had. You definitely mixed it with your love and beauty," says Darius.

He's flirting, making TiAnna giggle.

"Yeah it's pretty thick," she says.

But I don't think Unc Rae-Rae likes Darius. He glared at him. But daddy just lifted his eyebrows lookin' at me like, "You got him hooked too, eh?"

Later in the evening

Luanne puts Brittany and Jayden to bed and doesn't return. Daddy and Unc Rae-Rae head to his den to talk, I guess. I walk by there a couple of times and don't hear any arguing. It's so quiet I hope they haven't killed each other. If they're getting along miracles do happen.

When I get to my TV room, I swear Darius and TiAnna are whispering. They stop when they see me. Maybe my paranoia's working overtime.

Darius leaves around midnight, so me and TiAnna decide to go to bed. Since TiAnna's being here is no longer a secret, she has her own room – the room on the other side of the TV room. But she still hangs in mine – sleeping in my queen bed next to me. She gets anxious and sometimes has nightmares. It's gonna take her a while before she feels really safe and not like she has to look over shoulder.

It's around 1 o'clock in the morning and we're still talkin', staring up into the skylight above my bed. I've yet to see any stars. What's the point of a skylight if you can't see nothin'?

TiAnna's laughing, thinkin' the same thing I bet.

"What's up with the window Tip. Have you seen any stars?"

"Girl paleeze," I say. "It's gone from blue to gray sky."

"Ha. Maybe it's for spotting flying saucers. Maybe one of those little green men will come knock on the window and say hey. What would you do if they green and fine?"

"Huh. Now wouldn't that be somethin'." I say.

I almost say something stupid, but stop myself from sayin', it probably wouldn't be an alien just some pervert. I know TiAnna is far from healed but her talkin' about crazy shit makes me happy.

She's glad she's here but she misses her brothers. Unc Rae-Rae tells TiAnna her daddy and brothers miss her too and want to see her. If she feels up to it, he'd be happy to fly back to Portland and take her to Atlanta for the holidays. T says she'll think about it.

"What's up wit' your stepmom?" she asks.

"Maybe her former lover made her feel uncomfortable," I say.

"Hm," TiAnna says.

I had already told her what happened between Luanne and Darius.

"That AB negative shit is wacked T. Y'all related you think?" I say, jokingly.

"Not funny Tip. Don't be tryin' ta give her ta me. She's yo' kinfolk."

"Ok I'll stop. But strange, huh? She's not a match? There's more to the story she ain't sharing."

"Well Sherlock I'll let you figure it out. I'm going to sleep." TiAnna rolls over and pulls the blanket up around her.

I scoot over next to her, lean over and give her a big mushy kiss on the cheek.

"Ugh Tip. Goodnight."

I laugh and lay back down with my hands underneath my head. I can't sleep. Got too much on my mind and some of it's about Luanne. I've never known her to be so damn quiet. Not once did she say somethin' mean or be a smart ass. And she was nice to me and T. Even gave us both a hug. Maybe having Unc Rae-Rae and Darius here helped. But still, when it comes to Luanne, there's always somethin' more. I wonder what she's hiding this time.

5

New mama in The House

Christmas Eve in Atlanta

Everyone hears the news about Judge Simms's being investigated – his cases are suspect. This is big news in Atlanta. The Judge wronged many people like Raymond Ellis who feels vindicated when he hears the news.

Whereas Christmas Eve in Portland

The news doesn't fair well with Robert Ellis. His brother's out of jail and the papers he had Tippy sign, giving him guardianship over her $100 million estate – and without her knowing – could be overturned.

Christmas Eve in Miami

Jeremy and Stephanie hear the Judge Simms news. This worries Stephanie especially when she overhears Jeremy on the phone talking to his mother about how his uncle and Tippy's father made him sign an agreement, keeping him from Tippy. His mother of course is still in denial about her brother, so he decided to stop talking to her about it. But he feels it's time to tell Tippy what happened.

Stephanie knows it's time to make her move. This is Christmas Eve, a time of good will, good cheer and all. "Jeremy and Tippy getting stuck under the mistletoe most certainly would interrupt my chances of being Jeremy's wife and baby mama."

"Tippy give me a call," Stephanie hears Jeremy say.

"Good she's not there," Stephanie says under her breath. "I have to intercept her return phone call."

Stephanie walks into the back bedroom where Jeremy is stretched out across the bed. She lays down next to him and begins rubbing his chest, playing with the curly hairs.

Jeremy is not responding because he's in deep thought – about Tippy and what he's going to say. How can he tell her he went along with the agreement to stay away from her in order to save his career and her? Would she understand or think he was being selfish? Tippy has always been supportive of his dream, so he's hoping she'll forgive him. After all, he still loves her.

Jeremy couldn't let Tippy's father commit her or send her to juvie for mistakenly getting wasted at her birthday party. After running into Bobby Franklin a few months later, he jacked him up. Bobby told it was all a set-up. Said Judge Simms threatened him with a case which would put him away for a while. Judge Simms struck again.

Jeremy's glad his uncle finally got caught. ATL will be better off without him and Jeremy could care less what happens to him.

Stephanie rolls over on her left side, extending her right leg over Jeremy, then sits up straddle position across Jeremy's groin. Kneeling on both knees, she begins humping up, down, back and forth – while caressing Jeremy's upper arms.

"Mmmm," Stephanie mutters as she continues to dry hump. She's admiring his muscles. Jeremy is Sagittarius – his birthday is

December 10 – so he tattooed the Sagittarius zodiac sign on his right upper arm. Then she sees the damn tattoo of the Gemini on his left upper arm, which she got him to admit is Tippy's birth sign!

She remembers seeing it the first night they met and had sex. She ran into Jeremy at a Miami U football launch party, which she attended with a couple of female students from the Fashion College. She knew Jeremy would be there.

Jeremy played hard to get, but the more he drank the looser he got. Because she had been a ho for years, she knew guys like Jeremy. The one's trying to forget their problems by drinking too much booze and or having too much sex. She stuck with him all night; got him to talk about his recent breakup with his long-time girlfriend. The one he planned to marry one day.

Stephanie moves to what she knows how to do best. She moves down below Jeremy's groin, unzips and pulls down his pants and boxers. She engages in foreplay for a moment then opens her mouth and swallows his penis whole. Back and forth, lick here, lick there, Stephanie waits for Jeremy's penis to harden. Jeremy grabs the side of Stephanie's head, following the motion of her mouth – up down.

"Ooo suck it hard," says Jeremy.

Stephanie is sucking hard and licking his balls when she hears his cellphone vibrating, which is on the bed inches from her. She reaches over and pulls it closer. Still satisfying Jeremy without missing a beat, she looks at the screen. It's a 503 number. She figures it's Tippy. With her thumb she pushes the answer button, then sets the phone near her and Jeremy, who's now making loud erotic noises.

"Suck me harder Stephanie. Harder, harder. Whew!"

By this time Stephanie is undressed. She pulls Jeremy's penis from her mouth, lifts up and with her vagina over his penis she sits down, allowing him to enter her. She notices the phone is still on answer. Hoping it's Tippy, Stephanie goes into action.

"Oh Jeremy, you feel so good," she says humping him faster.

"Ooo you feel so damn good. Fuck me harder girl."

"Ooo Jeremy. Come wit' me baby!"

When they both climax, the phone hangs up. Stephanie falls forward onto Jeremy's chest. She feels like a winner. Turkey-baster or not she will be a baby mama soon. They just had unprotected sex and Stephanie is ovulating. She put an end to the Tippy and Jeremy story – for good.

6
Being Real

Dinner on Prescott

I'm missing TiAnna who's gone home for the holidays. Me, I've decided to have Christmas Eve dinner with Darius, leaving daddy to tend to his twins and Luanne. She's moving back to Atlanta for good and daddy still refuses to allow the twins to go.

Darius brings up Judge Simms during dinner. He also says he's had no further contact with his mama.

"I'll never forgive my mama yo," Darius says. "But hey enough of the feelin' sorry shit. Huh. Judge Simms gettin' busted is gonna help you out big time."

"You think?" I say.

"Naw. I know so yo. Makin' a move on your daddy's company is gon' be a piece a cake. So, keep learnin' everythang you can about daddy's bizness."

I've been working a few hours after school with my daddy. As his special project assistant, I've been doing research for him like learning about competitive strategies and the business's long-term strategy. I'm also taking some business courses online through PCC.

Darius has been building up my ego, sayin' I'm really smart. He believes I can run daddy's business. Running the business is my best option because my $100 million is wrapped up in the company and could take a while to recoup. I'd have to sell off the company piece by piece. The scary part is if RJ Designs goes under, I'd lose everything.

Darius's support has really helped me over the past few weeks. I know he's hoping for something more between the two of us, but he's been good about not pushing too hard. Our friendship has been good for us since we both have mama and daddy issues.

Hm. My phone is vibrating again. Jeremy? What!

"Got your damn nerve!" I say letting his call go to voicemail.

"Who dat?" says Darius.

"Not for you nosey," I say.

I'm annoyed, but at Jeremy for calling me out of the blue. Haven't heard from him since my birthday party in June. He didn't even call to see if I was okay.

"Okay shawty. I ain't tryin' to be in your bitness. Your face went real ugly on me," says Darius, raising his eyebrows.

"It's my ex Jeremy okay! I haven't heard from him since my birthday in June. He can go straight to hell!"

Darius raises his eyebrows. Why is Jeremy calling? Does this mean I have to add get rid of Jeremy to my full list of things to do? Shit. I may even have to make a move on Raymond Ellis. He's been tellin' Tippy to be cautious. So far, my girl's defending me. Huh. T's gone for a while. Maybe tonight I can get my mack on. So here I go.

"Shoot. Having you would make my world," says Darius out loud. "Yo Jeremy gotta a problem. He don't know what he let go."

Now I know this is true y'all but still. I was wondering when this Darius was gonna show up. Ha. Wonder what Shonny would say if I was doing her cousin?

I don't really care. We barely speak anymore. The last time we spoke she tells me she's Lesbian, Lucinda is her fiancé and they plan to get married in the next couple of years.

Lesbian or not, I'm feeling like maybe Shonny's rushing things. What if she finds out she's not Lesbian? Maybe she's just bicurious? I don't tell her my feelings. She says she truly understands herself now and has always been attracted to females.

At one point I thought I wanted to marry Jeremy but that's changed. I have no desire to marry anyone anytime soon I remember telling her. She just said, "I hope you'll find someone who'll makes you happy like Lucinda makes me," she says.

Okay y'all
I'm sidetracking a little here
Since Shonny's been gone from Abraham Lincoln, it's been much lonelier. I'm hoping TiAnna can join me soon. Since I was arrested at school and paraded through the halls it's been intense. The white kids really stare now.

"You know they hatin'," said Julie. "Most of them are druggy's, some are sellin' and do things that could put you bein' arrested to shame. The only difference is they don't get caught. If they do, they have parents well connected to the DA, police chief and city commissioner. So, they get away with it. It's who you know in this small town with a few big fish."

It was like that for us in Atlanta. We had the hook up, especially with daddy's friend Judge Simms. He's gone now though and good riddens.

OK Back to Darius

"I hope I don't make you uncomfortable," Darius says.

"Naw," I say. "I'm glad you're my friend. I like talkin' to you."

"Yeah me too. But I wish I could be more yo."

I spoke too soon. Now he's pushing it. I don't want to hurt Darius's feelings. I need his help. So, I just say, "You never know. But right now, I'm feelin' a little confused about relationship things. I thought Jeremy was the one; he's gone and I don't know what I did. Then I meet your brother; he's gone right in front of me." I don't say the words killed or murdered. We both know what happened.

"Then I meet AJ. I thought he was cool, even though I'd never dream of being with a white boy. Then he flakes out on me again. Invites me to his concert then says he changed his mind. Maybe it's best we stay friends nothin' else after begging me to forgive his white ass, making me feel all insecure and shit. Like something's wrong with me. I meeean. I'm the bomb!"

"You know you jiggy wit' it girl. It ain't you yo," Darius says. He reaches over and grabs my hand. "You are hell of a lady. If you ever choose me I swear fo' God, I'll treat you like the queen you deserve."

I want to pull my hand from his. But I don't. At least he makes me feel better. Someone recognizes me for the queen I am. I take another bite of the gumbo he made along with some hot water cornbread. I'm surprised he can cook like this given he was raised by a white mama.

"You're very sweet Darius. And you can even cook, ha!"

"I can burn just about anything," Darius brags. "I learned young 'cause I ended up fendin' for myself most of the time. I'da starved if I waited for my mama..." he pauses, blinks back a tear and then says, "And my uncle's wife ain't no Betty Crocker."

Darius is really trying to hold back. I'm feeling 'im so I lean over and kiss the side of his left cheek.

"Uh-huh," he says, grinning.

Ooo. What did I do? I shouldn't be sending him mixed messages. Dang. Darius leans over, gives me a small kiss on my lips. Hm. How do I get out of this? Ooo and my twot-twot just squealed. Staying a virgin is getting tougher given my raging hormones. I better go wipe the vaginal liquid dripping into my panties.

"I'll be right back. I gotta pee," I say.

I take my cell phone with me in case fool Jeremy calls again.

Mm mm mm. I can't wait to hit dat, Darius is thinking while watching Tippy walk away.

Sitting on the toilet
In Darius bathroom

I wonder why Jeremy called. Maybe I should call him to see what the hell he wants. Like T says, he may have a good excuse.

I punch in his number I still have on speed dial. Before it rings, I hang up. Calling him right now may be a bad idea. But I decide to go through with it so I press send again and let it ring this time. The phone picks up. I'm about to say hello when I hear moaning and groaning on the other end. I'm thinking it's a wrong number but I've never taken Jeremy's number off speed dial. It's also the same number he called me from.

"Fuck me harder!" I hear someone say.

Jeremy! What the hell! He calls me and I call him back even though he doesn't deserve it. And what do I get? I get him answering the phone while he's fucking some chick? What kinda sick joke is this? Then I hear some female talking nasty to him and calling his name, "Fuck me Jerry fuck me!" It's really him!

I hang up the phone and throw my expensive IPhone across the floor. Crash! It hits the floor. The back of it comes off and slides over hitting the side of the tub; the other half falls near the trash can. I drop my head into my hands and cry.

"No. I'm not going to cry over you no more Jeremy Simms."

I wipe myself several times with my feminine wipes, flush the toilet and wash my hands. I see some mouth wash on the sink, so I take a swig of it and rinse my mouth out. I rearrange my face from disappointment to everything's cool. Then leaving my phone where it fell, I head back to the dining room.

Darius has pushed his chair away from the table and he's leaned back with his long legs, stretched out in front of him. He's kicked off his slides.

"Want dessert," he says when I reach the table.

"Sure do," I say.

I walk over to Darius who's looking at me curiously, crinkling his brows. Throwing my leg across his lap and straddling him I sit down on his lap. Then I throw both arms around his neck.

"Sure do want some dessert," I say.

I kiss Darius on the lips, parting them, I stick my tongue in. Darius sticks his tongue in mine. It doesn't take long before we make our way into Darius's bedroom. Both naked and laying on Darius's king size bed, Darius is being very gentle, knowing this is my first time. Every step of the way he asks me am I alright, am I really okay with this. I nod, looking forward to saying good-bye to Jeremy and my virginity.

7

He Was Cold

4:00 a.m.
Christmas Day

H-e-l-l-o. Anybody here? H-e-l-l-o. Where the hell am I? It stinks like stale cigars and old cologne. And it's dark for real. Got my nerves screamin', my heart's going crazy. S-h-o-o-o-t. This must be a spell. No way I'd come here on my own. What's the dripping sound? Shit! Not on my hair! I just got a flat iron! Ooo! Down my face! Nasty! Damn cheap ass forty-watt bulbs. Stop flickering already, so I can see!

W-h-o-a hol'up. What's on the walls? Ooo nasty. Get me the hell out of here. Where's the door. I came in over there, I think. No, maybe this way. No, no this way. Wait. Who's that? Say something you ass! Who what the h-e-l-l... Wait! I know who you are! You killed my mother! I saw you! I saw you!

I'm awake

Darius is holding onto my arms gently shaking me. My eyes are closed but I feel his face close to mine. I can smell his cologne, hear his voice and feel his breathe as he tries to get me to open my eyes.

He's saying, "Hey baby yo. You're alright. I'm here."

When I open my eyes, Darius is sitting in front me. I'm so upset I don't notice right away he has on a jacket.

"You, wit' me Tip?" I nod and lay my head on his chest.

"Where were you?" I say. "Why do you feel cold."

"One of my fool ass homey's came by all drunk an shit. How you feelin'? Wanna talk about it."

Darius is holding me tight and rubbing the back of my head. I just made love for the first time and it felt really special. But now those special feelings are all gone thanks to having another damn nightmare. Something I haven't had in a while.

"I, I had the nightmare again."

"Yeah? You wanna tell me about it."

I take in a deep breath and close my eyes. I can feel Darius's chest warming through his jacket. His heart is beating normal now from when I first laid my head. I pull back from him, look into his eyes.

"I know who killed my mama Darius. It was Luanne."

6:00 p.m.
At the Atlanta estate

Raymond Ellis is there again to check in on his favorite patient. Dr. Stanwick is off for the holidays but left Dr. Lee Moore in charge. He finished looking in on the woman referred to as Diana Morgan.

"We are amazed with her progress," says Dr. Moore. "She's definitely a fighter."

"Thanks doc. Good to hear," says Raymond Ellis.

Diana looks toward the door when she hears Ray. She smiles. Ray reaches her bedside, leans over, kisses her. "Have I ever told you, you look as good as a bowl of Collard Greens on a Sunday?"

"Um ya uh yeah. Graaa eeens ahh Sun… day," Diana says smiling. Ray gently kisses her on her lips.

"It won't be long now my love," he says. "Not long."

6:30 p.m.

Back on Prescott

I can't go back to sleep and I ain't going home. Daddy's been calling. It's Christmas but I don't feel much like being with him. He finally gave into Luanne. So later today she'll be taking her twins back to Atlanta for a few days. The damn murderer's mama is dying! But she can't leave here. I gotta call the police so they can arrest her!

I let Darius call him to let him know I'm fine. I hear him also tellin' daddy I had a really bad nightmare. I know daddy is insisting on coming over. But Darius assures him I'm fine. And he'll bring me home later.

I stay over at Darius's for most of the day, lying in bed and won't eat. I know Luanne killed mama even though Darius tries to convince me otherwise. And he won't let me call the police.

"Baby I asked her flat out," says Darius. "She says no. I'd know if she was lying."

I'm pissed Darius is defending Luanne. He didn't even tell me he asked her about killing my mama.

"You're just protecting her because she's your woman!"

"Tippy stop!"

He got his nerve trying to raise his voice. Reminds me of daddy.

"Your daddy suggests we call Dr. Ryan. I'm inclined to agree yo."

Listen at this fool trying to use a word like inclined then says yo all in the same sentence.

"No," I say. "I wanna talk to my uncle."

Darius hands me his cellphone. He did rescue mine from the bathroom and put it back together for me. It's charging.

"Hello Unc Rae-Rae," I don't even say Merry Christmas. I just say flat out "Luanne killed mama I saw it in my dream. I saw it. We need to call the police."

Tippy had forgotten all about Dr. Ryan's request. She was to call her immediately once it was clear who killed her mother.

"Tippy listen," says Ray. "Luanne didn't kill Loretta."

"Yes, she did! So, you're going to defend her too?"

Raymond Ellis pauses not knowing what Tippy means, but he doesn't have time to speculate. He knows Luanne is not the killer.

"Listen to me baby girl. It wasn't Luanne. You gotta trust me on this. Luanne even has a strong alibi. She wasn't there when Loretta got killed."

"Where was she then?"

"Aw baby girl," my uncle says hesitating. "She was with your daddy at some hotel. They were seen."

So, this confirms it. My daddy was cheating with Luanne when she was still underage. When he was still married to mama.

"So, she didn't do it huh? Well they both may as well had. My daddy cheated on my mama and he's a pedophile. Well great! Merry fucking Christmas!" I say – the first time I said the word – and slam the phone down. If it wasn't Darius's phone, it woulda ended up like mine, sprawled across the floor.

Darius hears the whole thing. He wants to hold me and comfort me but I won't let him. This is real fucking bullshit! My mama's killer is still roaming free; I think it's Luanne but instead she's off fucking an old man – my damn daddy! I can't wait to get him back!

I'm coming for you Mr. Robert Ellis. Just wait. Next Thanksgiving you'll be the one getting served.

8
No LOL

It's almost time

Dear Mama:

It's almost New Year's Eve. I'll being making a whole new resolution. I'm determined as ever to find your murderer. Especially after my revelation on Christmas got shot to hell! It's hard for me to be back at home. Daddy has Darius to thank. He says it's important for me to play it cool. Daddy's hold over me could put me in the loony-bin for a long time. Then he'd be justified for stealing my money — the money you left me.

We spoke to an attorney Michael Billings about what daddy did. He's known for winning cases like mine. I told him I want to go after my daddy, overturn his contract on me and take his company.

Michael Billings has a dossier on daddy's company with my help — his investments, how much the company's worth, its Dunn and Bradstreet rating.

Every time I thank about it, it makes me mad as hell our $100 mil is making this company thrive.

TiAnna is still in Atlanta with family but will be coming back soon. Uncle Rae-Rae is bringing her and he'll spend New Year's with us. And get this — granddaddy is coming. I don't know what happened but daddy is going to allow it. Gramma wants to come but she's been sick. Granddaddy assures me she's fine. Her arthritis has been acting up.

Luanne is in Atlanta and won't be returning. She's giving daddy an uncontested divorce. With no wife and my $100 mil he's on cloud nine no doubt. And I think he's seeing someone else. I hear him talking on the phone sometimes and the way he talks, it ain't to a man.

Luanne blackmailing daddy into marrying her is still hard for me, but it's daddy's fault too. He did his dirty business right under your nose. For the longest, I wanted the killer in my nightmares to be Luanne. I wanted her to pay for what she did to our family so much so I deliberately began recreating my nightmares unconsciously, so Dr. Ryan says. Coming to terms with that has helped me to let go of my anger against Luanne and even Brittany and Jayden.

But when all is said and done, I'm my mama's daughter. I hope I make you proud.

Love LaTonya.

TiAnna phoned me shortly after she arrived in ATL to tell me some news. She hears Jeremy's gonna be a daddy and is marrying a biracial girl named Stephanie Matthews who's studying to be a fashion designer. He tried to call me a couple of times, after I returned his phone call, catching him fucking some girl. I now know the girl is this Stephanie person. I always knew Jeremy wanted a white girl. To save face he goes and gets a half black one so he won't have to admit he's into white girls.

TiAnna says she ran into Damon who says Jeremy's been trying to reach me. He wishes we'd connected.

"Damon doesn't look good," says TiAnna. "He looks really sad. Somethin's gotta hold of 'im. He told me there's more to the story and you should give Jeremy a chance to explain."

"What's there to explain," I say. "He was caught with his pants down. I'm done!"

"Yeah I know Tip. But you and Jeremy were the shit. Damon says Jeremy's got caught up and Stephanie is dangerous."

"Hm. Jeremy's a big boy. He can handle himself. Besides, he's not my problem anymore."

Me and Darius have gotten closer over the past few weeks. Sex no longer hurts and it's really good. Darius knows what to do when it comes to satisfying my twot-twot in every way. I also please him in every way too. We use condoms and pray they don't break especially when we really get into doing-the-do. We both agree we don't need kids right now. We've got a lot to do.

Darius's career is starting to take off and he says it's because we're together. He's been writing more songs for Fella Jiles and some other artists have inquired. Thank the Big G they're not rappers. Darius says I make him feel whole. And he's learning to love "Fo real yo."

I still don't know who killed mama. But after spending more time with Dr. Ryan I do know the killer is an older woman – I get the impressions she's black too. I don't share this with anyone for now. Not even Darius, TiAnna or Uncle Rae-Rae and not daddy.

New Year's Eve

And Unc Rae-Rae, TiAnna and my granddaddy have just arrived. I grab him first and hug him. Then TiAnna, who seems really down. What happened to my sis? Maybe spending the holidays with her family was too much. I look at Unc Rae-Rae, who looks concerned. He shrugs his shoulders not knowing what's up.

Daddy, granddaddy and Unc Rae-Rae head into the dining room for New Year's Eve brunch. It's a buffet this year and this time daddy has it catered.

"Say shawty, I need to holla at you for a minute," says Darius, grabbing me before I could move.

Damn. He's been buggin' since he's been here.

"Can we talk later please?" I say. "Somethin's up with T. I need to find out what."

"Yeah yo. But I'm next."

I see TiAnna walking slowly to the dining room. I run over and grab her hand, take her into the family room shut the doors.

She begins to cry. I grab her and hug her really tight and beg her to tell me what's wrong.

"So many things have happened Tip, I just don't know."

I know my BFF is still hurting. But she's been working through it with Dr. Ryan's help.

"My daddy gave me this," says TiAnna handing me the envelope she was holding in her hand. "You gotta read this shit Tip."

I take the opened letter which says:

My darling TiAnna:

I pray every day we find you. Me, your daddy and your brothers love you so much and want you home. God knows I am ready and willing to give up my life if it means they will set you free. I have made so many mistakes. One of the biggest was not telling you about Chelsea. But I didn't know how. It was my family's best kept secret; one I will never forget. Now because of my pain you are experiencing the same pain. I projected onto you and I am truly sorry.

I should've also told you about your daddy. My mama begged me to but I couldn't bring myself to tell you or him. Randall has done so much for me. He loved me despite my shortcomings. He stood by me even when I couldn't forget who I thought was my one true love. But because he fell in love with another woman — a woman who I despised more than life itself — I found myself fending for myself. If it wasn't for Randall we would have been lost.

I'm following my mother's advice now. I am through hiding the truth and telling lies. All I have done is hurt you and your father. My darling, Randall is not your biological father — he knows. Your biological father is Raymond Ellis, your best friend Tippy's uncle.

"What the hell!" I say. My mouth is stuck wide open as I stand there in disbelief. My Unc Rae-Rae is my BFF's daddy!

9

Daddies
Daughters

11:40 p.m.
Bring it on

As I am writing this truth, your real father does not know about you. Randall and I chose not to tell him. He had already inserted himself into the life of another woman which later caused problems for him and the family. I will not go into details on this because it's not my truth and not for me to say. But I will ask that you not hate your biological father nor your real father who raised you. Randall loves you more than life itself. You have always been his daughter and he's never treated you differently. Rather he spoiled you more than I would have liked (smile).

My darling, no matter what happens remember you are so blessed. Remember you have one of the purest souls I've ever known. I am proud to have been your mother. Please remember me often and hopefully with fond memories. Love your mother, Lydia

P.S. Stay close to Tippy. When the time is right, you will find out how important she is to you.

Me and TiAnna are both crying. This is way too much, especially for my BFF who was doing so well. I guess her father Randall had found the letter on the bed stand after Lydia committed suicide. It was addressed to TiAnna but he figured he would hold onto it until he felt she could handle the truth. He gave it to her while she was in Atlanta. Apparently, Uncle Rae-Rae knows now too. Randall went and saw him while he was in jail and asked for his help to find her.

"Tippy!" I hear my Unc Rae-Rae calling me. He's outside the doors. "What's holding you up?"

I look at TiAnna, who's saying nothing. I may be wrong but I figure it's time my Unc Rae-Rae make amends with his daughter.

"You can come in," I say.

My uncle walks in with his big charming grin, which suddenly vanishes when he sees the both us. TiAnna's still not speaking but it don't matter because I've appointed myself as her spokesperson and decide to hold nothing back.

"We know the truth Unc Rae-Rae or should we call you daddy?" My uncle looks at me, then TiAnna and back to me. He opens his mouth to speak but I cut him off.

"You know this is wacked. It don't matter how long you've known. Do you know all the suffering you've caused?"

"Tip, baby girl I wanted to tell you and TiAnna both. I was pushed into keeping quiet and even when I threatened to tell you, it never was the right time. But I love you both even though TiAnna I just found out about you not too long ago. Tip, your mama wanted me to allow Robert to raise you. They were having serious problems but she wanted to try and work it out."

My uncle doesn't realize I'm shocked as hell at what he's saying. He just keeps on babbling, "I blame myself for her. If I would have insisted, she leave your father she'd be alive. She didn't love him. I'm sorry but I'm not ashamed. What happened, happened. I know it hurt my brother and Lydia because I couldn't return her love. I love Loretta and always will. If you two hate me I'm cool wit dat. In my heart I've always wanted this day to come when the two of you finally know each other as sisters. You were drawn together for a reason and have remained friends. Life has a strange way of bringing the truth full circle," says Ray wiping his drowning eyes.

"What!" I say.

TiAnna places her hand on my shoulder, leans around and looks at me.

"Tip…" TiAnna says.

"What the fuck are you saying?" I say the word again and it feels good.

"Oh, baby girl, you didn't know. I thought… aw man. Your ma…"

"What, what!" I say. "All these years. Leaving me to wonder why my own daddy hates me. It's because of you he hates me! And my mama? What everybody says is true? She had an affair and with my own uncle? So, what else am I gonna find out! Daddy killed her or maybe you did it 'cause she wouldn't leave daddy! Or maybe it was you and Luanne!"

"Tip, Dar…"

"If you're getting ready to start with me about Darius don't you even go there. You have no damn right to say anything. I hate you and mama. You both made my life a living hell!"

My uncle reaches out to grab me, but I begin beating his chest with my fists.

"I hate you!"

TiAnna leans into my left arm, dropping her head to my shoulder, the same way she did the night of my birthday party – before everything went to hell. Only this time she ain't high and daddy ain't here to try and kidnap me like he did before; lock me up and steal my money! So far, he's gotten away with it and now I find out, he's stolen my life too! Robert Ellis is going down!

"No. No," says TiAnna.

The doors swing open and in comes my so-called asshole daddy, the thief, with granddaddy Oliver and Darius right behind him.

"What the hell's going on!" he says.

My fists tighten and so does my face. I'm breathing heavily, glaring at him, giving him a taste of his bouncer stance.

Robert Ellis ignores me and quickly turns his attention to his brother. He tenses up and shaking with anger, walks over to Raymond Ellis and gets right up on him.

I hope they beat the shit out of each other!

"What the hell did you say!" he says.

Mr. Rae-Rae slowly shakes his head but says nothing.

"You're not my real daddy! Now I know why you hate me!"

Darius raises his eyebrows and thinks, "This is what I'd planned to tell Tippy later –her uncle is really her biological father. Damn! The fireworks have already started and it ain't even midnight. I'm glad both you motherfuckas is getting told. It will make my plan go a lot smoother, especially if Unc Rae-Rae ain't around to ruin it."

"It figures!" my fake daddy's saying to his brother. "You been wanting to take my daughter from me for a long time. You already stole her mama…"

"Stop it daddy! Or should I call you Unc Rob-Rob!"

"I am still your father!" he says.

"No, you're not! And neither are you!" I say looking at my uncle. "Right now, the both of you make me really sick. I tell you what Mr. Robert Ellis, you can just get ready to write me a big check!"

Oh shit! Darius is shouting in his head. Tippy don't blow our plans to take down your scum ass daddy!

"And as for you!" I say pointing to my uncle, "Don't you ever speak to me again!"

Ooo that hurt! I love my uncle, I mean my daddy, I mean... shit!

"Well granddaddy I guess the party is over. I won't even ask how long or when you knew! I'm guessin' gramma knows too."

My granddaddy just stands there with his head down.

"Yeah. That's what I thought!"

I grab TiAnna's hand and push past those damn ass men who call themselves my family.

"If you don't mind, me and my sister have some packing to do. We'll be leaving with Darius!"

Once they leave the room is quiet.

"Uh," says Darius breaking the silence. "Happy New Year!" Then he turns about face and quickly follows the girls, knowing he's outnumbered. He's already feeling the knives piercing in his back. But it don't matter. He figures he's much closer to becoming the $100 million man.

Raymond Ellis makes it back to the hotel where he and granddaddy Oliver are staying. When he walks into his room, he's greeted warmly by his lover. He looks into her eyes, his face drained of color and eyes red from crying.

"I blew it baby. I thought today would be the day. The girls... I fucked up."

"My love," she says caressing his cheek. "You are always so impatient. They're just not ready yet. Don't worry, things will be as they should be. In due time my love, in due time."

10

It Ain't Over Yet

3:00 a.m.
New Year's 2013

"How's T?"

"She's asleep."

"You okay?"

"I dunno."

"You know I don't like it when you sad."

"Sorry boo. But I gotta get use to the fact my BFF is my sister. And my daddy ain't my daddy. My Unc Rae-Rae and mama… "

"I know it hurts. You really love your uncle like I love my mama. But then they betray us."

"Aw boo. I've been so caught up in my own stuff I haven't asked how you've been holding up since your mama accepted the plea bargain – 25-to-life."

"I'm cool baby. Besides you my family now. You make me want to do the right thing yo. Huh. Why you grinning?"

"I thought you always do the right thing D?"

"Well I'm talkin' about somethin' else. Like making you an honest woman. I'd like you to be my wife. How 'bout it?"

"Your wife huh? Like when yo?"

"Ha. You still sound silly. Just stick to the bougie talk yo. Your little white girl twang turns me on. I can have one without having one. Ha."

"Not funny. Besides it's called girlishcious."

"Ooo be gentle girlishcious. You know you pack a sting in yo punch. So shawty what up?"

"Uh-huh. I guess I can see myself being your wife."

"You guess. Dang don't sound so excited."

"Come here boo," I say. Then I plant a big, long wet one on his lips. "Mmmmm, now what?"

"Awww. Your girlishcious kisses are making me hot. Is dat a yes."

"Yes, under one condition."

"What I gotta do?"

"Marry me now."

"Like right dis second? You won't be 18 until June yo."

"Huh. I know. I guess I can wait a few months, unnnnless I get emancipated."

"True dat?" says Darius.

"True dat yo," I say, smiling.

Darius's cell phone rings. "Hol' dat smile. I'll make this quick." He picks up and says, "Who dis?"

"Darius this is your favorite detective. I know it's New Year's Eve, but my work is never done."

"Whatchu wont," says Darius, frowning.

"When you get some time, I'd like to ask you some questions about a man named Darrell Monroe. I believe he knew your mother?"

"And?" says Darius.

"His body was found. It appears he's been shot. We think it may have happened on Christmas Eve. You wouldn't know anything about it would you?"

8:00 a.m. that morning

Robert Ellis phones a mutual acquaintance – they met in Portland. He's got to find a way to enforce Tippy's contract.

"It ain't over yet my daughter. I know this is way too much for you. You need help," says Robert Ellis while phoning another friend.

On the other side of town, Darius has a plan but first runs by to check in with his homey to make sure everything's cool. He told the detective he has an alibi, so his homey needs to be ready. Then he heads to his next destination. Although resistant, he knows Tippy is miserable. He heard her crying in the middle of the night. And it made him sick. Maybe he can use Raymond Ellis's help since he and his brother Robert are on the outs. Can he trust him given how he feels about him?

Earlier, Raymond Ellis left word he and granddaddy Oliver would be leaving for Atlanta today. They hope Tippy will allow them to at least say good-bye. But she refused.

Downtown Portland

Darius parks directly across the street from Ray Ellis and Franklin Oliver's hotel. Before shutting off the engine, he contemplates on whether or not to broach Ellis at all.

"Maybe I should talk with Franklin Oliver instead. He's got clout and wants the best for his granddaughter. Huh. Maybe I should forget about makin' contact with either 1 of 'em. Let 'em stew. At least allow Tip to get over the shock. Sheeeit. Let me go talk to dem motherfuckas before I change my mi ...

Whoa! Who dat comin' out da hotel – daddy Rae, granddad and? What the ... who? Fuck yo! Naw it can't be!

Close your eyes Darius. Gotta be a bad dream. Now open 'em.

Whoa! Naw! Dats her. She 'pose to be dead yo! Got killed 9 years ago yo! Aw man. Naw dat's her. Dat's Tippy's mama – Loretta!"

Back at the Prescott house

Tippy is writing a letter to her mother.

Mama:

I guess I should start by saying Happy Fucking New Year! This is my last letter to you. Now I know the truth and won't need you anymore.

Our relationship was special so I thought. But you Unc Rae-Rae and daddy ruint it. I remember all those times me, you and Unc Rae-Rae were together – the family you really wanted.

Well the joke ends up being on you 'cause someone............ OMG MAMA! SHE DID IT. SHE KILLED YOU!

TiAnna calls Darius

"Darius. This is me TiAnna! You gotta come home. Quick!"

"Damn TiAnna. Slow down. What's going on? Who the hell's screamin'? Where's Tippy?"

"That's Tip screaming Darius. She's freaking out and I can't get her to calm down. Something's wrong!"

"Put shawty on the phone yo."

"Here Tip. Darius wanna talk to you," says TiAnna attempting to hand me the phone.

I'm sitting on the bed across from this TiAnna. My back's against the headboard, clutching my bent legs to my chest. I'm scared as hell and don't want to talk to whoever is on the phone. Instead, I frantically shake my head and yell at her, "No! I want my mama! I want my daddy! Where's Unc Rae Rae? Help me pleeeasee!"

"OK Tip. You're gonna be alright." TiAnna reaches out to touch me, but I push back. I may end up busting through this damn headboard. "Darius, Tippy won't take the phone. She wants her folks. Should I call 'em?"

"Hell fuckin' naw! Damn yo! I'm comin'! I got dis. Un-da-stand?!"

"OK Darius. Hurry! This ain't good," TiAnna says lifting her eyebrows. "I'm as scared as Tip. She acts like she don't know me."

After Darius ends his conversation with TiAnna, he starts the car reluctantly, putting it in gear with his left foot on the brake and right one on the accelerator slowly raising the engine.

"Dis some crazy ass shit," he says aloud. "Happy fuckin New Year! The fireworks are still bangin. Loretta's alive, Unc Rae Rae lied and daddeo is full of fuckin jive. I'll get back witchu Rae Ellis and you too mama Loretta. You supposed to be dead yo! Ah man. Let me get out of here before I kick all y'alls asses!"

Still with one foot on the brake and the other on the accelerator he presses down on it hard sending the wheels into a spin. "Eat my dust motherfuckas!" says Darius as he skids off.

Half-way down the block Darius slows to slightly above the speed limit hopefully not enough to get a damn speeding ticket. With Brannigan on his ass that's the last thing he needs yo.

Making it back to the crib in less than 15, he rushes inside. Tippy is curled up in a ball hummin' so he can't tell if she's gone mad or what. To Darius Tippy doesn't seem quite as wacked as TiAnna said. *I know my girl doe. She's prone to losing her mind. I've seen her in the zone. But I talked her back.*

Fully inside the room Darius creeps up behind TiAnna who's sitting with her back to him. *Damn broad don't even hear me. Sheeeit. I could be a burglar or a rapist all up on her before she even know what hit her dumb ass!*

"Yo girl. Move. Let me handle this," he says tapping TiAnna on the shoulder making her jump.

"Darius! You scared the shit outta me!"

"Yeah. You lucky it's me. You need to be on guard in case the enemy shows up yo." Stepping around her he moves towards Tippy. "Hey shawty. Whassup?" *She still don't seem to hear me. What the hell tune is she hummin'?*

Darius leans over the curled up Tippy and says "Hey shawty." She flinches and pulls back.

"See Darius. She wouldn't let me near her neither. At least she calmed down. I think we should call somebody."

"No yo! Like I said. We ain't callin nobody!"

My name is Tippy, right?

I'm looking at this TiAnna and green-eye Darius who appears to be in charge. I wanna say I don't remember either of you. Who are you people? Why am I here? Where's mama and daddy? Where's Unc Rae Rae? Y'all must be some of their friends, yet you seem familiar. I still wanna go home. I make eye contact with the green-eyed one and fix my mouth to ask.

Before I can he says, "My beautiful LaTonya. My beautiful shawty. Yo. I gotchu. I'mo always keep you safe. Un-da-stand?"

I wanna shout back no I don't understand. I can't get the words out. Why does he keep saying yo? What's up with the improper grammar? Grandma and mama wouldn't like it. And why did you call me beautiful? Are you a pervert? Maybe they kidnapped me and I don't remember.

"I'm here too Tip," says TiAnna. "You're gonna be alright."

Forget you TiAnna I'm yelling in my head. I want out! I look around the room for the first time so it seems. Then somethin' captures my attention. A mirror. Who's she? Wha - no! Can't be! I'm only 6!

11

When the Time's Right

12:30 p.m.
Downtown Portland

Whatchu gonna do Rae? I'm thinkin'. We're sitting in the car out front of the hotel ready to go, except I can't move from this spot. I'm glad I gave the Valet a large tip 'cause right now I'm stuck on stupid, overcome by anger. With my eyes piercing the windshield, I focus on the Portland drizzle while my tears slowly make their way out. If I'm not careful, I'll be the one flooding main street. Time to man up Rae.

"Loretta's right. We need to let baby girl be for now," says Franklin Oliver. "Let this news settle in."

"You mean leave her with my brother and Darius!" I shout. "My daughter ain't safe! Neither one of 'em! Naw! I'm taken 'em both outta here if I have to drag 'em out screamin'!"

"Umph. That'll go over well," says Loretta Oliver. "How do you plan to explain my reappearance after 9 years?"

"We may not have to," I say. "I think I saw that punk Darius parked across the street minutes ago. He knows who you are thanks to our daughter talkin' so damn much. Trustin' his no-good ass."

"You're imagining things again Rae," says Franklin. "Last night you thought you saw him after we left Ellis's house. We knew it wasn't him because he left with your daughters. My granddaughter."

"Being Tippy's your granddaughter, you should be concerned too!" I say, not letting up.

"Now Rae. You're giving into your emotions and for the wrong reason. You can't help the situation none if you don't keep a level head," Franklin warns.

"Look. I've played cool all these years. Watchin' my muthafuckin brother playin' daddy to my child because airbody wanted me to step back for their —" Suddenly, I remember the warmth of the only woman I've ever loved, sitting next to me in the passenger seat. She's staring at me with her beautiful brown wet eyes. She's hurting like me. Sheeeit. I need my ass whooped! Here I am pissing a bitch 'bout what happened at Robert's house. Tippy and TiAnna both found out I was their real daddy. Randall told TiAnna last week in Atlanta. Good ol' Randall who was my running buddy back in the day. He's raised TiAnna since birth. Took my place as her daddy and as a husband to my late ex-wife Lydia. She killed herself last year over some bullshit about a first daughter she gave away after conceiving her from being raped at 14. The child came back to give her hell. Kidnapped our TiAnna and wit' her pimp ass man Don Juan turned my girl out. Had her hoeing and hooked on smack.

Me and Lydia were married for a short time and still together when I got wit' Loretta. Lydia finally left me for having an affair and kept her pregnancy from me. Both Lydia and Loretta conceived around the same time. Yeah I was doing 'em both for a minute. Once Loretta found out she was pregnant she said she knew the baby was mine, but didn't wanna hurt my brother so she stayed with him. My damn selfish ass brotha who fucked around on her every chance he got. Like wit' the damn nanny Luanne who was 16 when my Loretta brought her to stay wit' them in Druid Hills. Luanne is a ho period and she got it honestly given who her daddy was and his bottom girl, her mama, known as Cheri. One day child protective services stepped in and took Luanne. She was 15. Her daddy dropped out of sight with a new young ho and her mama started using crack. We found out later Don Juan's new ho was Chelsea, Lydia's first child she gave away. Ain't that a bitch! Both my girls' mamas had to deal with crazy ass shit.

Luanne was nothin' but trouble. She seduced my brother when she came to live wit' 'em. He took the bait wit' his weak ass. Tippy caught 'em. Luanne goin' down on him. But Loretta stayed anyway and talked me outta going over there killin' the muthafucka and his stank bitch! Didn't matter to me she was 16. She was hired to watch Tippy! But noooo. Her and my brother doin' nasty shit in my Loretta's house and around my daughter.

"Loretta, I'm sorry baby. Here you are after 9 years. You made it through and came back to me and our daughter."

"Yes, I did my love. But we have to be patient. Tippy is in shock knowing about you. Can you imagine what she's gonna do when she finds out I'm alive?"

"Loretta, we had to keep you safe. We didn't know who tried to kill you," says Franklin.

"What you mean tried? Lydia almost killed our girl."

"She didn't and I'm alive and well. I have a chance to do right by our daughter. Mostly, I can make Robert Ellis suffer for what he's done to her all these years."

"Alright, enough talk. We need to get Loretta home. Mama needs her and the rest of us. She hasn't been feelin' well," says Franklin.

"You right daddy. OK. Rae? Tippy will be fine."

"Alright then, I'll be patient. For now." I lean over, kiss Loretta softly on the lips. Put the car in gear, head for the private airport.

Shontel "Shonny" Jackson

Me and Lucinda are hosting a New Year's Eve Brunch. Julie and her boo Jason just walked in. "Happy New Year Julie girrrl. How you been Ms. Thang? I see you and your boo still hangin'. You lookin' good Mr. Jason. I'll say." I lean back, admiring both of 'em. Jason's bouncing his head to the music playin' in the background. Hmmm. He does look good for a white boy – tall and athletic with shoulder-length wavy blonde hair and green eyes. If I didn't like females, I'd definitely give him a second look. Now Julie. She's a tall ass white girl with blue eyes and over-permed bleached blonde hair she wears right above her cheekbones. She don't turn me on at all. Not my type. She's cool though. One of the few white kids who spoke to me when I went to Abe Lincoln. I heard she also had Tippy's back.

"You the Ms. Thang Shonny," says Julie. "I hear you got engaged?"

"Sure did," I say, wiggling my left finger showing off a one carat diamond ring set in white gold.

Julie grabs my hand to take a closer look. "Ooo," she says, giving her boo the eye like *where's mine?* Jason's face gets a little flustered, attempting a smile. I wanna laugh. Girls fall hard for these boys when all they want is sex.

"Let me introduce you to my boo Lucinda. See the fine Latina over by the dining table?" I say pointing in Lucinda's direction.

"Mmmm," says Jason, grinning.

"OK down boy," says Julie. "She ain't into you."

"Sho you right," I say with my hands on my big hips. Now I'm grinning about me and mine doing our thing all last night.

"This jam must be off the CD Evolution of Anuff," says Jason, moving behind Julie, holding her waist and swaying to *Only One Me.* "It's bad ass," he's says, sounding like a straight up white boy.

"Yeah sure is," I say, singing the lyrics. Julie and Jason join in on the chorus. *It's only one me, it's only one me, it's only one me, it's only one meeee, I don't understand it, they just wanna see me falling down, It's only one me, it's only one me, it's only one meeee, I don't know the reason they don't wanna see me ballin' out.*

Some of the few friends we have left decided to show today. Me and Lucinda both came-out last year. People say they're cool wit' our thing. Yeah right. We soon found out who our real friends were. My mom is supportive. She's Buddhist so she don't judge. Lucinda's folks disowned her. Her Latin clan is much like many black folks. Homophobic. Fortunately, Lucinda is of age – she's 21 – and can take care of herself. She's got a fantastic job as property manager for a large real estate firm, which is how she got this house. They let her have this one for next to nothing. After I graduate, I plan to move in. By then, we'll be getting close to walking down the aisle. Maybe by Christmas or early next spring.

Lucinda moves under the mistletoe when she sees me coming. I join her and give her a big kiss sticking my tongue all up inside her mouth. Everyone is oooing, giggling, clapping.

"Lucinda baby this is Julie and Jason. Friends from Abraham."

"Hola," says Lucinda, giving them each a hug. "Welcome to our casa."

"Say sweetie," I say to Lucinda. "I'ma call Tippy and see if she and TiAnna still coming. Hopefully she'll be able to get away from conniving ass Darius for a minute."

"Shonny. This is New Year's," says Lucinda. "You should let him come too. He's your family."

"No he ain't! That Negro is trouble!"

"So how do you really feel about Tippy's new man," says Julie jokingly.

"Hmph!" I say throwing my head back, walking off to make the call. I ain't going to let the thought of Darius ruin this day. I wish Tippy would leave him alone. Can't say nothin' bad about him though. The last time I did, she read me good and she wasn't even wit' him then. We were at my cousin Jerome's funeral who got killed in a drive by last year. Darius's mother put a hit out on him – her son's half-brother! All for money. I think she also wanted to get back at Jerome's daddy who died a couple years earlier. Jerome's mom followed a year later after overdosing on sleeping pills. Damn Darius anyway. Jerome wanted to be a brother to him despite Darius's own daddy denying him.

I dial Tippy's number. The phone rings and guess who picks up? "Oh, Darius," I say, trying not to sound disgusted. "I was hopin' to get Tippy. You answering her calls now?"

"And happy New Year to you Shonny. My fiancé is sleeping. I'll tell her you called yo." *Click.*

"Oh no he didn't hang up on me. With his dang rude ass. Your fiancé? Tippy? Lord have mercy. What did you do? Hope you're OK."

I snap back from my thoughts because of the new bounce now playin'. Anuff's hit single *Dem Jeans.*

"Oh hell yeah," I say, turning back to the crowd. "Come on ladies," I yell. "Time to get our twerk on. Woohoo." I drop my big ass and twerk, causing the crowd to cheer and Lucinda to whistle. "Yeah sho you right. Who's up for a challenge?"

Over at Darius's house

"Phew. Glad my girl's out. Let's hope those pills Dr. Ryan prescribed keep her dat way for now yo."

"Who was dat on the phone Darius? Got you frowning," TiAnna asks.

"Nothin' for you to worry 'bout yo. Your task is to get y'all things together. We outta here in 20. I feel somethin's up. I don't trust nobody right now especially Tippy's damn daddies!"

"Ok Darius. But, I still think we should at least call the doctor."

"No damn way! Like I said yo, keepin' my girl safe is our number one priority. Un-da-stand?"

"I got it. I got it. I'll be ready in 17."

12
Outta Here

Heading to California

Me, Tippy and TiAnna hit the road shortly after I got to the house. Around 1:00 we was on I-5 heading south. In case they look for us, I switched rides with my boy Jodeci. I got his Ford Escape, which is pretty good on gas. Yo. I still can't figure why he wanna drive this cheap ass rig. Don't even reflect my man's cool ass personality. Dat's OK. He can be cool in my Range Rover. At least dude got insurance. As for my girl's convertible, I stashed it at my boy's place down the block and disconnected the tracker. I remembered Tippy telling me about dat when she first got it. Says her daddy installed it for her safety. Yeah right.

We don't make our first stop until we cross into California. I gas up in Redding, grab some water and snacks and head to the nearest rest area for a piss break. Both Tippy and TiAnna slept all the way, T up front with me and Tippy stretched out on the backseat. They start moving once the truck sets idle longer than a minute. I peak at Tippy through my rearview mirror, who just sat up, groggy from her meds. She rotates her head from side-to-side looking out each window, confused by her surroundings. Then she pins me down. I turn around, throwing my right arm over the seat and glance at T before giving Tippy my full attention.

"How you feeling," I ask her. No response. But I can tell her 6-year-old mind is working. I should find a place to get her some toys. A doll maybe? I smile. She don't. But she might if she knew what I was thinking.

"Hey girl," says TiAnna, joining in. "Wanna get out and stretch? Go to the bathroom?" Tippy nods. "Grab your coat. It looks cold out," TiAnna says, putting her own jacket on.

"I'mo let y'all ladies do your thing yo. We'll be ready to ride in 10. I picked up some snacks," I say, pointing to the bags on the floor in back. "We'll grab real food later."

Once the girls get out, I lock up. T grabs Tippy's hand, holding on all the way to the ladies bathroom and I run around to the men's, scanning our surroundings. Yeah I'm paranoid as hell. Luckily winter evenings come early, helping us to fade amongst the disappearing trees and slew of cars pulling in and out. This is a popular spot because it's close to the border. Nice. Everyone is minding their own bitness – get in, get out – even in the bathroom I barely get a nod. Cool with me. I finish up, sweeten my breath with mouthwash, then head outside and wait near the ladies room for the girls.

Me and Tippy
Turn up our noses

Once inside the girls' bathroom, it reminds me of how much I hate these rest stop toilets. They rarely keep 'em clean. The stained, dull white cement walls could use a good cleaning, trash cans need to be emptied and what looks like puddles of water in the corners should be mopped up. Hmm. I hope it's water. This bathroom has 10 stalls – 4 aren't working – and the wheelchair accessible toilet is the only one available. I take Tippy in with me 'cause she seems a bit nervous. I can't blame her. Even in the women's room, you can run into strange people. Like the tall thin blue-haired white girl with a Mohawk. She has white and pink feathers sticking out of the top of her hair, matching her long feather earrings and necklace. She's wearing all black and as cold as it is outside, this crazy looking chic is wearing a tight ass black leather mini skirt, tank top and high-heels with her toes out and no stockings. She's styling her make-up like Elvira and has a tattoo on each arm. Guess what it is? Yep. A pink feather. Now as white as she is, she can't be trying to pass as Native American. Maybe she's participating in one of those drumming circles. I hear lots of white folks love to drum with the tribes. I guess it makes 'em feel less guilty for what they did to 'em back in the day.

I pull the last 2 sheet covers from the wall mount and cover the toilet seat. Pointing, I motion for Tippy to go first. I'll squat when it's my turn. She pulls down her fuchsia jeans and sits. Smiling to myself, I'm thinking those fuchsia colored jeans is probably one of the few things she remembers. She's sitting with her head down and she's slightly rocking mid waist, holding her stomach, like she really had to go. Except when she's done peeing, she keeps moving.

"Are you OK?" I ask Tippy. She shakes her head. She must be cold 'cause I see her knees knocking. I take off my jacket and lay it across her lap with the bottom edge dropping right below her knees. My eyes drop to her panties down by her ankles. Raising my eyebrows I say under my breath, "Oh shit." Blood. Tippy started her period and she's got cramps. Girl still gets them bad even now. Damn. How do I explain this to a 6-year-old brain?

I reach into my purse for a pad. Today I have a couple along with tampons but can't use those. I kneel in front of Tippy and lift her chin up with my right hand so she can see my face.

"Bleeding," she says out loud with tears beginning to drop.

Huh. Now she wanna speak. Before I can talk to Tippy about what's happening, a lady in the stall next to us says, "Is everything OK?"

I start to say none of your damn bizness, but this ain't the time to get indignant. Darius says we gotta be cool in case Ellis has his peeps on our trail.

"Yes ma'am," I answer, turning up my noise. Hmm. She's taking a shit. What happened to courtesy flushing? I grab both sides of Tippy's cheeks with my hands and pull her close enough to whisper in her right ear. "Look you know you ain't 6 years old. You are a grown woman. What is happening to you happens to all women once a month. You started your period. I will explain more about this later. Right now let me help wipe you down, put this pad in your panties to soak up the menstrual flow. OK? She nods.

Damn. Between me helping Tippy and smelling shit, I'm fit to be tied. Finally I say to the woman, "Would you mind courtesy flushing please?" Without responding the woman flushes. "Thank god," I whisper. Tippy giggles. "Stinky," she says. I giggle with her. This makes her feel better, helping her to ignore this period fiasco. I wipe down her panties, throw on the pad and make sure she wipes herself good. When she stands up to pull her jeans up, I can barely get around her fast enough to drop my jeans and panties, squat and pissssss! Oh lord. I almost peed on myself.

That was some crazy shit

'Cause when me and Tippy get outside, we're still grinning. Darius is sitting on a stump and jumps up when he sees us.

"Happy to see y'all ladies ok yo. I was 'bout to come in there."

"Hmm. I'm glad you didn't," I say. "As you can see we're fine." I grab Tippy by the hand and we head back to the car.

Me and the girls
Get back on I-5

And soon pass through the grapevine, jam past the Sacramento and San Rosa exits and slide into San Francisco around 7:30. Here will get some real food instead of the chips, cookies, peanuts, pepperoni and Taquitos we've been munching on.

Earlier I decided we'd head over to the pier. I overheard a couple at the rest stop talking during their smoke break. Says it has good restaurants, street entertainment and kids attractions. Perfect I thought. Maybe I can score some brownie points. Make my girl feel more at ease.

TiAnna decided to ride in back with Tippy. She still ain't talking, but she's listening intently to TiAnna talk about female stuff. I keep hearing the word period every now and then. Damn, I'm thinking. I forgot about dat shit. Glad I don't have to deal with dat end of things.

In San Francisco

The cold weather doesn't stop people. The crowded streets lead us all the way to the pier. Glad to be on flat land down here. Those damn steep ass Frisco hills ain't no joke. After passing through the nearest lot a couple of times, a car pulls out of a stall facing the walkway. This puts us at the door almost. We park, hop out of the truck and get smacked in the face by the wind chill coming off the bay.

"Time to button up yo." Me and Tippy had good enough sense to wear our heavy coats from jump. We can thank cold-ass Oregon for dat. TiAnna grabs hers from the trunk, a knee length burgundy wool one in exchange for the short one she was wearing.

"Ha. Forget this trying to look cute shit," says TiAnna, adding a hat to her new outer attire. "Come on girl," she says to Tippy. "Let me help keep you warm." She locks her arm through Tippy's left and snuggles up close, shivering. Tippy giggles through her fuchsia neck scarf wrapped around her head, crisscrossing her mouth and neck. I fall in on the other side of her as she looks at me with those beautiful eyes. I smile, refraining from giving her my usual Darius gotchu wink.

Inside the pier, visitors, bright lights, shops, a myriad of attractions and street entertainers swallow us whole like a hungry gator. Out of my left eye I see Tippy's eyes widen as she scans her new environment. She giggles when one of those damn mimes approach us. I don't call what they do entertaining, but we stop and let him do his thing. Hey. They have something in common. Neither of 'em talking.

We decide to eat at a seafood restaurant where inside our waiter seats us at a table near a window, overlooking the water. TiAnna and Tippy take a chair next to the window with me still by Tippy's side on guard duty. I order Lobster Fettuccini, T orders fried Halibut and Tippy whispers to TiAnna she wants shrimp fried rice, which is one of her favorites. Her knowing this gives me hope.

After dinner, we spend the next hour touring the aquarium, feeding the sea lions and riding the merry-go-round. We play darts and I won Tippy a big brown Teddy Bear. She smiles and hugs him tight. I hold back from saying, *I want Teddy to remind you of just how cuddly I am.* TiAnna's looking at me smiling. She's probably thinking *Negro please.* But hey, I'm horny as hell. No telling how long this setback will last. Until then, no fuckin'!

Around 9:30 the crowds start to dwindle as the pier prepares to shut down. We run to a cafe and grab dessert to go – me a Butterhorn and a cup of coffee. Tippy and TiAnna order strawberry shortcake and hot chocolate. Tippy told me once the 2 of 'em love strawberries. Another good sign. We make the grocery our final stop, so T can purchase some personal items for Tippy. I buy more snacks.

Me and the girls

Are back on the road by 10:30. We have another 6 hours of driving before we reach Oxnard where my Uncle Dan lives. Uncle

Dan, mom's brother, is expecting us. I didn't have time to go into details but told him I'd give him the lowdown once we get there.

A half hour later, the girls finish smacking and drinking coco. TiAnna crawls up front, giving Tippy back her space. She lays down and pulls the blanket up over her head and goes right to sleep. TiAnna covers up, cocking back her seat.

"You OK?" she asks. "You want me to drive?"

"Naw yo. I like driving. Helps me think."

"Well cool. I'ma be snoring here in a minute."

"Do your thing yo. By the way, good looking out," I say, tapping the side of her arm with my right fist. I think she heard me before she started snoring like she promised. I do appreciate TiAnna's help with Tippy. I hope we can continue double-teaming my girl back to health.

13

Help's a Comin'

January 2, 2013
Downtown Portland

Mr. High and Mighty sitting behind the bench is piercing me with his eyes as if I'm gonna crack. No sir. Not a chance in hell. I've come too far with the upper hand and I intend to keep it. This is serious bitness. My future is at stake.

"Mr. Ellis," says the Honorable Multnomah County Judge Munson. I acknowledge him with a nod. Then the judge says, "I know this was a tough decision. It would be for any father. However, I am inclined to agree with you and Dr. Ryan. Therefore, your petition to have your daughter LaTonya Loretta Ellis placed on a 72-hour mental health hold for further evaluation is granted. Since you do not know where she is at this time, we will issue a warrant for her arrest. Upon arrest authorities will take the defendant directly to the mental health facility. Is that reasonable Dr. Ryan?"

Dr. Ryan turns to Robert Ellis sitting to her left. She meets his eyes briefly then back to the Judge. "Yes, Judge Munson that is reasonable. Mr. Ellis and I thank you for your assistance. We all want what's best for Ms. Ellis."

Ellis nods in agreement with the good doctor. This time he even shows the judge some emotion. Draw some water to his eyes.

"Courts adjourned," the judge says.

"All rise," the Bailiff announces.

Outside the courtroom and away from extra ears, Ellis walks over to Dr. Ryan. Her face is stern and he can see she's doing her damn'dest to hold back her anger. Whatever.

This is my game to win Ellis is thinking. He then says, "Well congratulations counselor," and extends his right hand. The good doctor ignores his gesture. "Now now. We must keep up appearances." He grabs her hand and shakes.

Scowling, pulling her hand away she whispers, "You got what you want so I would appreciate it if you would leave me the hell alone."

"Ha. Your check's in the mail. If I were you, I would enjoy it," says Ellis grinningly. "We all got we want." Then he walks away leaving Dr. Ryan to fume some more and wish like hell she could spit in his face.

If only. Huh. She got herself into a mess years ago and thank goodness it was to my advantage. She has no choice but to help me keep my daughter locked away from her $100 million trust I borrowed. All for the good of RJ Builders and Designs. I'm sure y'all calling me all kinds of S.O.Bs and shit. But look here. I plan to pay it back. Someday. Hmm. Wonder where my darling daughter is. Damn! Time to phone home girl. Time to phone home.

14

No friend of mine

January 2, 2013
Back in Portland

"Well hello Dr. Ryan. Or shall I call you Sheila."

"What the hell do you want Robert!" I say tersely. I shouldn't have picked up the phone, but whatever he wants, I need to hear him and be done.

"Now, now. Is that anyway to speak to a friend?"

"You're not my friend! Now why the hell are you calling me? You got what you wanted."

"Now look here Sheila. We ain't out of the woods yet. Not 'till you pick up my daughter."

"Robert! The police just received the warrant so hold your horses. LaTonya will be in custody within the next hour."

"That's what I like to hear doctor. As long as you play by the rules, we all agreed on, we won't have anything to worry about."

"You made your point Robert. So please leave me be."

"Righto Dr. Ryan. I'll be in touch." He hangs up, finally.

"Damn him!" I say, tossing my phone near the bottom of my feet curled up on the sofa. I haven't even had time to pee!

Not more than 10 minutes ago

I stick the key into my front door and walk into my waterfront abode after having to succumb to an emergency court hearing the day after New Year's. I kick off my heels, throw my coat and bag on the dining room table, one of the first pieces of furniture I cross when I enter. I am so tired I can't find the strength to take off this $700 navy blue suit.

"Good thing I don't have a social life. The highlight of mine is my townhome, but she's clear out on Hayden Island where the traffic getting here is horrendous. Generally, I manage a smooth sail from downtown across the Marcum or Fremont Bridges, depending on the time of day, up I-5 heading north until I get close to the Jantzen Beach exit. My exit is the last one before you hit the bridge leading into Vancouver. This stretch of freeway heading into Washington State is famous for the before you cross the bridge bottleneck. If the bridge goes up, wait time can turn into an hour during rush hour for Washingtonians. This means I'm stuck too, along with other Oregonians who live, work and visit the island. We are forced to endure the pain and suffering caused by those damn Washington travelers. Sitting in traffic, I often play a game I invented called "Count the Oregon license plates." That's how you know who's jamming the highway – them! They travel to and from daily, using our services, taking our jobs and as a thank you, continue to say NO to building a new bridge. I hope they legalize marijuana, which is one of their ballot initiatives. Maybe they'll smoke enough to stay at home. Personally, I'm all for instituting a toll. This will at least give me satisfaction for impeding on my get home quick time, especially when I still live in this state and pay high property taxes for a house I rarely see. Assholes! There. Venting out loud makes me feel much better."

I don't know how much more of this I can take. I've broken the law not once but twice. Tippy is at the mercy of her father because of my stupid sister. I should have never let myself be talked into this. What we started years ago could land us in prison.

The police interrupted my plans

I'm wit' my girl. We was even thinkin' 'bout taking Darius's Range rover out for a spin. So, I let them muthafuckas knock for a while before I answer the door. When I do, I don't even say hello and I'm standin' here in my draws and a T-shirt showin' no respect. The cop standing in front of the other 2 starts talkin'.

"Hello. My name is officer Ludlow with the Portland Police Department. We're looking for a LaTonya Loretta Ellis. We have a warrant for her arrest."

"Ain't no LaTonya Loretta Ellis here," I say defiantly. I'd smack the stank outta this smug muthafucka and his pawtna's but I can't let today be the day they kill anotha brotha.

"Well sir. We understand she is here and has been since New Year's Eve. Please tell her to come out. If not, we are bound by this warrant to come in and retrieve her."

"Like I said officer, no one by that name is here. Just me and my lady."

"And who is your lady?"

"Ain't your business officer. She ain't done nothin' wrong and neither have I."

"Now look here son. We can arrest you for interfering in police business. I hope we don't have to take this up a notch."

Ooo man, I wanna lunge at 'im. Fuck all this tryin' to be calm and shit. Always makin' excuses to kill brothas. They want me, but they ain't gunna get me. Jodeci too slick for dat.

"Babe, be cool," says Trisha my lady. She walks up and stands beside me, wearing tight blue jeans and a T-top. When they see her, they probably wish they could say something smart about this white girl with this dark chocolate, handsome brotha. I am buffed, which comes with the territory. When I let peter loose on my girl, she hollers louder than a muthafucka.

"I'm cool girl. These blues just havin' a hard time wit' no LaTonya Loretta Ellis lives here shit."

"Well she sho better not be," says my girl tryin' to sound soulful. She don't need to do dat to please me. All she gotta do is spread 'em wide when peter comes callin'.

"Ma'am I'm officer Ludlow and we have a warrant. We were told this young lady was here with a gentleman by the name of Darius Broussard. Heard of him?"

"Darius ain't here neither officer Ledlaw," I answer for my girl, purposely saying the officer's name wrong. He's really gettin' me riled up. If my girl wasn't standin' next to me rubbin' my back makin' me all horny an shit, I don't know what I woulda down by now.

"Baby just let the officers in so they can see they're not here. They can't touch nothin' else. Right officers," Trisha says.

"Sheeeit, I don't trust them mutha -"

"Babe," Trisha interrupts, punchin' me.

"Here's the warrant ma'am. You can see for yourself what it gives us permission to do," says Ludlow.

My girl grabs and reads the paper word for word. She ain't no dummy y'all. She's smart. Has a Paralegal Degree and works in the DA's office. And she's studying to be a lawyer. Huh. I got my ear to the ground. So, if a nigga get messed up, she can help. I ain't stupid now. I know how to pick 'em. I did finish high school. Uh-huh. Went to Jefferson back in the day some 10 years ago when we was hot. I even played a little basketball until I found out not every nigga can go pro. But every nigga can game and slang some dope if he need to.

And that's what I do. I sho can't rap, can't get no job 'cause I ain't settling for slanging burgers. I ain't starving for noo-baa-dee and don't give a damn what they say 'bout a brotha neitha. Don't want us to slang, give us some decent jobs.

"It's cool baby. If these officers do somethin' else outside of this warrant, we'll sue 'em," my girl says with a big wide smile lookin' dead at Ledlaw.

So, in come dem muthafuckas and we follow 'em just to make sure. Me on Ledlaw, Trisha on another and my partner Stank on the third one. Stank was in the living room chillin' when we came in. He a mean dude and ugly too. We call him stank 'cause he gotta fucked up attitude. Mad all the time and he hate cops. One shot his baby brother in the leg back in the day. Says he tried to resist arrest after he got caught with a little bit a dope. Not enough to get time just a fine for selling a dime. Huh. Now you see why I can't be no rapper.

Stank's baby brother can't walk but on one leg 'cause his right one is paralyzed. Doctors fucked it up operatin'. I think they did it on purpose. Dude didn't have no insurance. Back then I wish I'da known Trisha. I coulda helped Stank get his brother some money for them doctors' malpracticing. Oh, by the way, my full name's Jodeci Watkins. Not for real doe. I gotta birth name but I ain't tellin' y'all what dat is. My girl don't even know. Sheeit. I don't trust 'er all like dat. Anyway, I got my reasons for keepin' to myself and it don't concern none a y'all nosey muthafuckas! Ha! Maybe one day I'll tell you what planet I'm from, but for now, mind yo bitness.

The officers complete their search and plant themselves in our front room. "So y'all mutha – uh – officers satisfied?" I say lookin' at Trisha. She's shakin' her head. She probably wanna say nigga please but she ain't got it like dat neitha. I tol 'er don't take the black talkin' shit too far. Say the wrong thing I won't be responsible for my actions. And she betta not try dat suin' me shit.

"Do you know where we might find Mr. Darius Broussard or LaTonya Ellis? This is his house?" That Ledlaw asks some silly ass questions. Do I look like I'ma tell him? Yeah dey ova there. Go get 'em. Stupid cop.

"Naw. I'm just a roomie. We don't keep tabs on each other." Ledlaw looks at me like he's tryin' to figure if I'm lyin'. I am but so what. He can threaten me all he wants too. We ready for 'em.

Ledlaw hands me a card, which Trisha quickly grabs 'cause I be damned if I'ma take dat cop card.

"If we hear from them, we'll tell them to call you," Trisha says politely.

"Thanks," Ledlaw says,

Once the cops step outside my front door, I slam it as hard as I can. Sho felt good.

I grab Trisha and softly kiss her on the mouth. Then I slap 'er on the ass and tell 'er to meet me upstairs for an afternoon snack. After she's outta sight I head back into the livin' room.

Stank is on the phone. "Alright man," he says. "We covered yo ass. The next one's on you." He hangs up.

"Wha'dup?" I ask Stank about the call.

"Settlin' in," says Stank.

"My man Darius," I say. "He love dat girl."

15

Ain't karma truth?

January 2, 2013
Druid Hills – Atlanta

I'm sitting with my lady Loretta in one of the smaller TV rooms of her big ass house she once shared with my brother. Her parents bought it back from Robert, so Loretta could be in a familiar setting when she left the hospital. Doctors say keeping comatose patients in their own home can sometimes help. Loretta's parents hired a new staff. They still live here, which helps this place feel less like a museum. Hell. There's something to be said about having an average

American house like mine with 3 bedrooms, 1 bathroom and an ensuite.

We're watching the news about Church on the Way. Pastor Bradley and his wife got busted for child sex abuse, pornography and victimizing their foster children. Loretta was almost a victim when she was 12. The son-of-a-bitch tried to seduce her, but Loretta's mama – Mrs. Joselyn Oliver – told her she was imagining things. The pastor left Loretta alone thanks to her father who was also responsible for the Bradley's getting out of the foster care business years later. Joselyn begged Franklin to keep things quiet to avoid a public scandal. Frankly, I don't think she gave a damn about the church and the children. They were just collateral damage.

Joselyn Oliver is one of the most prominent Black Republican women in Georgia. She believes her name and status is more important. Franklin, being the good man that he is, did what she wanted. He had a long chat with the pastor, who tried to blame Luanne, who was 15 at the time, but she had video evidence. She gave the video to Loretta, who gave it to her mama who handed it off to Franklin. Joselyn also didn't care much for Luanne anyway, and like I say, the other children were just victims of their own circumstances. According to the gospel of Joselyn, their parents are to blame. Finally, the Bradley's get busted after all these years. Joselyn's association with the church – well – she hasn't been active for the past several months. She became ill before all this went down and believes this happened because the Lord was tryin' to spare her good name. Unfortunately, Joselyn has breast cancer. Same thing my mama had and died from.

"This is good news baby. I'm glad they got the bastard. I ain't never got over what he tried to do to you."

Loretta attaches her eyes to mine, smiles and says, "You loved me back then and didn't know me yet Rae."

"Yeah but I know you now and you're hurting inside. I feel you Loretta," I say putting my arm around her.

"I'm feeling you too," she says teasingly.

"Well how 'bout this," I say with a grin. "We go upstairs and do some real feelin' before your mama gets up from her nap. She'll be callin' you over, taking your attention."

"Ooo Rae. You're not jealous?"

"Naw baby. She needs you especially wit' her facing surgery."

"Yeah. Mama losing both her breasts is gonna be tough."

I lean closer to Loretta and pull at her yellow sweater. "Hey baby. I don't mean to be heartless, but all this talk about breast got me wanting to play doctor. Girl you can wear a knit sweater." I drop my head down and kiss one of her breasts then the other, looking up with pleading eyes.

"Come on here," Loretta says. She stands up, grabs me by the hand and pulls me along back up to our love nest on the east wing.

Outside of Atlanta in Conyers

"Mama you gotta be kiddin'. Robbie yo real baby daddy? He nothin' but a low life! Didn't mind me suckin' his dick when I was 16!"

"So, will you find her for me Luanne? Y'all still cousins. I need her to know who her real mama is and I didn't mean no harm. I tried to go back and get her but she was gone."

"Her name is Chelsea huh?"

"This is what they tell me. She's who Don Juan left me for. My baby was no more than a girl herself."

"She Robbie's baby too. Cain't wait to tell 'em mama."

"No! Please! He got too much power. No tellin' what he'll do to squash that secret. He was sleeping wit' a ho."

"OK mama. Calm down. I won't tell Robbie nuttin. Get some rest." I sit wit' the woman I call mama 'till she falls asleep. I will find

Chelsea like she wants. As for not tellin' Robbie the truth, I can't keep that promise.

Jeremy Simms

Here in Miami it's 65 degrees and warm enough for me to lay out on my back balcony with shorts on. Every now and then a breeze passes through the surrounding exhaust fumes. Such is life living off campus. I'm still close enough to the political science building where I take some of my classes. I jog the 2 miles most of the time. Keeps me in shape so I can run fast down the field and make those touchdowns.

Right in the middle of chillaxin' my man Damon calls in from ATL. "My man wassup," I ask answering the phone.

"Keeping warm," says Damon.

"Yeah that's right," I say. "Y'all dealing with typical ATL weather. Cold and wet."

"Yeah man," says Damon. "Hell we may even get some snow."

"Ooowee," I say. "You coulda been down here enjoying the sun like I am right now. Shoot. We got sun, white sandy beaches with turquoise water and Mm, Mm, Mm beautiful women. Miami's the truth man. Even in January," I say, bragging.

"Miami already got you Jeremy. You put 'em into the Bowl."

"Yeah man. Your boy's on higher ground, but the team could use a strong linebacker like you Damon. If we had you, we coulda been one of the teams fightin' it out over at the Gardens instead of Notre Dame or Alabama. Our boy Carl Woods gotta a ways to grow into your shoes man."

"He a'ight man, but you right though. He not like yo boy here Damon."

I can tell Damon is grinnin' from ear-to-ear and I'm glad. We haven't spoken much since he paid me a visit last fall. He even skipped out on me the next day saying he had to get back to ATL right after he met up with his girl Delinda's baby brother who landed his ass in jail out in Dade County. He's up on drug charges wit' 2 of his gangbanging boys. They came all the way to Miami to pick up some dope. Silly fools. Because of Delinda, Damon's tryin' to help a brother who don't deserve his help. He's a gangbanger to the core who ain't gonna amount to nothin' because he don't want nothin'. He's goin' down on this one for sure.

"I'm cool wit' Miami anyway Jeremy. The Trayvon Martin shit got me mad as hell. Stand yo ground? Self-defense? Bullshit! I'm betting on Zimmerman gettin' off."

"Let's hope not Damon. A not guilty verdict would cause a hella mess around here. I gotta enough to deal wit'."

"Huh no lie. How's Chel, ahhh Stephanie."

"Man Damon. Her being pregnant ain't cool. Now, if she were Tippy, I could handle being a young daddy."

"Look Jeremy, you make sure you get a paternity test."

"I still get the feelin' y'all didn't take to each other when you were here. What happened Damon?"

"Man, she gives me a bad vibe. Watch yourself. You're still rebounding anyway."

"Well Damon after how I left things wit' Tippy, I deserve what I'm getting I guess."

"Naw Jeremy. Nobody deserves that. So beware."

"Dang Damon you sound like you know something. What's the deal?"

"Just watchin' out for you man. We're boys Jeremy from way back."

"Thanks for lookin' out. Say Damon, I'm headin' out to Vegas in a couple of weeks wit' a couple of friends to let loose. You should come along. We'll be down there for a weekend."

"A'ight man," says Damon. "I'll make a note. I could use some releasin'."

Damon Studdard

After I hang up with Jeremy, I get to thinkin' about the shit wit' Stephanie who is Chili, a stripper and an ex ho. She disappeared when Don Juan got killed last year. The ATL police still looking for her. I want to tell Jeremy the truth but she's got me pinned against the wall. Please don't judge me y'all. I do plan to come clean. Jeremy's gotta know the real deal. Chili is way too dangerous.

In the meantime, I gotta deal wit' the latest news from my girl Delinda. Earlier today she told me she was pregnant. I held this bit a bad news from Jeremy given he has his own shit. I also didn't wanna hear him say I told you so. Jeremy calls Delinda a hoodrat. She lives with her mama in the projects and graduating from high school this year. She is about the best thing to happen to her crackhead mama and criminal brother.

Delinda a'ight. She can be a lotta fun and we have good sex. We do use condoms so I'm pretty puzzled by this whole thing. I don't believe they just break. I figure she got scared because I was lookin' at colleges around the state. Bet she thought if she got pregnant, I would take her along and one day marry her. Marrying ain't what I want with Delinda. My mama sure don't like her. She believes Delinda is using me for a way out – her meal ticket. OK. Maybe. I do have a bright future ahead in football. I'm going to the NFL no doubt and do commercials on the side. Your boy ridin' high off an energy drink spot he did last year. Got to flex my muscles and throw a football around. Hell, I'm a good catch. I'd keep my temper in check if I didn't have to deal wit' Delinda's crazy ass. I am also a little romantic. I bought her flowers once. I believe on her birthday. Don't take much to please her. All the other guys she's been wit' ain't gave her nothin' but a dick.

Mama and Jeremy's mama are friends. They go to the same church and always talk about their sons marrying church girls. Jeremy's mama was proud when he got wit' Tippy. It hurt her as much as Jeremy when the shit went down thanks to her now infamous brother Judge Simms. The payback train has finally reached his stop for the shit he's pulled on everybody.

Mama wants me to date Marietta James who is a real devout Baptist. Marietta is going to Atlanta University like me. She's sticking close to home cause of family so she says. Deep down she thinks I'll cave. Ha. Hate to break the news to her. There are too many honeys at the university and I still have crazy ass Delinda to deal wit'.

I go to church wit' mama sometimes 'cause she practically twists my arm and makes me feel bad if I say no. She says I should be thanking God for all my benefits. I tol 'er I do every day, in my own way and don't believe I have to go to church. Especially since Marietta accosts me every time I go. She can be as pushy as Delinda. Sits right next to me like we're together. Damn. A brother can't even breath, take in the sights and look at some of the other honey. Like Angie. The way she be lookin' at me I bet she gets down.

Marietta a'ight lookin' but she ain't someone I can have fun wit'. Sow my wild oats like wit' Delinda who's now pregnant and I don't have the heart to tell mama. Delinda says she's not getting an abortion. I don't know if I like the idea neither but to have Delinda as my baby mama ain't somethin' I'm lookin' forward to.

Delinda is actually beautiful, dark-skinned and built like a brick shit house. She don't wear weaves but keeps her real hair straightened, which comes to her shoulders. Yeah. She one of the good-hair sista's. But Delinda's downfall is her temper she got from her wacked mama. Delinda is mean as a Rattlesnake. Always tryin' to cuss me out over some bullshit. I had to get at her a few times – shut her down without smacking her. If this is payback, it sure is a bitch times 2!

The search begins

"So, Mrs. Ellis, you say this Chelsea is probably Stephanie and she is currently living in Miami?"

"Yes detective. I want her found. I'll pay any amount," I say. "And you can call me Luanne."

"Good then Luanne. I got most of what I need for now. If anybody can track her down, I'm your man."

16

I spoke to soon

January 2, 2013
4:30 a.m. Oxnard, Cali.

Me and the girls make it into sleepy Oxnard early morning. Funny this city doesn't change much when she's awake – for real. Living here, I found the city of 200,000 people real boring. She reminds me of Portland. The black population here is also small. On the upside, this coastal city brought out my sunny disposition when I could see my way clear to LA for a weekend – less than an hour's drive by car or bus.

Inside Uncle Dan's house

"Thanks for putting us up Uncle Dan," I say, coming back into the living room of their new 3-bedroom home. He and Aunt Jenny purchased this house in a new development finished last year. My uncle says they were offered a really good deal and bought it regardless of the extra space they don't need.

Years ago, they opted not to have children, which leave the extra bedrooms for Jenny's family when they're in town. When I lived with them, we shared a 2-bedroom townhouse on the other side of Oxnard. With only one bathroom, things got a little tense. I used that as my excuse to run the streets until Uncle Dan tried to clamp down on me. I refused to fly right doe and had a difficult time showing respect to any authority figure. I blamed my father for my fowl attitude. My hatred for him led me into the streets doing shit I had no bitness doing. What got me started down that road was this black dude Leon I met in school. He was trouble, but hell, so was I. Leon's mama planned to send him to Compton to live with his older brother. He invited me to go. Says I needed to get away from all these white folks and learn about my black side. The next day, I decide to trade-in Oxnard for Compton and left with Leon and without saying good-bye. I was 16 yo.

In Compton, I stayed with him at his brother Langston's house, who turned out to be gay and had another dude living with him. I tried to ignore them as much as I could. Sometimes yo I wanted to yell "take dat gay shit elsewhere" especially when they got to huggin' on each other. Damn homos. But I was in dair house, which was real nice but in a rough area. Langston tried to get Leon to fly right. They'd end up arguing and Leon would call him all kind of fags and shit. Pissed me off 'cause he was on the verge of getting us kicked out. Too keep the peace we hung in the streets and got introduced into a crew. We was always up to no good and had to watch our backs 24/7. I still remember the face of the Mexican who threatened to take me out next time he saw me. A few months in I decided to get out. I reconnected with Uncle Dan.

"Are the young ladies settled?" Uncle Dan asks.

"Oh yeah," I say. "They was barely woke when we came in."

Uncle Dan gets quiet. He's in his robe and house shoes and kicked back in his recliner with his arms folded across his waist. Uncle Dan is a big, tall dude, weighing nearly 300 pounds. He's a foreman for a construction company, making good money. Enough for him and Aunt Jenny. They've been married for 15 years. Aunt Jenny is an elementary school teacher. For a white woman in her 40's, her face is flawless and she doesn't need make-up. She once told me the students were enough kids for her. They probably keep her looking young.

My uncle bends his eyebrows and stares right into me, waiting for me to tell him what's up. So, I tell 'em everything, including Loretta being alive. At first, he thought I was makin' the shit up until I went on the Internet and showed 'im some stuff, including who Tippy's father was. I also tol 'im you won't find pictures of my girl doe cuzz she witnessed her mama's murder when she was 6. Uncle Dan believes me now. He sees how hard I'm tryin' to hold back the tears.

"Damn Darius. How do you get yourself into these dangerous situations? There's gotta be someone in the criminal justice system who can help."

"I wish dat were true Uncle Dan, but her daddy know eeh-vree-baaa-day. Yall can't hold us for a minute I'll make a way. I got cash."

"Darius, you're family and my sis, you can't count on now. You stay as long as you need to. I'll talk to Jenny in private. We'll come up with somethin'."

"Thanks Uncle Dan. This means a lot yo."

Upstairs where the girls are

Near the bathroom, the door is cracked and I hear TiAnna talkin'. She comes out the bathroom and I'm standing there ready. I ask, "Who da hell was you talkin' too at 6:00 a.m.!"

She steps back nervously. "Dr. Ryan," she answers. "She left me several messages and I called her. She's also my shrink too Darius."

84

"Damn T!" I'm shaking my head furiously, wanting to slam-dunk this wacked broad. "Please tell me you didn't tell 'er where we was!"

"No. She asked but I said we were on our way to Atlanta."

"You gotta be kiddin'! Are you dat damn stupid! Shit! They can track us off those damn cell towers. Girl do you know what you did!? Huh!? My boy watchin' my house told me dey got a warrant to lock Tippy up in the nut house! Who do you think authorized it?"

"Tippy's daddy not Dr. Ryan," T answers.

"Da hell she wouldn't yo! She did along wit' Tippy's daddy! I knew dat shit! I knew it all along. Dey in cahoots!"

"Darius, I, I didn't – I, I'm sorry," says TiAnna. Darius has me scared and I can't stand him yelling. I want to hit somethin' bad and I ain't talkin' about the walls.

"You ain't nothin' but trouble girl! First you stab some crazy muthafucka to death and ask me to clean it up yo! Now I gotta clean dis shit up before they take away your best friend yo!"

Uncle Dan and Aunt Jenny come running up the stairs. My uncle walks over to me and Jenny stays near the staircase. "Darius! What the hell."

TiAnna backs away and runs into the room she's sharing with Tippy. She comes back out with her coat and purse, dashes past me, Uncle Dan and practically knocks Jenny over as she descends the steps and out the front door. SLAM!

I don't care. I hope she stays gone. Y'all may think I'm bein' cold but dealin' wit' 2 wacked broads is makin' me crazy. My girl dat's cool but takin' on her friend? Damn. All was going so well.

I tell Uncle Dan what just happened. He agrees we should take every precaution. He mentions that he and Jenny own a vacation home in Tahoe City where me and Tippy can stay as long as we need too.

I pack our things thinking of a plan dat could set me and my girl straight. Headin' over to Nevada might be our ticket to freedom. As

Amanishakhete

for TiAnna, if she shows before we leave fine. If not, she on 'er own. Darius Winston Broussard ain't gonna sweat yo.

17

Rougher than tougher

January 3, 2013
Tahoe City, Nevada

I gas up before we leave Oxnard and drive this baby straight through to our off-season destination. Our afternoon arrival catches the last bit of warm sun. First, I stop in town to grab a few things from the store. My girl's sleeping. For her safety, I snap the child locks on before running in. I'm expecting the tinted windows to keep the sun from disturbing her rest.

In hindsight

I know T's sudden disappearance is affecting Tippy. Things were starting to feel familiar for her. I tried to explain. Rather than tell her about our argument, I'm surprised she didn't hear, I said T had to get back to Atlanta for family reasons. She'd be checking in soon. I tell

Tippy about what was going on in Portland and to keep her safe, we had to make a quick move. I show her, her diary and photo album and say we'll go through this little by little, to put the pieces in place.

At the urging of Uncle Dan, I did try calling TiAnna a few times. She never answered but she did send a text, "Take care of my BFF. I can handle myself." No doubt I'm thinking. What she experienced in ATL made her tough as nails. Maybe parting ways is for the best. The girl could snap at any time, making me or Tippy her next victim. My uncle says he'll keep the welcome mat out for her and call me if she returns.

Aunt Jenny helped Tippy get ready – shower, change clothes. TiAnna did talk to her about personal stuff, but I asked auntie to make sure she was cool on how to handle the period thing. I don't want the responsibility. In the past when she had cramps doe, I would rub her stomach and back. Offering this as an option may make her uncomfortable.

Inside the store in Tahoe

I get some stares. Probably don't see black men much in d'ese parts. I have on my best smile, nod and say "Hello how are you?" to everyone I pass. Uncle Dan told me before we left to drop his name to alleviate suspicion. Folks here know Dan and Jenny Broussard. He said he'd make a call ahead to friends and tell we're coming. They'd pass our names around.

At checkout, the lady says with a smile, "Good time to visit. Not as crowded."

"Yeah. My Uncle Dan agrees."

"Dan?" she says, trying not to sound nosey.

"Dan Broussard," I answer.

"Ohhh. Dan and Jenny are wonderful people. They were here over Christmas."

"So he said. By the way my name is Winston. I'm came with my wife Lisa."

"Nice to meet you Winston. I'm Sheila. My husband's name is Dan too."

I smile and say, "Well that's easy to remember." I pay for the items in cash. I got my uncle's credit card doe. For now, we cool.

The house is located on the other side of the lake winding around a narrow road. I drive slow staring at all d'ese big-ass trees and big blue lake. Up ahead, I see a road off to the left where I turn and follow the narrow passage with more tall trees hugging us on both sides. In back against a hillside is a light green, 1-bedroom cottage. A hiking trail begins in front, hooks around and up the hill. This is probably what my girl needs. Fresh air, quiet and a taste of the outdoors to bring her mind back to reality.

I pull the truck into the garage adjacent to the house and park alongside Uncle Dan and Jenny's blue little car, one of those cars dem hamsters be riding in on TV. My uncle says when they come here for extended visits, they choose to blend in, using a car with local plates.

We enter through the recently remodeled kitchen. Uncle Dan says he decided to use his contracting skills last summer overlooking the purpose for him hanging here, which is to kick back and relax. He painted the walls beige, put in granite counter tops, hardwood floors and a bay window above the kitchen sink, facing the backyard. He took out the backdoor and put in a sliding glass one. In the far right corner, he built a breakfast area for 2 and then trimmed everything in white – the cupboards, window seals and matching appliances. This suits Aunt Jenny's traditional taste.

We go through the entrance to the right, leading into the front room. It's a little chilly in here, so I turn on the gas fireplace.

"My, my," I say shaking my head at the place. In here is where Uncle Dan needs to put in some work yo. I look over at my girl right beside me. She still ain't spoken, but she did just wake up. She spots the purple couch across from the fireplace, goes over and sits down with her coat on. She sits sideways, pulls her feet up and stretches out, dropping the right side of her head on the sofa back. I follow her over and offer to take coat but she shakes her head.

"I'll get your blanket," I say. On my way to the bedroom on the left side of the house, I glance at the rest of the décor – a couple of purple cushy chairs, a wooden coffee table on top of beige shag carpet and old pale pink wallpaper. Wooo!

After setting our bags down, I go through and grab my girl's wool fuchsia blanket and Teddy. Did I mention this blanket was her favorite? Tippy begged me not to tell anyone yo. She's been dragging the damn thing around since childhood. She says she was 5 when her mama bought it for her, during a time she discovered how fuchsia crazy she was. Now y'all see how much I love dis girl? How many men would be wit' a girl who carries around a favorite blankie? 'Cause she's worth a $100 million you're thinking. Naw for real. I've grown to love dis girl more than y'all know. Fuchsia blankie an all.

"What do you think about this place?" I ask Tippy, laying the blanket over her and handing her Teddy. She don't say nothing but stares at me wide-eyed, lookin' wacky and shit. Dang. I should've remembered to get her a doll, a coloring book and some crayons. Ha! OK y'all I'mo stop.

I sit down at the other end, near the bottom of her feet. She tears up. I hold out my left hand. She hesitates but then gets up and scoots over to where I am. She lays her head on my chest. I put my arm around her and squeeze gently. She's crying bold tears now. I let her do dat without talkin'. I think we sit like dat for about a half-hour except she stopped cryin'.

Finally, I say, "You gonna be alright shawty. I won't let anyone hurt you. I'll keep you safe. You work on getting' better. Remember the wonderful and strong person you are and what we mean to each other."

"K," she says to me softly. This makes my eyes water but I'mo hold back. I gotta be a man and win the battle for both our sakes.

Chili, Chelsea, Stephanie. Who?

Miami's my home too and I've come too far to give up now. I'm pregnant and want Jeremy to be my baby's daddy, but I'm not sure he is. There's only 2 other possibilities and I can't bear the thought. Don Juan is gone for good and Judge Simms I can't have. He's around and not doing so good. All his conniving and scheming caught up wit' 'im. Don't matter to me. He was still one of my best and we allowed ourselves to get close. We broke the rules. Thanks to him I'm able to live freely as long as people who know where I am keep their mouths shut. I often worry about how long a mouth can stay closed. I'd better be ready to call-in one last favor.

1/4/2013
I'm riding the LA high

I was on the first thing smokin' from Oxnard this morning. I can take care of myself. Got cash and can handle bizness.

For right now, I'ma stay high. This is one good thing Chelsea my so-called sissy taught me. Stay up so you won't hurt. I must say, I feel much better. The past few weeks have been hell. I find out daddy ain't my daddy. My daddy Rae is Tippy's daddy who she didn't know was her real daddy until recently, not long after I found out about 'im. Mr. Raymond Ellis, Robert Ellis's brother, who Tippy thought was her daddy but ain't cuz he's been a complete asshole all her life.

In times like these, I miss Virgil. He's locked up but answers my 9/11 when he can. He helped me escape rehab and meet up wit' Tippy in Portland. Leaving that place was my best option. Just wasn't helpin'. All I could do was think about gettin' high to ease the pain of findin' out I won't be able to have kids. I ended up with a bad infection, which made the abortion I had even more necessary.

Amanishakhete

Whissss. Oomph. Haaa. That was a good hit. Mmmm. Better save some for later. Can't blow all the money. Gotta have some for this fancy hotel on Sunset.

When I first entered through the door downstairs, I was greeted by white and gold walls and chandeliers with red velvet décor as the dessert. There was also a fine black bellhop who grinned at me and handed me a flyer. He spoke with an accent – probably Nigerian. "Hello lady," he said. I could tell he wanted some of T. Naw y'all not for me.

I reach over and grab the flyer I laid on the nightstand when I got in. After looking at it I yell out, "Oh hell yeah! I got plans. DaMenace is performing here in LA tonight! Time to get girlishcious!

18
Feelin' it

January 4, 2014
Hollywood

I'm hold up in a 5-star hotel, chilling before my concert. Unfortunately, I can't get my chill on right 'cause I'm here with the wife in name only. She's pissin' the hell outta me on purpose. Holdin' me hostage. Made me drop the divorce in return for her droppin' the charges on Tippy, who whooped her ass deservingly.

Darius was probably the mastermind dat's why I'm keepin' my ear to the ground. I don't trust 'im at all. He may be Jerome's brother but dey ain't nothin' alike. Jerome had a good heart. Tried to save Darius 'cause he got a raw deal thanks to dey daddy. Dat don't give Darius permission to fuck wit' everybody else. Especially not dis white boy. I am DaMenace no joke.

"Uri dis my night! Don't start no shit! Ain't about you, ain't gonna be!"

"Hmph. You need to come on get and hit this," Uri says wit' her hands on her hips, rockin' 'em back and forth.

She's one of those Persian's with thick long brown hair, golden skin and a bangin' body. She even got them full sista lips and a pair of deep set eyes. She ain't bad to look at but she's a liar and a skank. I don't want no part of a woman like dat who lied about bein' pregnant when she can't even get pregnant. All to try and trap a boy. Wit' dis latest stunt, she got me even more wound up. I can tell you dis doe, I ain't stayin' locked up forever. I do plan on ditchin' dis bitch soon. Den I can get on wit' my life.

"You think you gonna wear me down. Ain't no way. You can bet dat. Sheesh. You livin' in la la land Uri." I walk out of the room and into the bathroom to take a shit. Maybe I'll even jack off. "Don't bother followin'. I'm lockin' the door."

"Lock on then!" Uri yells at me as I gladly slam the door in her face. "At least you ain't wit' Miss snooty bitch from Atlanta thinkin' she all that. Hmph."

I hear her but I'ma leave dat alone. Our time together will be over soon enough.

On the east coast
Around the same time
Stephanie called me talking shit. Like she can faze me with her threats. Not a chance. She really don't know the real me. I have no problem protecting me and mine.

"A mutual friend told me your conviction was overturned 'cause you paid him to get your records tossed on a technicality. I've been told where to look for the dead presidents. You feel me?" she says in a soft voice.

I answer her back snidely, "It's a rainy night in Georgia and I feel a chill comin'. You got anythang else?"

"Oh, I got plenty," she says. "When I come callin' be ready."

"Ha, ha, ha. OK darlin'," I say. She hangs up the phone before me and without saying goodbye. She didn't need to tell me who she was. She can't out fox the fox nor catch the wolf and I'm both. Bring it on baby. Bring it on.

Now back to Hollywood

It's almost show time. I make it to my dressing room with Uri close behind. We lucky there's room in here for her ass to sit in the corner and me to kick back on the sofa. I got my stage gear on — holey jeans, a wife beater underneath my jacket and red high top tennis shoes with moussed up hair and a diamond in each ear. I'm ready to go when they call. Until then I'ma keep my eyes closed with a big smile on my face, making Uri wonder.

"Ooo baby hurry on home to me wit' yo fine self," I say out loud for Uri's benefit. "DaMenace is waiting." I got more to say except the guard's knockin'.

"Wassup!" I yell out.

He lets himself in. "Say man," he says. "You got company. A girl name TiAnna downstairs says Tippy told her to stop by and say hey.

Tippy tol' me 'bout this TiAnna but I ain't never met her. Tippy was gonna bring her to my concert last winter wit' Boss Amanishakhete. Dey got sidetracked, meaning Uri got in the way. I notice Uri out of the side of my eye, squinting her nose and lip. She gets mad every time she hears the name Tippy. To mess wit' her I tell my guard to let the girl in.

A few minutes later in comes this milk chocolate, slim little thang wit' a short do, decked out in a burgundy mini-dress and matchin' pumps. She got on sunglasses. She's probably high. Otherwise, there's no need to wear 'im. *The lighting in here matches the mellow darkness of the moonlit night* blah, blah. Dat's actually lyrics to one of my soulful tunes.

I stand and slide over to her tryin' to remain a gentleman. I ain't had none in months, so little DaMenace is showing out – hollering, through my jeans. Don't matter dat Uri's eyes is piercing my back. I'll dry off the blood later. Right now, I am mesmerized by Miss TiAnna's beauty, making me forget all about Tippy until she mentions her.

"Oh and how's she doin'?" I ask with little concern.

"Sheee awww'ight," TiAnna says slowly.

Yeah. She high. I would be too if I didn't have to go on stage in a few. I only smoke dank doe which she ain't on.

"Sheee says uhh sorry she couldn't come."

Hmm. Is she talkin' 'bout last year 'cause I ain't invited Tippy down since all dis shit happened. Actually, I had to cancel and she cussed me out again. I wasn't expecting to hear from her. So, I say, "Oh OK den. No sweat. Glad you could come and enjoy what I g -" Can't finish what I got to say 'cause baby slams me with a kiss, plunging her swirling tongue inside my door. Baby don't stop I'm screamin' inside my head. And I don't mean the one up top. After one final thrust she exits, leaving me droolin' like a crazy white boy hot for a sista. I'm pleadin' through my eyes hoping she'll take mercy on me.

"Meet me at Charlie's in Hollywood after dis. We can talk more 'bout mutual acquaintances," I whisper, keeping the conversation between us. Uri ain't invited. I kiss TiAnna on the cheek, step back and smile. Hell. I might dump Uri's ass tonight if I can hit dis.

I make it to the stage area

And my dick is still hard. Fella Jiles is finishin' up with his hit song Mindless Intensity. The one Darius wrote. Thinking about the enemy makes my dick go limp. Betta make note never to play any of Darius's music when I'm wit' a honey.

"All right y'all! Ready for some-of-dis and some-a-dat?" announces the emcee. The crowd cheers makin' me jump up and down like a wrestler does before hitting the ring.

"Move over Eminem, take a seat Robin Thicke. Make room for your blue-eyed boy Daaaaa Meeenace!

TiAnna still hangin' out

I thought I found a quiet place, but I hear DaMenace blowin' all the way back here. Let me hurry and hit this, so I can get my groove on. Glad I'm in the ladies' room by myself. I need just one more line to keep me up. Uh-huh. I'ma have him tonight. "Swisssss. Mmm. Nice." I wanna take another hit, but I got company.

"Hmm. Whachu want? Shouldn't be sneaking up on folks. Know tellin' what might happen. Didn't yo mama tell you the world is full of crazies?" I say, looking in the mirror at the person standing behind me.

She puts her hands on her hips like she's bad ass and says, "Hmph. Take your sadiddy-ass on back home wit' your girl. You may wanna ask her about me."

I turn up the left side of my mouth. "No need to hoochie. My girl tol' me all about your fake ass. Tryin' to keep a man who don't want you."

"Excuse you," she says tapping the back of my right shoulder.

Ooo snap. I'm like Tippy. 'Oh no she didn't.' I got somethin' for her ass. Let her keep on.

"Uhh, do I make myself clear?" she says.

"Real clear," I say, putting my medicine back in my waist-strapped purse. I turnaround and push past her like I'm leaving. Without her noticing, I reach into my bra and pull out Susie. Then I turn back around facing her back and grab her hair with my left hand. Snapping her head back, Susie makes one clean slice across her neck.

"Ooo looky. What's wrong girl? Say somethin'. Oh you can't. You chockin' and your neck is split droppin' pretty red blood. Hmm. You sure is makin' a mess," I say. I shove her and she stumbles all the way down to the last stall where I push her in with my right foot. Her head hits the stool first – BAM – before she falls to the floor. I close the door, run back to the sink and rinse the blood off my weapon, gloves and floor as much as I can. Clean Susie goes back into my bra. I pull myself together and get out of there quick, passing 2 drunken white girls coming down the hall. They're laughing and horse-playing distracting them from fully noticing me. I look back right when they push open the bathroom door. Moments later, I hear the end of a scream as I make it around the corner.

God you've shown me mercy

I died that night because she killed me while my little girl watched. Thank you God for protecting her from the one who harmed me.

Yes I died that night so I thought. Rather, you lifted me up and showered me with blessings of love and forgiveness. Your spirit kept me breathing but let me sleep until I was of the right mind to live out my destiny.

I lived a lie– and still do. I allowed a beautiful soul that chose me as her vessel to suffer for years at the hands of a devil-soul who lost his heart long before me. My little girl lives in her own private hell wondering why I left her. I thank you for the love of another who shields her from the burning flames and who prays for me to rise above the pain, the hurt and the lies.

I died that night but you anointed me. I have arisen with strength and safe from the killer who no longer exists on this plain. She's at peace but not those close to her. I fear their hatred will push them to seek revenge. So I pray in your holy name, God keep us safe and remove us from their path of destruction. The devil-soul must be stopped. Mine is your vengeance and I shall not fail.

Back in Portland

They ain't showin' me no respect. The judge, the police, Dr. Ryan they all messed up! Now I gotta do this myself. Track their asses down.

"Pick up the damn phone Ryan! You're gonna have to face me sooner or later! Uh wait. I'm getting a call. This had better be her." I click over and say, "It's about damn time you called back."

"Hello Robert. How you doing?" says the soft smilingly voice on the other end. It's not Dr. Ryan. She sounds like — but can't be. We buried Billy Paul's Mrs. Jones 9 years ago!

19

It wasn't me

January 4, 2013
Los Angeles

At least they can't blame me for Uri's murder. I was on stage. Your boy was smokin' when the guards cut me short. Called me off stage so 5-O could tell me what happened and question me at the same time. I didn't answer any questions but said, "Can you let a fella breathe first? You just told me someone slit my wife's throat."

They holding me in a room backstage and won't allow me near the crime scene. I sent the guard who got close enough to return with some info. He says, "Man, it's crazy down there. Cops are all over, especially down near the bathroom entrance. They got yellow tape across the door and them damn reporters sniffing around." He also says dey been askin' for me. I ain't commenting or speaking to none of dem vipers.

The cops called in a doctor and coroner to examine Uri's body. She bled out in one of the stalls. I sit for about an hour before 5-O decide to show dey face again. Whoever killed Uri musta been a pro 'cause they took her out with one clean cut. They also have possible witnesses. Two white girls say they passed a black girl in the hall. They didn't get a good look but thought she was wearing a short red dress. My heart stops when dey said dat but I don't react. Dat's what dey want. Dey already tryin' to figure how to blame this on me 'cause I'm the spouse. At least here in LA dey don't know me and Uri's volatile history. The girl these potential witnesses saw puzzles me. TiAnna was by earlier. The dress she had on was burgundy doe. She may have been high but she don't look like she'd kill anybody. Hell. Tippy wouldn't hang wit' anybody dat crazy. I decide to keep dis to myself until I find out what went down.

Finally 5-O says I can go. They leave the room and the guard comes over and hands me an envelope. Inside is a note from TiAnna wonderin' what the hell is goin' on. She mentions she's headin' back to her hotel and I'm welcome to stop in at Room 356.

"Man I need you to get me outta here unnoticed. Got someplace to be." The guard nods and motions for me to follow him. He takes me in the opposite direction from the crowd gathered at the foot of the stage. Rather than use the exit we came through earlier, the guard leads me down a back staircase opening up into a long musty tunnel. A car will meet us on Lincoln Street. VIPs, who want to avoid crowds and camera's come this way. Celebs though coming through the front entrance where they will be greeted by reporters and fans.

"Sweet," I say.

Along the way I think about Uri. Sure we didn't get along. But I wouldn't have wished this on her for nothin'. Whoever did this is a cold muthafucka. I plan to find out who killed Uri. I'll decide den what to do.

1/5/2013 back to Atlanta

Yeah, I'm girlishcious Miss T, flying first class on Delta flight #1955 with no one in the seat next to me. Good thing 'cause I don't want to annoy anyone with my giggling about what I did earlier. Bitch got what she deserved. Had my friend arrested and tried to punk me. Last night AJ told me she was blackmailing him.

"Excuse me Miss. I'm Jonathan your host. May I get you anything?" the steward asks all bubbly. "We have 3 choices for lunch. Would you like to see a menu?"

Jonathan definitely has my attention. Dang he's so gay. Got me thinking about my girl Tommy. "No food for me right now Jonathan but you can bring me a soda," I say. *I could use something for this hangover I'm thinking.*

Speaking of Tommy

He moved out recently. I mean, he got put out. His mama was peeking out the window and caught him kissin' his mystery boo who dropped him off one night after a football game. Tommy sent me an email and says he's hurt by his mama's rejection but glad he doesn't have to keep quiet anymore. He didn't have to tell me or Tippy. We already knew.

I text Tommy this morning after me and AJ rolled outta bed. I needed a place to stay since I decided to return to Atlanta but not to my family's home. Tommy invited me to stay wit' him and his boo who I can't wait to meet.

Here comes gay Jonathan

Who says, "Here's your soda ma'am. I'll be close by if you need anything else."

He put my drink in a wine glass with a slice of lime on the lip. Ain't this cute. "Thank you, Jonathan," I say, purposely giving him a flirtatious wink. He grins and walks away. I lean back and close my eyes. Lucky me. I did get a chance to experience DaMenace.

Once I got away
From the concert

And back to the hotel, I was reminded that everybody in L.A. is always on celebrity watch. Someone shouted, "Brandy!" LOL. I ignored the comment and kept walking. Had to be a white person who said it 'cause I don't look like Brandy.

AJ comes by an hour later. After he tells me the story about Uriella, I give him a big hug. Celebrity central helped my acting skills. I even manage to drop a couple of tears. AJ talked and I offered my support, hoping like hell he don't ask.

He mellows out after we smoke some weed. I also slip into the bathroom to freeze my nose. Then we screw all night. Doing-the-do wit' AJ was a'ight. He good for a white boy and he wanted to eat my coochie, but I wouldn't let him. I have my reasons.

Anyhoo, I was already turned up and hadn't felt that good since Susie killed Joshua.

20
Whole again

January 5, 2013
Atlanta Hartfield Airport

Tommy's mystery boo wasn't who I thought. She and Tommy picked me up from the airport. We get to the car and he introduces me to his pawtna. I can't help but stare at the tall skinny dark-skinned black woman whose gotta be about 40. Her name is Patrice and she's got a lot of make-up covering her long ass nose, round golf-ball eyes and flat forehead. Her blonde wig is styled like that dead actress Marilyn Monroe.

On the drive to Tommy's house I occasionally glance at Patrice who catches me when she looks through her rearview mirror. Hmm.

Tommy's 18 and considered grown under the law, but this female is way too old for him and strange. There's somethin' weird about Ms. Patrice.

Thirty-five minutes later, we arrive at Patrice and Tommy's in Norcross. They live in a nice neighborhood in a large 2-story brick house. Everybody's lawns are well-maintained. Tommy says this is a new development and the homes here – he emphasizes – are pretty pricey. Once inside I'm greeted by sea blue walls with white trim, holding a staircase off to the left. The staircase is also trimmed out in white and white carpet. Wow. White carpet? Now y'all know better. Good thing they laid the foyer floors with dark brown tile for people to wipe they stanky feet.

Patrice offers to take my things to the guest room upstairs. She mentions I will have plenty of privacy and will have my own bathroom. Before she leaves, she looks at Tommy grinning. Reaching up, she pulls off her wig, exposing her close-cut reddish-blonde afro.

"Well holla-me-bad," she says, flippin' his head like a traditional gay boy. "I'll let y'all cuties catch up." Then she switches off up the stairs. Miss Patrice is a drag queen.

"Come on here girl," Tommy says. "Stop starin'."

Ooo. He caught me. Tippy use to get annoyed with me for staring at folks and not caring. I figure why hide. If I wanna stare, I'ma stare.

I start to follow Tommy into the living room opposite the staircase and off to the right of the foyer. I stop at the entry, lean my head in and quickly look around at the spice brown walls. Then down at the floor. Shit. Here go this damn white carpet.

"Tommy want me to take off my shoes?" I ask after noticing he had kicked off his.

"You can if you don't mind. Unless of course yo toes is lookin' rat-tat-tacky."

"Please. When have you known my feet to be rat-tat-tacky," I say mockingly. I kick mine off to the side and step inside.

"This carpet show is warm Tommy."

"Ain't it. Patrice had a floor warmer put in. Makes the place more cozier along with our fireplace. Perfecto for days like this. Girl Hmph. You know how cold and crazy Atlanta metro can get in the winter."

Tommy curls up on the brown leather chair. I choose the loveseat on the other side of the end table, sandwiched between both of us.

"You want some libations Miss T? Girl we ain't got no weed. Patrice can't stand the smell honey."

"Naw. I'm cool," I say even though I'm not. I could use a hit of somethin' but I didn't dare bring it with me on the plane. I did the last before I left LA and right after kickin' AJ out. He hung his head like a sick puppy. Like I tol'em, the sex was good but time for us to both move on. He tried to kiss on me anyway and I read his ass. He's lucky that's all he got. He finally left. Ugh white boys. They so damn clingy. Those white tricks use to be the same way. Had the nerve to say "I love you," after they raped me. I think I'll consider dissin' AJ, payback. My Susie killing his wife was an added bonus. White boy may end up getting blamed anyway.

"Girl, tell me what's going on with Tippy. On your text you said she flipped the hell out!"

"Naw Tommy. You first. I wanna hear all about you and Miss Patrice." I'm stalling but do want to hear about this ol' dude Tommy call himself messin' with.

The first thing out of Tommy's mouth is, "Honey the sex is good." He jumps up from the chair and drops his ass twerking.

"Girl there's more to tell, so get comfortable. I'll get us some snackaroos and soda. You sure you don't want anything? Patrice drinks gin."

"Yeah maybe I will. I'll take mine with ice," I say.

"Ooo," says Tommy turning up his nose. "Gin with ice? Well ohhhkaaay. You the one drinking it. I shall return." I make my signature exit – pose with my left hand on my belly and the other dropped by my side. Toss my head back and sashay away. "Holla-me-bad!"

Patrice is so foul

"Girl, I wouldn't worry about her. Tommy says she be talkin' to the same shrink as Jeremy's crazy ex. Hunnnaaay. He be tellin' me everythang. I'll keep you posted."

"Thanks Patrice. You my girl. On my end I wish Jeremy would stop resisting."

"Having his baby oughta be enough Chili. What's wrong with him?"

"Jeremy's like no other man I've known Patrice."

"That's 'cause you ain't been wit' nobody except for that dead muthafucka Don Juan."

"Now Patrice."

"Now Patrice my ass! Good riddens! Always bruisin' you up and shit. No wonder your belly was hurting. Good thing you only had an ulcer."

"I know huh. Scared me, making me think I had cancer or somethin'."

"Thank the good Lord."

"You ain't tryin' to be religious are you Patrice."

"Now look ho. I do believe in God. I just don't go to his churches. His so-called people don't like my ways. God loves my gay good-lookin' drag queen ass no matter what them damn Christians say."

"I'm glad for you Patrice. Maybe I'll believe one day. Right now I got to keep up the pretense and don't want to be forgiven for it. I deserve this after the hell I've been through."

"You right honey. You wouldn't have gotten anything outta the deal if not for Judge what's his name."

"Yep. He's the only man who was good to me. He was still a trick doe."

Judge Simms rescued me from the life right after someone killed my Donny. I can't say I miss him. There was no love. I was just his bottom ho, who was able to talk him into bringing my so-called sissy into the picture and who he ended up liking. Says he remembers seeing her long time ago standing out front of a black college in East Atlanta. He says she made eye contact, turned up her bottom lip and stared at him with her hands on her hips. Donny says in the backa his mind he chose her. Hmph. I shoulda realized what was up when I pointed her out to him shortly after I suggest we kidnap her ass and turn her out. He was way too eager although he resisted the shit earlier.

"So the bitch is back in Atlanta. Wonder what she's up too Patrice?"

"Like I said don't worry. You just take care of my baby, you hear me?"

"Yes, yes mama Patrice. I'll call you soon." Right when we hang up Jeremy walks into the room.

"Who's mama Patrice? Thought your parents were dead Stephanie?"

"Uhhh, Jeremy. You startled me. Uhhh that was a friend from school who's always acting like she's my mama. She's been concerned."

"What's up. Everything OK with the baby?"

"Yeah baby," I answer walking over to him. "Other than feeling a little tired and stressed."

"Maybe you oughta take time away from school. Take care of yourself better. I told you I'd be here for you."

"You've already been good to me Jeremy. I couldn't have a better father for my baby."

LaTonya 2

My baby daddy tries to not show his sadness when I talk about our baby. He wishes I wasTippy. Damn! This has gotta stop. Rae Ellis you can get ready to help me out. I haven't figured out what I'm gonna have you do, but you'll do what I ask, or go down for real this time.

21
Makin' sense

January 21, 2013
Tahoe City to Atlanta

"Look here Rae yo. I can disconnect right now and you'll never see your daughter again. Un-da-stand?"

Yeah I'm threatenin' 'im. I got the upper hand. Lyin' muthafucka. I ain't tol' 'im I saw Loretta. He helped hide her all dese years, making my girl suffer. She probably sittin' right next to 'im listening to our conversation.

"Now as I was sayin' before you interrupted yo. I trust you'll want to meet wit' me. Here what I gotta say. Oh, by the way, I wouldn't try no surprises. Your brotha already failed."

Darius is pissin' me off

While I'm over at Loretta's in Druid Hills. I'm already mad as hell we missed them in Oxnard by a nanosecond. I was talking with my boys about our next move when I got this phone call.

Loretta sees me tense up and begins to stroke the side of my left cheek with the back of her right hand, her way of saying take it easy. I love when she caresses me. Calms me so I can think. I breathe deep before I respond. When I do, I refrain this time from showing my annoyance but still determined.

"Darius, I'm concerned for both my daughters' safety. My brother can't be trusted when it comes to Tippy."

"Sho you right yo. I suppose you heard yo brother is plannin' to lock my girl up in some loony bin? She's scared as hell."

"Yes, I heard, which is why I want to protect Tippy as well as TiAnna."

"For real? You sure you not in on it too Unc Rae Rae?"

Ah hell! I'm 'bout to lose it no shit! Loretta better get to strokin'. "Darius now you bullshitin'. I don't play those types of games. I'm the one who watched over her all these years despite my brother. You just entered the picture." I stop myself accusing him of bein' a con, taking advantage of the current situation. What happened on New Year's Eve drove a wedge between me and my daughters. I'm not gonna let him make matters worse. "Look Darius this conversation is going' nowhere. When and where?"

"How 'bout I text you in the next couple a days. Make sure Tippy's cool wit' all dis."

"I guess what I'm hearing is I don't have a choice but to wait for your call. Will Tippy be coming along? How about TiAnna?"

"I can't speak for TiAnna. As for Tippy, it's always been on her yo. Cool? We out."

Darius hangs up leaving me fuming and feeling helpless. Sheeeit! Not cool. I'm Raymond Allan Ellis. I'm the man who's always a step ahead. Can't lose my grip. Hell naw!

"Sweetie look at me," Loretta says grabbing my chin, turning my face towards her. "You can't let him get to you. That's not your style."

"True, but the little punk brings out my worse."

"Down boy. You know how I feel about bad Raymond although I found him sexy too."

Baby got me cheesin'. "I pulled you when I was bad Rae."

"No sir Mr. Raymond. I pulled you with my heart."

"Huh haaa. Yeah you right Loretta. Your heart did captivate my spirit. Made me want to do right."

"Mm hm. Hard-headed is what you and Robert T. have in common."

"Maybe. But brotha got me beat on being cruel and heartless."

"What's he up to now?" Loretta asks.

I've been keeping Robert's latest plan from her. Keep her from worrying needlessly since I don't intend to let him succeed in locking Tippy up.

Loretta laughs and says, "I would've asked him myself, but I thought spooking him a little would be a better touch."

"What are you talking about Loretta? What did you do?"

Loretta spits out another laugh. This one gives me chills. "I called Robert. The man who could've stopped Lydia."

Speaking of Robert Ellis

I'm thinking how anxious that damn phone call made me. So much I stayed away from the office today. I'm in my sauna after working up a big sweat in my home gym. Earlier, I threw on my boxing gloves and tried to knock a hole in the punching bag. One of the joys of having my own workout space is I can unleash my anger without scaring anybody. For my age, I've built my muscles up pretty good. These fists look like they can stop someone as crazy as Mike Tyson. Each time I hit the bag I say, "Damn Republicans. Take that. Pow! And this. Pow! TKO!"

I take a moment to cool down and reflect back on the unsub who called the other day. She sounded like Loretta. With Tippy AWOL I can't help but wonder who close to home is trying to play games with my head.

The night Loretta got killed, no one else was at the house except for Tippy who was in her room asleep. I checked in on her when I first arrived. We'd given Chester and his wife the day off to be with their grandkids. Luanne, well, no need to bring up a past mistake I ended up having to marry. Glad the nightmare is over.

Loretta wasn't upstairs, so I went looking for her and heard loud voices coming from the downstairs parlor. I approached from the west entrance, peered in without being noticed and saw Loretta and Lydia standing almost neck and neck. They were yelling at each other sista-style – hands on their hips, rolling their necks and shakin' a forefinger in each other's face every now and then. Despite Loretta's proper diction, she can get down when she wants to. Quickly assessing the situation, I determined they were arguing about Rae. Lydia accused Loretta of still sleeping with my brother. Loretta laughed and said, "Yeah you're right and we're not going to stop despite Robert Ellis or you."

Well damn me! Not long ago we moved past her and Rae's indiscretions despite the fact I found out LaTonya wasn't mine. Loretta admitted she secretly dated Rae while we were planning a future together. Hell, I only introduced her to him once. He was at mama's house the night we stopped by. Rae's sorry ass got to grinning and carrying on with my fiancé right in my face. I ended up cutting the visit short, which annoyed Loretta. She accused me of being jealous and told me I had no reason. Ha! The joke's on me!

Me, I tried to be a stand-up guy and married Loretta without hesitation. I couldn't wait to have my own family. I have to admit during our marriage I did slip up a time or 2. Most foolish was the time with Luanne when she was only – anyway – Loretta was suspicious, but she didn't have any proof until Tippy told her.

Admittedly, I thought Luanne was the basis for our problems. Luanne did mention Rae would stop by when I wasn't home. She claims they were up to something. I told her she was wrong – not my Loretta – despite the fact I had betrayed her. After the incident with Luanne, Loretta comes clean about her and Rae. She says she had a DNA test shortly after Tippy was born and found out Tippy was Rae's, not mine. I slapped the shit out of her! I wanted to kill her ass! I opted to leave for a few days and only came back because my daughter was having a rough time. She was still daddy's precious little darling.

I suppose Loretta and I should've called quits especially after I found out about LaTonya, but my pride wouldn't let me. So, I took back control over my wife and daughter by convincing Loretta to stay for our daughter's sake. This was the beginning of my payback to Mr. Rae, who she promised to stop seeing. Rae also agreed not to pursue legally establishing paternity. I had a long talk with him and dared him to make a move. His response to me was "I'm cool unless you give me a reason too. Then all bets are off." Rather than argue with him, I called my friend Judge Simms to ensure he stayed clear of me and mine.

You see why I act the way I do? You may not believe my actions are justified, but I don't give a damn what you or anybody else thinks.

On the night in question, I witnessed Lydia strike Loretta with the round cement paperweight she picked up from our coffee table. Loretta stumbles and falls back on the couch. Lydia ran right up on top of her and struck Loretta in the forehead. Then she pulls a knife from her bra and goes to work. About the 5th time in, I backed away. The blood and Loretta's soft cries for help was making me sick but I didn't intervene. All I thought about was Loretta and Rae, talking and screwing behind my back. Made me look like a damn fool.

Then I heard another scream. This time oh shit. My daughter's yelling, "Stop! Leave my mommy alone!" Tippy's screams brought me back. I yelled from the hall, "Tippy!" I stood for another moment, giving Lydia time to get the hell out. I came around the corner in time to see the backend of Lydia running out the front door.

Once back in the parlor, I see my baby girl – her head on her mama's stomach. Loretta wasn't moving and I didn't want her too. So I stood there, making sure she'd die. I thought I saw her take her last breath. Then like a good daddy should, I ran to my daughter's aid. She had passed out from shock. I grabbed her up and held her close for a moment then reached down to check Loretta's pulse. It was real faint. I figured by the time the ambulance came, she'd be dead for sure. I only made the call because I felt a little guilty. After all, my precious darling would be growing up without a mother.

22

Head of the game

January 22, 2013
6:00 p.m. Tahoe time

"I've been doing a lot of thinkin'," I say to Tippy who's sitting across from me at the kitchen nook. "We should make the move. In your head you may not remember but you insisted we get married. You wanted to be Mrs. Broussard real bad."

I wait for my girl's reaction. She stops midway between taking a bite of her Jambalaya, glances at me with a blank stare then back to her food. At least her taste buds ain't changed. This is one of her favorites from my chef's bag of tricks.

"I called your stepmama. She's gonna have to sign the papers since you still 17."

Seeing Tippy scrunch her brows makes me suspect the word stepmama confuses her. I've been slowly telling her things but haven't said anything about her real mama being dead or alive. I did say she's unavailable and will talk about why later. I also told her I called her uncle. This made her smile. I lied and said he wants me to keep her safe. He'll be checkin' in.

"You and yo' stepmama, Luanne, got along real good before all dis happened," I explain continuing the lie. "She's keeping an eye on your daddy for us. Like I told you, we can't let him find you. He wants to lock you up and throw away the key. Un-da-stand?"

I was gonna blackmail Rae into signing her over but meeting up wit' him would be a big mistake. He'll probably have a rescue squad at bay to grab her and TiAnna. Me and T haven't spoken. A couple a times the phone rang and I'd answer to silence on the other end. One time I said to the silent caller, "Hey TiAnna hope you are OK." Then the phone went dead so I knew it was her. I'm assuming she's cool. Good thing.

"Will she be here soon?" My girl asks. She speaks a little bit and her memory's been coming in bits and pieces.

"I wanted to talk wit' you 'bout it first shawty. See if you up for company. I figure we meet up in Vegas, dress up and go see a Justice of The Peace."

Tippy shrugs as she takes the last bite. "This was really good, thank you."

"You're welcome my lady. How you feelin'? Want me to put on a movie?"

"Ooo. Can we watch the Johnson's Family Reunion again?" She says, bouncing up and down in her chair. "Ha! They're funny!"

"Yeah I like dat one too." I get up grinning, move from the table and over to her. She jumps up and grabs my hand. Pulling me on, she skips and I walk back to our cozy cove to watch the corny Johnson movie for the umpteenth time.

1/23/2013
Atlanta 10:00 a.m.

"Mama pass yestaday moanin," Luanne says to Darius who just called from Tahoe.

"Whaat? Sorry to hear dat. You said she was sick. Can I do somethin' for ya?"

"Naw. I got thangs handled. Da kids wit' Robbie."

"Huh. At least you don't have to worry 'bout yo kids wit' him. Sorry muthafucka!"

Lol. "Know he ain't yo fav but he good ta mine. Set me up nice for givin' 'im a divorce."

"Well he should pedophile muthafucka! He needs to turn over my girl's $100 million he stole. Speaking of which, I need your help yo."

I tell Luanne my plan. At first she resists but den finally agrees. I don't tell 'er 'what's goin' on wit' shawty's brain doe but dat we're hidin' out from her Robbie. I can trust 'er wit' dat. Yo. She don't care nothin' 'bout Tippy but she'll keep thangs on the QT for me. We agree to meet in Vegas in a couple a days after she finishes up wit' burying her mama.

Den I phone Rae to tell 'im change of plans. He tried to go off on me but I shut 'im down wit', "Tell you what. I'll take care of our girl so you can keep focus on Loretta. Oh and hey, tell 'er I said hello yo." I hang up laughing. I'm loud enough to where shawty runs into the bedroom where I've been makin' my private calls. I stop when I see her standing by the doorway. She has a big smile on her face.

"I was wonderin' where you went," she says. The movie is over."

"Wanna watch it again?" I ask.

She nods frantically and says, "I'd like some popcorn too please."

"Sure thang," I say. I get up and follow her out. She makes herself comfortable with her blankie. I hit play on the DVD then make my way to the kitchen stopping to look over my shoulder at Tippy who's as content as can be. Yo. The future Mrs. Broussard is giggling away anticipating the adventure ahead.

That afternoon

LaTonya 2

At Lennox Mall in Buckhead

I run into Damon Studdard out front. He and Jeremy use to bromance until Jeremy moved to Miami. Damon stayed in Atlanta wit' his wacked girlfriend Delinda. Rumor has it she's pregnant. Poor Damon. I guess he and Jeremy got that in common. Why do crazy bitches always get the good guys? I shoulda gave Damon some play rather than be so into Virgil. Yeah y'all. Damon wanted me bad and he was wit' Delinda. I'da reciprocated but woulda had to hurt the girl.

Mm, Mm, Mm. He still looks good. I wanna drag him over behind those bushes on the side of the parking lot and fuck him real good before I head back to Tommy's. Too bad Delinda's pregnant. Susie could handle things. Release Damon from his demon. Then he and I could kick-it! Susie ain't that cold though like the sons-a-bitches who messed me up wit' they shit so I can't have kids. Damon lucky I like him for real 'cause I'ma spare him the hell I go through. Having to take expensive meds and all. Between my daddies I don't have to worry about the cost. They set me up online with direct bill and my meds are mailed to me or sent to a nearby pharmacy.

"Hey beautiful whassup?" Damon says when I reach him. He gives me a hug. Ooo he smells good.

"Ain't nothin' Damon. How's life been treating you?" I let him loose, not wanting to and readjust my shoulder bag.

"How much time you got?" he asks. "Anyway, I should be asking you. Last I heard you were in Portland with Jeremy's still in love with ex."

"Now my turn to ask how much time you have Damon."

"Well then T, how about we grab something to eat and catch up? I could use a friend. Are you driving?"

"Yeah. I'm driving Tommy's new red mustang his new boo bought for him."

"Tommy's new boo? Boy I'm definitely outta touch. We could meet at LaCapone down the street. We've missed the lunch crowd so we'll have the place almost to ourselves."

"OK Damon. I'll meet you there."

Lunch at LaCapone

We ask for a table in back and follow the waiter through the quiet café along the same mauve colored walls and checkered floors and sit at a booth on the same worn cushioned seats.

"I guess some things never change," I say to Damon looking up at the ceiling. "They still have crazy upside-down stop lights for lighting. I'm glad they're on pause."

"Yeah. Me too. Staring up at the constant flashing of red, yellow and green can give you a head trip. It's a cool concept although it don't ring Italian."

"Oh right. You've been to Italy Damon."

"Yep. Both me and Jeremy played in an international league for a week."

"Quite the experience for you and your boy no doubt."

"For me anyway. I got in some extracurricular activity. Felt good. No Delinda. Jeremy huh. He was too in love. Still is," says Damon. All of sudden his handsome face turns sour. Like me, he was rooting for Jeremy and Tippy. Things change unfortunately.

"How's Jeremy anyway?"

"Hmm. Trying to do right by his fake ass girl who got pregnant on purpose. Ah hell. Let's talk about something else," Damon says, breaking into a grin. "Tell me about Tommy and his new boo."

"Ooo Damon. You're not going to believe this. When I first met him, I mean her, I mean anyway I thought she was some old woman. But turns out she's an old man about 40 I'm guessing. He was dressed in drag and goes by the name Patrice."

Damon's mouth drops and eyes widen. "Patrice?" he asks on stun.

"Yeah Patrice. Why you know her Damon?"

"I sho in the hell do! Patrice is best friends to Chelsea who is now Stephanie!"

"Stephanie who Damon?"

"Jeremy's Stephanie. She's faking her identity right under everybody's nose including yours!"

Randall Johnson in Atlanta

"Our target has a good friend by the name of Patrice who lives in Norcross. She's living there with a gentleman by the name of Tommy Crumbs," says Jerry Lang the private detective I hired to track down Chelsea. He's a good friend of mine who use to serve on the ATL PD as an undercover cop working the ho stroll.

"You work on pinpointing Chelsea's exact location, I'ma go fetch my daughter."

"I'm on it, Randall. I'll be in touch," says Jerry.

Earlier, Rae also called me about TiAnna's location. Now I'm hearing there's a connection to Chelsea. Our direct bill, which I have yet to review, updates my daughter's address to Norcross. Before this one, we traced her to Oxnard, California but by the time Rae's team got there she, Tippy and Darius were gone. Darius's uncle and aunt said they all left in the middle of the night without telling anyone. I'm sure they told Robert Ellis the same thing. He got there after we did. Ha. With all his money he can't beat us street smart Negroes.

I have no qualms about killing anyone who come after mine. Rae's the same way. He's crazier than me. I never understood how someone like Loretta could go for him. Lydia neither. When Lydia came to me, I was at least off the streets. I was working a regular 9 to 5 and willing to play the good husband and daddy role to Rae's child, TiAnna, whom I love more than life itself. She's my favorite even over my own. And Lydia. I miss her dearly no matter what our problems were. Now she's gone thanks to a ho who was her unwanted daughter. Chili, you tore my family apart. You'll pay!

Amanishakhete

At LaCapone's
I can't believe the shit

Damon breaks it down. He plans to tell Jeremy despite what may happen with those photos. I suggest he hold off until the baby is born in case it's Jeremy's. Don't want the bitch to do something crazy. Actually I want time to make my own plan before it all goes down. Susie's getting antsy. Hmmmm? What am I gonna do about this Patrice and Chelsea BFF shit? Obviously, Tommy don't know about the situation. All he is, is a piece of young ass for that nasty she/he. Miss Holla-me-bad need to leave my friend alone or bear witness to Susie's wrath.

23

Bitter sweet

January 22, 2013
5:00 p.m. Stone Mountain

At my parents' house, mama's downstairs in the TV room. I lean over, hug her and she kisses my cheek. Plopping down next to her on the rust-colored sofa, I'm reminded of the late nights I'd fall asleep here, coming in after curfew. Like Jeremy I'm an only child, a son who was a mama's boy. I'm too old now except I can't help miss her spoiling me. Years ago Daddy scolded mama about her dottiness and said, "Let my son be a man. Stop all the 'my baby boy' shit." I ain't no Jody, but I do stay here most nights. Over on campus I have a roomie Tyrese who's a pussy-hound. Almost every night he's jumpin' off wit' a new chick, making me wonder how he gets any studying done. Anyhoo, his sex habit wears on my nerves, so I asked to be moved. I'ma hang here until it gets handled. Daddy suggested I get my own apartment near the University. Naw I don't think so. Delinda would be in my business. She's already hinting around about us living together. Uh, uh. I ain't going there wit' her. I don't care how crazy her mama is and I ain't scared of her brother. I told Delinda don't start no shit and there won't be none.

"Mama, uhhh. I gotta tell you and daddy something. I thought he'd be home."

"He got held up suga. You can talk to me can't you?" Mama's looking at me curious squinting her eyes and shit. I'm hesitant about telling her my situation without Daddy being present. Neither of my parents like Delinda, but daddy would keep mama calm.

"A new painting?" I ask, pointing to the art above the fireplace. The scene depicts 3 fashionably-dressed black women with black hats and yellow dresses, standing outside a barber shop. "Reminds me of a small country town you see in those old movies, where black folks go to church every day and hit the juke joint at night," I say grinning.

My avoiding talking about what's up annoys mama a little. She says, "OK Mr. I think I'll wait 'till your daddy gets home. Must be bad news."

I shrug and say, "Depends. But I am interested in your beautiful painting."

"Hmm. I'll keep my high-blood pressure medicine nearby. For now I'll leave you alone."

"And the painting?" I ask again.

Mama's face breaks into a big smile. "I'm the artist."

"Whaaat. You painted that mama?" I jump up and walk over to the fireplace to get a closer look.

The painting is pretty good even with the few flaws. Mama had a hard time with the women's facial features. The noses look off center and the slanted eyes make them look Asian. I don't think she meant for them to look like that.

I'm proud of mama – Mrs. Marietta Studdard. Over the past couple of years she's been doing her own thing. She retired early from the Stone Mountain School District where she taught middle school for the past 15 years. Mama said she loves teaching but got tired of kids getting crazier every year. Since she's been outta there, I gotta say she's got her swank back. Don't get me wrong, mama always kept herself up, except now she's lost all her 50 pounds of fat. She works out at the gym 3 times a week and mall walks with some of the ladies from her art class where she's been learning oil painting. This is something she's dreamed of doing from the time she was a little girl. Even got a certificate from an art school after she graduated high school. But her parents insisted she get a degree with wider career options, so she chose teaching. Mama comes from a family of educators. They were happy when she decided to get with their program.

"Me being an art major didn't quite cut-the-mustard for them," mama would often say.

That's why she doesn't get on me too much about career choices. She's OK with me wanting to play for the NFL, but also encouraged me to get a degree to fall back on. I followed her advice and chose Sociology as a minor and Psychology as a major. Daddy would've preferred me following in his footsteps and go to law school. I can't see myself being an attorney. My degree would allow me a chance to counsel some of these bad actors coming up the ranks. Hopefully help detour some of our young black brothas from being a number in the system.

Jeremy and me are fortunate. Both of us come from 2-parent homes with working parents who are still married. My dad D. James Studdard is partner at a law firm in Atlanta – Blakely, Studdard and Wakefield. They practice corporate law mostly but also handle white collar criminal cases. Like now he's all wrapped up in the criminal case against his good friend Judge Simms.

"Mama I'm proud of you," I say. Walking over to her, I bend down and kiss her on the cheek. She grabs my hand.

"Sit." She pulls me down not giving me a choice. "Who knows what time your daddy will be home. You know he's involved with the Judge Simms's case and been putting in extra time."

She pauses, tilts her head sideways, looks at Damon. "So, Damon James Studdard Jr. tell me what's going on. Whatever it is has been messing with you."

"Ah mama."

"Ah nothing boy. What's worrying you has to do with Miss Delinda doesn't it?"

Man. Almost like she's reading my mind. Well I'm her son.

"Ok mama, but you gotta promise you gonna be cool. Deal?" Rather than say yes, she looks at me sternly scrunching her forehead and lips.

"Well you see it's like this mama." Before I can finish I hear a familiar voice at the top of the stairs.

"Hey sweet pea. Your Mr. Goodbar is home!"

Ah hell yeah. Saved by the bell. Pops is in the house. Maybe Mr. Goodbar can sweeten his sweet pea up a little more before I tell 'em both the news.

1/25/2013
On Hayden Island in Portland

I'm talking with my sister who is damn calm considering.

"Yes. I'm aware Sheila."

"You certainly are calm about this. I'm going out of my mind. I wish we'd never gone down that road all those years ago."

"Well we did and there's no turning back. Maybe it's time you take in some of your own counseling," Uh ha, ha, ha, ha.

For my older sister Delores to make light of our situation concerns me.

"There, there Sheila. As long as you help Robert put away his daughter we're in the clear."

"What I'm doing is highly unethical. His daughter is getting close to discovering the truth and he doesn't want that to happen."

"Look Sheila. Get over yourself. You having a conscious all of a sudden isn't very becoming."

"This was not how it was meant to be Delores. I really wanted to…"

"What? Be a good psychiatrist? Help people? Well you have. You've done your part. But now it's my turn. You owe me Sheila. You owe me! Thanks to me, our father, who killed our mother, is dead! Dead! Dead! Dead! If he had lived he would have killed us too! Don't you ever forget!"

"Not a chance. You'll always remind me about you being forced into making a deal with the devil."

"Right! The very one I had to marry at 18 and who paid for your degrees. I'd say they came in rather handy wouldn't you?"

Delores is right. Not long ago I was second-guessing the decision we made. We're all to blame for our circumstances today.

Long time ago
In Wisconsin

It was just the 2 of us – me and Delores. We grew up in rural Wisconsin on an aquaculture farm where our father raised and sold Large Mouth Bass and Trout. Mr. Luke was his name and that is what he insisted me and Delores call him. He certainly wasn't a loving man, but he was a breadwinner and quite successful.

Rita our mother was a stay-at-home mom, which Mr. Luke demanded. He was quite controlling as well as abusive, which we often witnessed up until the day she threatened to leave and take me and Delores with her. Rita lived to regret her decision. You see Mr. Luke had a good friend Dr. Daniel Michelson a prominent psychiatrist. He placed Rita under psychiatric house supervision, trumping up a diagnosis of paranoid schizophrenia and prescribed medication, making her lethargic and immobile. When Mr. Luke wasn't forcing Rita to take the medication, he made Delores do the honors. So for months, we'd watch Rita in that state until one day when it all changed. Delores decided to stop giving her the medication. She replaced the little blue pills with some sugar pills she got from the corner grocery in town. When Rita came back to life, we hatched a plan to outsmart dear old Mr. Luke.

I was 16 then and Delores was almost 18 the day me, Delores and Rita attempted an escape. That day was October 28 a cool, sunny fall day. A day when Mr. Luke had business in town. But he must have known something was up because he came home early. When he came through the door, we were standing there with Rita who had suitcases in both hands. Mr. Luke wasted no time. He ran over to her and slapped her. As she started to fall he grabbed her by the neck, strangling her. "I told you I'd kill you if you ever left didn't I!" he yelled. Delores and I stood by watching Mr. Luke's face and neck turn a blood red as he strangled our mother lifeless. By the time we, or rather Delores, decided to step in, it was too late. Our mother was dead.

All was quiet near our creaky stairway where Rita lay except for the sound of Mr. Luke's heavy breath, standing over her body. From where I stood near the door, I could see the hate in his eyes and no remorse. Delores, who had run out during the event, returned with Mr. Luke's favorite hunting rifle. The one we learned to shoot using birds and rodents for target practice. The very rifle Mr. Luke insisted his girl's learn how to handle and protect the homestead. I guess we could say this was the time to put protecting the homestead in action.

Delores stood behind Mr. Luke. He didn't hear her come up, so didn't know what was coming. Delores cocked the trigger and – POW - blasted him in the back of the head. The explosion of blood shot from Mr. Luke's head, his knees buckled beginning his slow descent down, down, down until he met Rita, whose eyes were wide open. She unwelcomed him to her bodice, knowing even in death she couldn't escape his evil touch. Kaplunk. He fell right on top of her his head resting right below her chin.

Turning my head from the two dead bodies, I looked at Delores. She was standing there with the same hateful look Mr. Luke had; she too, showed no remorse. The 2 of us stood there in silence. We exchanged no words but in our minds we knew what Delores did would cost us. We just didn't know how much until Dr. Daniel Michelson came to collect.

After I hang up with my sister Sheila

I call my lover to tell him what's up. When he answers he asks, "How's my beautiful Miss Delores today?"

"Your beautiful Miss Delores had to dance a 2-step today with her sister," I reply.

"I'm intrigued. But you'll have to tell me what you mean later. I'll see you tomorrow."

"Really?" I say smiling. "You know it's been too long."

"Mmm sure has. I'm ready for some dreary coastal weather. It'll keep us inside. Make sure you keep the fire hot." Ha, ha, ha.

"I'll do that lover."

"Say baby, I gotta bone to pick with your sister," says my lover. "She's not answering her phone."

"Don't worry. I've got her back on track," I say. "How about you? Have you tracked down your prey?"

"No but getting close. I missed them by an hour down south. My sources say they are not too far away. Up in the Sierra's somewhere." My lover pauses and takes in a deep breath.

"You OK?" I ask.

"Yeah beautiful. I'm alright. Just can't shake a feeling I have. I received the strangest phone call the other day."

"From your brother?"

"No. But he's on the same trail," my lover responds. "He seems to be one step ahead, but I have no problem closing the gap if he gets in my way. This is way too serious for me. You know I could go down."

"Well lover. As long as we have each other's back, we'll stay in the clear."

"You got that right beautiful. What would I do without you?"

"You'd be a dead lover," I say jokingly. My lover chuckles a little, but we both know what I'm capable of.

24

Catch us if you can

January 26, 2013
Portland

Believe it or not y'all, I ain't been right since Uri's death. Maybe 'cause it's still fresh in my mind, or 'cause of the way she died. So when I'm not on the road, I stick close to home, my crib out on Sandy. She's worth the time spent here now.

With the money I've made, I paid off my mortgage. I also increased security here by putting up a black iron fence around the property, replacing the wooden fence out back. My Latino boys put a fresh coat of paint on the walls throughout – a light-green mint color – and put down indoor/outdoor carpet with dark green, cinnamon, gray and white stripes. I even got rid of the old funky couch and bought a dark gray living room set. Rather than have a coffee table, I placed 3 big Ottoman's in front of the couch, introducing one big chair on the left side of the couch to the other big chair on the right. Like the couch, the chairs are solid and wide enough for me to squeeze a honey in their wit' me. For entertainment, I bought one of those 3D floor length flat screens wit' surround sound. Good thing I'm in a house. The shit gets loud.

I've been keeping things on mellow since my brother's high school party here last winter, when all dat shit went down wit' a girl hollering rape. Occasionally, I have some of the local rappers over to fuck around in my recording studio in what was once my garage.

Then there's days like today I could use some noise besides my own. My ultraconservative, right-winged parents ain't said nothin' nor have they expressed any condolences. They didn't like Uri and her kind – she's Iranian.

My brother did go with me to Uri's funeral yesterday, which I paid for. Her parents, who hate my guts, had her buried out in Beaverton somewhere with their other dead family members.

Uri comes from a pretty big family. I tried my damn'dest to stay clear of 'em. The elders came here from Iran years ago and made a go of it. Uri was born here in Portland with the rest of her 7 siblings, cousins and shit. As far as I'm concerned, they're all wacked. Could be terrorists, which is why I spent a boat load of money to send Uri off to wherever in style. I think her family appreciated it. Especially the food, which I paid her uncle and aunt to cater. They own a restaurant in Hillsboro. Hopefully we can all be at peace, at least call a truce. We all want the same thing. Uri's killer.

"This morning, on a damn Saturday, I had to speak to Leonard Gross my criminal attorney." I'm telling this to my buddy Roscoe who stopped by with some bad-ass dank. I ain't seen Roscoe since Jerome's funeral last year. Although dude gets on my nerve wit' the way he stutters and shit, this helps me get my mind off things.

"He charges way too much for giving advice."

"S-s-soo, do dem damn p-pigs still think you guilty?" Roscoe asks.

"They say I ain't a suspect. But I don't trust dem muthafucka's which is why I went to see Gross. He tells me not to worry but give him $10,000 as a retainer in case shit go down. Good thing I'm working. Doing more gigs."

"Sheeeit man. Least you got Gross. He's bad ass." says Roscoe.

"Ha! Roscoe you high as hell. You know how I can tell?"

"Because my eyes is red and I'm noddin'. You got something to snack on?"

"I can tell you high 'cause you ain't stuttering. No wonder you like to smoke weed."

"Man I don't stutter."

"Oh yes you do and you know it. We all do."

"Whatever man," Roscoe says brushing me off with his hand. "Gimme somethin' to d-d-drink," Roscoe says laughing. "I'm just playin' but for real doe."

"I'm on it. Here take another hit," I say handing the joint to him.

I ain't gone but a minute, but when I return from the kitchen, Roscoe's head is leaning to one side. His eyes are half-closed and his mouth is wide open with drool rolling down the left side of his mouth.

"Hey wake up," I say pushing on his shoulder. "You got spit running all down your mouth and shit." I throw some napkins at him I brought in with the corn chips, ranch dip and soda. I think the dip is still good. Don't remember when I bought it but snacks go real fast around here since I smoke a lot of weed.

"Say Roscoe, have you heard from Buster? Muthafucka done disappeared since snitching on Darius's mama. He's just as guilty doe."

"Naw man. Last I heard he was down south somewhere. Probably Atlanta where he can get his freak on and stay under the radar."

"Even doe I don't believe in snitching, I'm glad we got Jerome's killer. Can't believe it's Darius's mama. No wonder he fucked up in the head," I say to Roscoe.

Roscoe picks up another handful of chips and pushes 'em in his mouth. He says, "I wouldn't know. Jerome loved his bro doe."

"Yeah, yeah whatever," I say. "He still a chump who can't be trusted. I hope Tippy gets hip to his madness. TiAnna told me all about his ass." Then I go off topic and ask Roscoe, "Do you think Buster is a fag?"

"Yep. For a fact he is," says Roscoe.

"Ohhh reeeally," I say snidely. "Y'all…"

"Don't even g-g-go th-there man! D-dat shit ain't cool!"

"OK my man. Calm down. I'm just fuckin' wit' ya. You wanna smoke some more weed?"

"Naw I'm cool. But Buster, h-h-he ain't cool. H-h-he did try something once. We was all h-high an sh-shit. I busted him dead in his f-f-face! Ma' fucka h-hollered like a bitch!"

Now I'm laughing. Can't help myself. Roscoe's face is all scrunched up. Mouth all tight. He's mad as hell. "Don't tell me no more man," I say shaking my head, trying to stop laughing. "What is this world coming too?"

Roscoe stops munching long enough to fire up another joint. He takes in a few hits, holds, blows out the smoke and settles back in. Then he says, "The world coming to an end we get more faggots coming out da closet."

"I ain't got nothin' against 'em Roscoe. But all dis talk about fags is making me tired all of a sudden. Let me turn on some noise. DaMenace is in da house."

1/26/2013
4:00 pm in Norcross

When I pull up in front of Tommy's house, I see a familiar face standing on the porch talking to Patrice. "Shit. It's daddy. He found me. I should just dri – oh hell – too late. He sees me. Here he comes." The closer Daddy Randall gets, I can see he's aged since I last saw him in December. His hair is all gray. No more salt and pepper. He still got a belly and ooo pigeon-toed like a mutha. His mama and daddy should've bought him some corrective shoes when he was little. He's worried about me. But as y'all can see, it ain't like he can't find me.

I get out of the car. Daddy rushes over to me and gives me a big long hug, laying his tear-stained face against mine. He lets go and wipes his eyes with his right arm sleeve. Placing each one of his big thick hands on each side of my upper arms, he lowers his head close to mine. He says, "Ask me why later but you're going with me. You're not safe here."

Out of the corner of my left eye I see Patrice. She's on the phone talking, looking dead at me. Probably got that bitch Chelsea on the phone! Sissy!

"No need to ask you why daddy. I'll be ready in 5."

"With my help you'll be ready in 2," daddy says.

Me and daddy head towards Tommy's to get my shit. Patrice ends her conversation when we get close. I wish holla-me-bad would start something. Susie might forget we got company.

25

All about me

January 26, 2013
It's afternoon in Vegas

Damon is chillin' with me in the penthouse at Bellagio. Me, Damon and my teammates Jeb and Dietrich, who came in with me from Miami, went up on this place. It's badass. We have a panoramic view of Vegas, including our fill of the bright lights and neon signs coming from the casinos. I haven't been here in years. With the exception of a couple of new casinos, things ain't changed. Even in January the place is hoppin' with some of everybody.

Me, I'm done with the drinking. We started on Friday night when we got here and partied 'til this morning. It's around 2 in the afternoon on Sunday and me and Damon just came to life. Ordered a late breakfast through room service. As for Jeb and Dietrich, they got caught up with some broads they met yesterday. We ain't heard from 'em but I ain't worried. They're grown enough to handle themselves.

I'm glad my man Damon came down to keep me company. I wasn't up for a one nightstand. I got enough female problems thank you. Damon understands where I'm coming from. With both of our girls being pregnant, he needed a break too. He finally told his parents about Delinda. His mama like mine ain't happy one bit. From what I hear, our mamas have been commiserating with each other. Knowing the 2 of 'em, no doubt they're devising a plan to one-up our baby mamas.

Until breakfast showed up, we didn't know how hungry and hung-over we were. We barely said 2 words until we chugged down most of the pancakes, eggs, sausage, hashbrowns, biscuits and gravy. Oh and fresh squeezed orange juice for Damon and a V-8 for me. My stomach is queasy like a mutha.

"I get the picture they had sort of a falling out," says Damon. "Hmm." He pauses, rubbing the top of his right eyebrow. Something he does when he wants to say something but doesn't. Like he's holding back or hiding something. Damon's my main man but since he came to visit me in Miami, he's been holding back a little more than usual.

"Annnd? Come on Damon spill."

Damon rubs his eyebrow again then says, "There's a whole lot of shit going on."

"Like what Damon?"

After a brief pause he says, "TiAnna says Tippy ain't herself. She didn't go into details but. Uhhhhh. I get the impression she may be in trouble and that Darius dude is taking advantage."

"Of course he is!" I say agitated. "He's probably after her money! Don't let me see his ass."

"Hollup Jeremy. You don't even know dude. Besides you ain't wit' Tippy no more. Or have you forgotten."

"I still love her though," I pause to breathe. "Ahhhhhh," I say stretching my arms up. "I'm so damn full I can't move."

"No shit," says Damon. "Should last me 'til dinner."

"Wit' yo big ass. Whatever it takes to be a linebacker I guess huh?" I say to Damon. He chuckles and nods. "About my girl, I mean Tippy. I can't help but worry. She may have had a setback. I wish I could find out somehow. Let her know I still love her."

"And Ch, uh, Stephanie. What about her?" Damon asks.

"What about her? Like I said before Damon. It ain't like that and won't be like that between us. I'll take care of mine – if it is mine – and that's that."

Damon holds his head down avoiding eye contact with Jeremy. Telling him about Stephanie is on his mind but he's inclined to follow TiAnna's lead. Leave it alone for now.

6:00 p.m.
We're in Vegas yo

And it's about me dis time. Me and my girl checked in at the Stratosphere. Luanne showed up about an hour after we got here. She hasn't said much. I think she's still reeling from shock. My girl's been really nice to her. Talking like they don't hate each other. On the way down, I schooled my girl on some information. I gave her enough details to keep Luanne at bay. Not the real deal about their relationship. Luanne ain't crazy though. She knows something's up. She keeps lookin' over at me like "nigga this is bullshit and you know it. What's really going on?" Thankfully this little gathering is coming to a close. We have a 6:30 appointment with the justice of the peace.

9:00p.m.
The pilot calls in

"Sir. We've got about 45 minutes outside of Vegas."

"Earn your keep and make it 30! No one gets away this time! No one! I hope I've made myself clear!"

"Very clear sir. Very clear."

1/26/2013
9:05p.m.

I don't understand. I can't remember past being 6, yet I'm 17. So we did the marriage thing anyway. He says he's my husband and I'm his wife. I wish we could have left the consummation part out 'cause now I feel really bad. Like I did something wrong. Mr. green-eyes is asleep lying next to me. I'm glad. He can't hear me crying. Green-eyes would only say it is because I lost my mind temporarily. He says I will be OK as long as I stay with him. But I don't feel OK. I don't want to be with him either.

I get up quietly and put on some clothes. I grab a jacket and my bag and head for the door. I get a little scared when I open it. Should I? Or should I just stay here and wait it out? My memory's got to come back. Familiar places and people keep appearing in my head. I think they're memories. Like right after the wedding, I got all sad but tried not to show it. Then all of sudden a picture of this guy flashed in my head. He had a big smile and Basset-Hound looking eyes. He was throwing a football. I was clapping. Then. Nothing.

I think I'm going to take my chances. I took what money green-eyes had out of his wallet. I'm sure he can get more. I also found the other phone he's been hiding from me. I think it's mine. If not, it's mine now. I look back at green-eyes who's still sleeping soundly.

"I'm sorry," I say softly. "I gotta go. I may not know me right now. But I don't feel safe anymore."

Outside the cool night air is nice and ripe for a jacket. I watch the lines of people crossing in front of me and cars covering the streets. Hmm. Where to? Maybe I should find another hotel to hide out in. Or maybe I'll go to Atlanta. Whatever. I better decide quickly. I'm feeling anxious. Like something's about to happen. And it won't be good.

I turn left and walk towards more bright lights. Ahead I see these beautiful fountains shooting up from the ground turning all sorts of beautiful colors. I smile when the color fuchsia splashes in and dances along. She's inviting me to play too. There is where I should be.

9:07p.m.
Preparing for landing

Gotta keep my employer happy so we made it here in good time. We've also identified the target's destination. Once we hit the tarmac we'll call the boss to let him know we should have everything in tow within 15.

9:17 p.m.
I could stand here

I feel at peace for the first time. All is well until...

"LaTonya," I hear him say. He's standing right behind me. I can't move. I won't move. I won't even look his way. Instead, I lower my head. Maybe he'll move along. Thinking he made a mistake. Not a chance. He touches my shoulder. I flinch slightly. Yet, I still don't move. Funny, I don't think I want to. Then his hand leaves my shoulder. I can feel his movement. He steps back then slowly steps to my right. He's coming around to face me. Closer. Closer. Here he is facing me.

"LaTonya," I hear him say again. This time I take my chances. I slowly raise my head, wondering who the man behind the gentle voice is. When I meet his eyes I laugh. "OMG!" I say. "It's you. The Basset-Hound."

26
Too slow Joe

January 26, 2013
9:20 p.m. Stratosphere

Who the hell is knocking at the door! Woke me up from a good sleep. The best I've had in a long time. Fiiiinaaally. I got to make some good loving to my new wife. She was smellin all sweet an shit. I reach my hand out to stroke her. But she ain't lying next to me. Where the hell? She's not in the bathroom as far as I can see.

"Yo Tippy," I say loud enough for her to hear but damn sho hoping whoever's at the door don't. I wait momentarily before I call out again. Still no answer. "Where the hell is dat girl?" Shit! She better not have gone out. She was curious about that crazy rollercoaster up top. I tol 'er, "hell no we ain't riding that shit! I ain't fixin ta die and you neither yo!" Maaaan. I hope she didn't go back up dair on her own. As wacked as she is, she'll draw attention.

Knock, knock, knock. Yeah, yeah, yeah. Damn! I hope it ain't about her. Better answer it.

I roll out of bed butt-naked, grab my sweats and the complementary white robe that came wit' da room. I made sure we got the best wedding suite. I had lots of fuchsia flowers delivered before we arrived. They add a splash of color to this beige and cream. I even had 'em sprinkle some flower peddles across the bed along with some chocolate hearts. A nice touch. Yo. Darius Winston Broussard the romantic. We also got some champagne for me and Diet Snapple for my girl. The other day she asked for some. Her memory could be on its way back. I sure as hell am hoping.

When I get to the door, I look out the peek hole. Ah naw. Somethin' done happened now. There's 2 policemen and another white man in a suit. Wait. Hollup. What the hell is Brannigan doing here?

9:22 p.m.
Outside the Bellagio

"They're on the move. Shall I follow?" I say to my boss.

"No. Leave 'em alone. I'll take it from here. What you can do though is keep the men posted around the perimeter. Watch the exits in case we have unexpected company," he says.

I assure him, "We got someone watching in case they make a move this way. Right now they're focused on the other target. You know him as you say, he won't say anything."

"No. That little punk won't spill. Ain't his style. Besides he thinks he got the upper hand. He won't get away with it. I'm out."

After finishing up with my boy on the phone, I immediately send a text. The person I am texting is someone I can trust. It was pure luck he was at the right place at the right time. His help will come in handy.

9:23 p.m.
At the Bellagio penthouse

The message I just received is about my girl who I brought back with me after running into her outside. OK. She's my former girlfriend so Damon likes to remind me. Either way, I'm glad she came. She's in trouble as I suspected. The message says keep her hidden until we get out of Vegas. In 10 minutes, we will head down and meet a private car and driver who will be waiting for us out back. This means my playtime in Vegas is over. OK by me. I wasn't having much fun anyway. Not until I spotted Tippy. Good thing I left my wallet upstairs and had to come back and get it. Otherwise I may have missed her. Even with the delay I almost passed her up. I was on the other side of the path away from the fountains. What caught my eye was this beautiful young lady in a fuchsia leather jacket heading up the walkway to the right of me. She ran over to the fountain and started jumping up and down like a little kid when the colored lights and water sprouted up. Gotta admit the Bellagio got it going on with this fancy water show. Everybody comes to watch the performance. My girl had her back to me but I said to Damon, "She looks familiar." I walked over to the fountain to take a look. The closer I got the more nervous I got. I knew I knew her. In case I was wrong I didn't want to look like a fool. But I took a chance. Low and behold it was her! When I stood in front of her, she called me Basset Hound. We both laughed.

I talk Tippy into coming with me; she didn't hesitate. I grab the handle of her suitcase on rollers. Damon follows us back to the penthouse then left us alone to talk. At first she told me her name was Lisa. Then she finally came clean. She lost her memory. Something I already knew. She says her husband told her to keep quiet. Yeah she told me everything. That muthafucka Darius, who I wish I could find and whoop his ass, married my girl earlier this evening. I couldn't believe Robert Ellis would let that happen. But come to find out, he wasn't the one to give his blessing. Luanne did.

How she got away with this, I don't know. What I do know is this shit can't be legal since Tippy's only 17.

Damon plans to stay in Vegas until tomorrow like we had planned to keep up appearances. Before he left the room he did say he had something to talk with me about. Later though. He knows Tippy's my priority right now.

Another text comes through. Time for us to leave and Tippy is really happy. I'm taking her back to Miami with me. Not home to my place though. Wouldn't be a good idea with Stephanie busting in and out pregnant an all. We have another place all lined up. Iron clad to my understanding.

Once we're about 50 miles safely away from the city, I get a phone call. "How are things?" he asks.

"All is well sir," I respond as I look at my girl who's huddled next to me. She fell asleep with her head on my shoulder. I left her alone.

"Cool," he says. "Make sure it stays that way."

What he means is he don't play when it comes to our girl.

"You can count on me sir to watch over her," I say assuring him.

"Right. We'll talk," he says.

All's quiet on the road. The driver is taking us the scenic route leaving me to wonder how he can see. It's dark as hell out there. I can't see nothing. At some point, we'll hop a private jet at an undisclosed location. Rather than worry, I lay my head back against the warm leather seat. Like all limos we've got comfort, lots of space with amenities. Real nice. Quiet. Smooth. Hmmm. I break into a smile. Imagine y'all. Me and Tippy together again. As we should be. Gotta say I'm grateful for this moment. Thank you God. Thank you Uncle Raymond. Good looking out.

27
Can't win for losin'

January 27, 2013
2:00 a.m. at the Vegas strip

No. Not theee strip. The Vegas air strip yo. We preparing for take-off. You not going to believe dis, but I'm being arrested for kidnapping. Being sent back to Portland in handcuffs. The Vegas PD released me to Brannigan and his officers. And yo. Get dis. Brannigan threatened to charge me with murder. Says I can join my mama. He's lucky these cuffs stop me from kicking his ass. Short greasy-haired white muthafucka! Lookin' like a broke wino wit' his big red Rudolph nose. Bet he drinks vodka every night. I can't believe he's still trying to find a way to pin Darrell's murder on me. Not a chance in hell. Who says I did it? Besides I have an unbeatable alibi.

As for my wife, I'm kinda glad she took off when she did. I'da been in jail and she'da been locked away. I wish da hell I knew where she was doe. Her uncle gotta be behind her disappearance. He beat me dis time but I will be back.

Whether she wit' him or not, no one's talkin and me neither. Her things were gone from the hotel room so they really couldn't prove she was wit' me. As for our marriage license, I had it mailed to my private P.O. Box in Portland. Once I get back I plan to stash it in my safe deposit box over at the bank.

"So Mr. Broussard, you still wanna claim stupid," says Brannigan once we're in the air.

I look over at him and smile. I can't let 'im win. Gonna follow my attorney's advice. Mr. Perry Mason himself. Leonard Gross. White man stay busy. I hear he's also representing DaMenace. What're the chances?

"You think you're a slickster don't you?" Brannigan asks.

I knew he wasn't done. He's tryin to fuck wit' me. Get me all mad an shit so he can get somethin to stick.

"You ain't changed since you tried to kill your daddy. An upstanding citizen I might add. You're certainly not a chip off the ol' block."

Ahhh here we go. Can't help but scrunch my face and tighten my mouth. I'm angry as hell. Rather than respond though I keep quiet for a minute. Then say, "Yeah you right about dat yo. I ain't a chip off the ol' block. I'm a better man. One who's still alive. I got da world envious of my disposition. Even you."

I turn my head and stare out the window. I'm done talkin. Done had my say. Yo muthafucka. You welcome to say somethin' else. I ain't hearin' you. My wife is on my mind. I really miss you shawty. I do love you. My heart aches thinkin' about how much. Best believe you mine forever. Ain't no one taking you from me.

1/27/2013
Early on Sunday morning

I'm sitting by the fire facing the beach. It's low tide along this foggy coastline, allowing only the tips of the waves to be seen. The sand is still wet where the tide came and left. Down near the ocean I see the early birds, joggers, masters and their dogs roaming wishing I had taken in a morning stroll. Maybe it would've helped my foul mood. Yet, here I sit drinking my 4th cup of coffee. And for what? I don't need the caffeine. I've been awake all night and not for good a reason. I was all wound up and couldn't get my groove on. I kept going limp. This morning my anger decides to stick around, which doesn't make my lady happy. I can't even enjoy the nice breakfast she made. She makes a hell of a spinach and sausage quiche. This time she added raspberry crepes to the menu and French potatoes.

"I don't like seeing you like this Robert," my lady says. "What can I do to make you all better?"

She's standing next to me with her hand around my shoulder. I grab her other hand and pull her down in my lap.

"You're still light as a feather," I say stroking her white face. Delores is probably the whitest woman I've been with. That's because she is a white woman. My first wife was black but she had fair skin. My second wife was biracial. I guess you could say I like cream in my coffee. A little or a lot.

"What's the plan?" she asks.

"I don't know," I respond. "The boy ain't talking and they have nothing to hold him on. The detective suspects he's lost track of her too. Hell. She didn't just disappear without help from my brother no doubt. Could've sworn we had him beat this time."

"What do you think happened lover?"

"I think he played us. The people we kept tabs on were decoys. Took us around the block and back and the real guards tracked the prize. Yeah beautiful. We got played."

"Oh Robert, I'm sorry. I want this to be over. You haven't been yourself. I've missed you."

"I know beautiful. Please be patient with me hear? I got to get clear of this. Otherwise your man is gone." I lean up to kiss her. She parts my mouth with her tongue, sliding it around my mouth. The warmth tickles me inside, making my Robbie get hard. Maybe he'll stay right this time. "How about I work on making you not miss me?"

Delores giggles. "OK lover. Get to work."

1/29/2013
It's Miami calling the Judge

Making me long for the good ol' days. But I've got to stop this before it starts again.

"As much as I want to, I can't," I say to her. "I've got too much heat on me. You know I had to call-in every favor. Even with influence, I don't think they'll let me go. But at least I can do my time in one of those posh federal prisons. We just have to figure out how much less time I can do."

"I know. I know. I'm worried about my baby. He needs a father. Jeremy's getting more distant by the day."

"You know the sex of the baby already? You just got pregnant Stephanie. Or is there something you're not telling me?"

Yeah there is something I'm not telling you I'm thinking. You're the father. But I can't let you be. Like you say, you have too much heat on you. And my son needs Jeremy. Not a washed up judge who can't help me no more.

"Look I'm not trying to start something. All I want is solid information on Raymond Ellis," I say.

"Like I said. I don't have anything for you. We made a deal and I suggest you stick to it. You don't want to end up where I'm going. Right uhhh Stephanie?"

"Yeah," I say and hang up the phone without saying goodbye. Shit. What the hell am I going to do? Jeremy still refuses to marry me. At least Tippy is out of the way. She's still with that Darius dude. And my sissy. She's resurfaced. Glad Patrice is keeping an eye on her.

"This shit is getting old," I say out loud, looking around my quaint one bedroom condo. She's posh though. I made sure I got the best near the fashion institute I'm attending. But right now, even this European style homestead ain't keeping me happy. I need my man and now.

2/15/2013
In Druid Hills

I'm sitting with mama in her bedroom. I opened the curtains to let in the beautiful day God has blessed us with. February has brought in a cold front to Atlanta. The past few days we've had heavy rains and a few storms. But today, the sun is hovering above my parents' estate, poking spotlights off of the crystal clear lake.

Mama's in bed sick from another round of chemotherapy. Last week, she had both her breast removed. Once she feels strong enough her doctor plans to schedule her for breast reconstruction. My mama's illness has been hard for me to accept. Especially the possibility of her not beating this thing. But she has too. We've missed too much time together especially our mother, daughter talks. Some of those talks were filled with disagreements. You see, mama never wanted me to marry Robert Ellis. She didn't think he was good enough for me. Daddy went along with mama like he always does. He's definitely the doting husband who does anything for Mrs. Joselyn Oliver. From feet massages, to bathing her in warm bubble baths and keeping her secrets, if she felt exposing them would make her look bad.

As it turns out mama was right about Robert T. He's an angry man who was that way before I met him. He was arrogant and selfish and still is from what I hear. Robert cares about no one but himself.

It's no secret mama wanted me to marry Atlanta Republican and U.S. Senator Stanley Rutherford. Stanley is in his first term as senator after spending the last 6 years in the U.S. House of Representatives.

When it came to Rae, both mama and daddy loved him. He won them over. I have to say, Rae is one of the most loving people I've met. Despite his flaws and hidden profession, he's always been there for me. He listens and allows me to be me.

I remember the first time me and Robert T. fought. I should've taken note of his meanness. He went from the loving man I fell in love with to Mr. Hyde. I can't believe we got into an argument over whether he should wear a white or beige shirt underneath his navy blue suit jacket. He wanted to wear white. I thought the beige would add some life to the boring conservative suit he chose to wear. His fraternity brother, James Wilson, who is his partner and the "J" in RJ Builders and Designs, was getting married and we had planned to attend the pre-wedding banquet. Robert T. of course was the best man. As it turns out I ended up not going. Robert said some hurtful things. He called me uppity and over-bearing like my mama.

"Just because I come from the poor side of the tracks, don't mean I don't know how to dress!" he said. "I may not have rich duds like you but I do the best with what I have."

"What does that have to do with me making a suggestion about what shirt you should wear?" I asked him. "You were the one making a big deal out of what to wear."

"Who asked you?" he snapped back.

"Well excuse me," I said snidely. "What's got you all bent out of shape."

Then he says, "I tell you what. You can go on home and I'll take my broke ass over to the banquet hall. Capeesh?"

Rather than continue arguing with him, I stormed out of his raggedy, small one bedroom apartment. "He has a lot of nerve," I said aloud riding down the rickety elevator. I was hoping the thing didn't break down again like last week.

Robert T. and I got stuck for about 10 minutes between his floor on 6 and the 5th floor. The elevator alarm bell didn't work so Robert

T. tried to pry open the elevator doors with no luck. He got so angry he started banging on the elevator walls and doors. I couldn't get him to calm down. All he kept yelling about was how he'd "be a millionaire one day and never have to worry about this shit again!" Robert T. was so determined about his millionaire dream he even carried a personal check he wrote to himself for a million dollars. He showed it to me when I first met him. He said he kisses it every day.

I didn't mind the determined part of Robert T. It was his flipping attitude toward my family and our wealth. Wealth he feels we didn't really earn. But wealth passed down "from whitey to his slave bastered." Robert T. absolutely has no respect for my family history despite the fact my great, great grandfather was the reason why our family's business is so successful. Funny. As much as Robert T. hated me for having more money than him, he didn't pass up the $10 million cashier's check I handed to him to start his business. Because of it, he was able to claim 65 percent to James's 35.

Once outside Robert T.'s apartment, I was faced with having to walk alone to my car parked about a half-block down. His apartment was located in the seedy part of downtown Atlanta. Fortunately, it was early evening and I left my real jewels at home. Before visiting Robert, I would remove my beautiful diamond rose ring and earrings along with my gold antique watch passed down from my great-great grandmother Shelondra Oliver folks call my twin. I didn't want Mr. Broke to accuse me of flaunting.

About 2 steps from my dark red Mercedes coupe, a car pulls up alongside of me. "You and your beautiful car should be more careful around these parts." It was Rae Ellis. Giving me one of his big fine smiles he says, "Has anyone told you, you look as good as a bowl of Collard Greens on a Sunday?"

28
Outside again

February 16, 2013
In Portland

My attorney got me out on bail 2 days after arriving back in Portland. Muthafucka Brannigan and the Portland PD tried to keep me locked up yo. Robert Ellis was behind all this. Lucky for me they can't prove Tippy was wit' me. Girl took everything except she didn't find her Diary. Good deal yo. Wouldn't want her to find out to soon about the half-truths I've been saying about her stepmama. When she does, I'll say that it was for her benefit. I've already set it up pretty much by telling her about her evil daddy.

My man Jodeci didn't tell nothin'. You couldn't pay him enough to snitch. I trust this nigga wit' my life yo. He and his girl still here. I don't mind since I'm in and out. My house got empty rooms that need fillin'. I may have to soundproof blood's room doe. He and his white girl love to fuck. They be loud as hell!

Instead of sitting around listening to the 2 of dem, I grab a coat, head out and jump into my own ride. I handed Jodeci back his keys when his car showed up this morning. I had to have the damn thing shipped back.

I don't know where I'm going but I need to clear my head. Think about what I'mo do next. I can't file a missing person's report. But I did hire a private detective to find out where she may have gone. My attorney was able to subpoena the hotel footage. All it showed was Tippy leaving alone. She must've met up with whoever once outside the building.

On MLK I stop at the carwash. I figure I can get my frustration out on washin' and waxin' my ride. I pull into the only open stall I see next to a familiar looking white boy. Yep. It's him. DaMenace wit' his no rappin' ass. Y'all may like him, but I think the wigga sucks. He ain't from the hood. Just a white boy from small town Portland who ain't been nowhere. Dat's why he's got some wacked lyrics.

I hop out of my car and walk over to the change machine located between his stall and mine.

"I see y'all made it back in one piece," he says when he sees me.

I raise my eyebrows. What do he mean by dat. "You keepin' tabs," I say half grinning.

"Naw man," he says. "TiAnna mentioned she left y'all down south."

What da hell? He done peeked my interest. "You saw T?" I ask.

"Yeah," he answers. "She stopped by my concert in L.A. Afterwards we kicked it. She was a nice distraction given what happened to Uri."

My head is spinning for sho. Dat damn girl sho gets around. Runnin' her damn mouth. And she was in L.A. when Uri got killed. I read the papers yo. Said her throat was slit clean. One end to the other. What a coincidence.

"Sorry 'bout Uri man," I say.

"Yeah I bet," DaMenace says sarcastically.

I don't respond. I'mo have some respect for the dead. Uri did help me out.

"Let me go get dis done before the rain." As I walk off DaMenace says, "Say hey to Tippy for me." I can feel him grinning behind me. Thinking he's dissing me yo. Don't matter doe. The Tippy you'll never have is Mrs. LaTonya Broussard. Now dat's gangsta.

2/16/2013
Back to Atlanta

"How the hell?" My mouth drops wide open. I'm so surprised I can't even finish my sentence. Virgil is standing in front of me on my doorstep. With his head slightly tilted downward, he's looking up at me with his dark devilish eyes. Grinning like a little kid who just got caught doing something wrong, acting all innocent. I never expected to see him again. At least not on the outside.

"Bebè caliente," he says grabbing my hands and pulling me outside. My arms quickly cover his neck and I jump up, wrapping my legs around his waist. He's twirling me around and we're laughing. He sets me down. We kiss. Tongue action.

"You know I missed you girl."

"Me too. I missed you V." Ooo. No more holding back the tears. I let 'em pour.

"No, no bebè. No crying. I ain't going nowhere."

"You promise?" I say pleadingly looking into Virgil's eyes. "I can't do this no more. Everything's all wrong. I'm all wrong."

"No, no. You're a good woman. My woman. I ain't gonna let nothing else happen to you. Got it bebè?"

I nod allowing my head to drop sideways to his chest. Virgil feels really good and warm. And he smells so damn good. "Where you staying?" I ask him.

"Where I was before. My mom kept my place for me."

"Mamacita loves her some Virgil."

"Yeah she do. Being the baby out of 7 comes with perks."

"I'm sure being the only boy ain't got nothing to do wit' it. Ha," I say laughing.

Mr. Fine 5'8 steps back to admire Miss Girlishcious 5'5.

"Why don't you come take a ride with me? Mama made me a feast. Had it ready for me when I got home."

"Virgil. You mean you just got out today?"

"Of course. You know you was the first on my list girl."

"Weelll, OK." I say hesitantly. Not because I don't wanna go. I'm afraid of what might happen. Me and Virgil still haven't done the do. I want to, but we'd have to be careful. This would mean I'd have to tell him why.

"Hey bebè. Why so hesitant?"

"Got stuff on my mind is all," I say. "My head don't be right most days."

"Dat's why I'm taking you with me. So get your things. No arguing."

"Ok. Let me go grab some stuff. And leave daddy a note. He won't be back till later."

"Cool. I'll wait for you in my ride."

I lean around Virgil to see what he's driving. He's still got his Cadillac SUV. "I see you still rollin' in style."

"Got to be. Now go on. I'll be waiting," he says swatting me on the butt.

"Ooo stop. I hate that shit," I say.

"OK bebè I'll leave dat alone for now." Virgil turns around and jogs down the stairs to his car.

When I get inside the house I'm thinking about how horny Virgil must be. Which is one reason he wants me over. I guess I should be grateful. He could be screwing one of those bitches he don't think I know about. I guess he figured he had to get some from somewhere waiting for me.

Amanishakhete

I can hear Virgil now, "Come on Bebè I'm 'bouts ready to bust."

So I'd give him some head. Got schooled by my girl Tippy. Ha. Yes I did. I laughed when she told me what happened the first time she sucked Jeremy's thang-thang. Except, I don't feel like doing duksick neither. Thanks to Don Juan and sissy, I did enough sucking dick to last me a lifetime. Yeah. Thanks to them, I got a lot of health worries. Can't have no kids, but that ain't the half of it. You see y'all I got HIV. Thanks to them.

29
Bold Move

February 16, 2013
Miami Beach

Me and Tippy remain tucked away in a house in Oceanside, one of Miami's posh communities. Tippy's Uncle Ray leased the 4 bedroom property and paid extra to have the walls re-painted in fuchsia. The place has white carpet throughout with fancy white and black marble floors in the bathrooms and kitchen. This place looks like it came out of one of those upscale home and garden magazines. But it's for Tippy's benefit. This place definitely has a severe feminine touch. Even the patio furniture lends itself to her theme. Tippy felt it too when she first walked in. She kicked off her shoes and ran around like a little kid. Then off she goes to play in the sand right below the house.

Amanishakhete

Being here puts me in a romantic frame of mine, but I keep things friendly. My girl still hasn't recouped much of her memory past the time she was a little girl. Deep-down she knows who I am and we had it going on. But I don't want to spook her. And I wouldn't wanna piss-off Raymond Ellis.

Unlike my dinky apartment, which I've barely seen over the past couple of weeks, this place comes equipped with private security, housekeeping services and a personal chef. It also has enough rooms to house round-the-clock mental health care staff. Rae also flies in Dr. Evelyn Anderson, Tippy's original psychiatrist. She was surprised to find out that Dr. Ryan and Robert Ellis had commitment papers drawn up. Rae Ellis is convinced the 2 of them are in cahoots. Frankly, I believe it. Robert Ellis has always had control over Tippy. More to do with money than a concern about her mental health. This is why I stayed close to her in Stone Mountain. A second set of eyes. Those same eyes, including Dr. Anderson's and Rae's, keep Tippy's whereabouts on the QT. Robert Ellis will meet hell-fire coming anywhere near us. Personally, I wouldn't mind getting a piece of 'em.

During the day, I still attend classes. I also avoid seeing Stephanie, but I do check in by phone. When we do speak, she whines about how bad she's feeling. Says morning sickness is kicking her ass. Maybe. But I think she says it to keep me locked in. She's knows I'm committed as long as we get proof the baby is mine. I ain't saying I don't trust her. But what do I know about her really? Nothing. She claims she has no family. Grew up in foster care. Abandoned by her parents. She doesn't say much after that. Makes me wonder what she's really hiding. Anyhoo, given Tippy is back in my life, me being a potential father to another woman's child sickens me. Deep down I pray the kid ain't mine. Especially since I made damn sure we used condoms. Well except that one time around Christmas. My soul was feeling pretty raw. Made me slip-up. Sheeeit. Now I may have to pay the piper. Ain't cool. Ain't cool at all.

Ω

Today, I finished my last class at 3. Boring ass American History. I'm a political science major so it's part of my degree requirements. Other than that, I do like politics. Next to a career in football, I often think about a career in government relations. But this is far as I'll go. No running for office in my future.

Around 4:00 I'm back at the ocean. I see a couple of extra cars parked in the driveway. All have Miami tags so I assume it's the staff.

Once inside I hear faint sounds of chatter, coming from what we call the group room. The mental health staff use it for counseling sessions with Tippy. The room is located on the left side of the house adjacent to the living room, which opens onto the patio. When I step into the living room, I stop momentarily to take in the view. Even in February you can count on the sun shining in Miami. I spend a lot of quiet time in here. Gives me a chance to meditate, get my mind together when Tippy is asleep. I often ponder what may happen once Tippy regains her memory. And she will. For now, I take one day at a time. This is the advice Dr. Anderson offers me in my side counseling sessions with her, since I'm also sort of serving in a caretaker capacity.

Sudden laughter snaps me back to reality. Curious, I head to the group room. The door is open so I peak inside. In here, tinted windows stop the sun from bouncing through. The moonlight effect has me thinking romantic thoughts again. I quickly divert my attention to the group huddled in a circle near the corner windows. Seated at the arch of the circle, facing me is Tippy with her uncle on her right and Dr. Anderson on her left. Next to Dr. Anderson is Granddaddy Oliver. On his right and with her back to me is his wife, Joselyn who's wearing a red scarf around her head. Mama told me Mrs. Oliver has cancer. She's probably hairless by now. Next to her and to Rae's left, is a middle-aged, light-skinned black woman. She's wearing her long brown hair, down over her left shoulder, which reminds me of someone. Whoever she is, I can tell she's fine from her side profile. I'm intrigued. But I don't want to interrupt. Instead, I turn to leave until I hear Tippy calling after me.

"Where you going?" she says.

I turn back. By this time, I have the attention of the entire group, including the fine black woman I was peeping earlier. Damn she looks like – I must be dreaming! The ghost of Loretta Ellis is starring right at me.

30

OK. Okay?

February 16, 2013
Atlanta

Right before we pull up in front of Virgil's, I get a phone call. The caller ID shows a 503 number. Shit! I hope this ain't DaMenace. I'm tempted to ignore his call, but I need to hear what's up with the police investigation. The last I heard, the girl's barely description of me was all they had.

"Who dat?" Virgil asks, trying to look over at my phone.

"Nobody for you," I say teasingly. After clicking in, I say "It's me if you know who me is."

"Yeah I know who me is yo."

Ah hell I'm thinking. I don't want Virgil to get too curious so instead I ask, "How are things?"

We pull up into Virgil's driveway and he shuts the car off. Leaning his left shoulder against the window, he turns his head towards me. Then scrunching his forehead, he sets his right hand on my headrest. Hmpf. He better not be tryin' to play the jealous boo. After all, Amigo's been locked up since last year. But rather than give 'em my "Latin Negro paleeze" look, I hold my expression as straight as an arrow. I don't plan on starting any shit. Virgil has been there for me.

"Things ain't good yo. But you know dat already. I believe you know where Tippy is and I expect you to tell me. In case you forgot, you owe me big time yo. Don't forget. A body can easily surface."

"Whoa slow your roll," I say, raising my voice looking at Virgil, bending his eyebrows.

"I ain't slowing nothin yo. They tryin' to get a nigga and shit. My wacked girl ran off and she had help. And you know who. And yo. What da fuck was you doin in L.A. with DaMenace? The night Uri got murdered. Bet you know nothin about dat, right? Look T. I ain't lettin' up until you tell me where my wife is."

"I don't know what you mean," I say to Darius, trying to be cool. "I thought y'all was still together. Don't tell me something's happened to —"

"Stop bullshitting yo!"

Darius is really pissing me off. Sounding like the night I ran off from his uncle's house. I want to cuss this Negro out but good. Say to his yo-ing ass, "I'm glad she's not with you!" Besides, I don't know where my girl is. Not exactly. I do know she's safe though. Damon gave me the lowdown.

"Look, I gotta get back with you later," I say, attempting to end the conversation. "I got company."

"Yo. I tell you what. We can meet up later. Yeah. I'm in Atlanta. And I aim to find Tippy before I leave."

"Hmmm. So where?" I ask, knowing I ain't meeting this Negro nowhere. "His threats don't scare me. I got my own ammunition, starring right at me. And he's frowning big time. "Look. I gots to go. You can text me." I hang up before Darius can say anything else.

"So bebe," Virgil says. "You gone tell me what dats about?"

"Yeah. But can we go inside? I need to taaa." Before I can finish, I burst into tears. Dang. I feel sick. Everything's spinning around me. So fast. "Blaahck."

"Ah hell. Throwing up all over my ride and shit. Betta be glad I love yo ass. What da hell got you so fucked up?"

"Everything's sooo wrong," I say, wiping my mouth and boohooing. "They fucked me up really bad. I hate me. I hate everybody. I'm dangerous Virgil. You need to stay away from me."

"Ha, ha, ha," laughs Virgil. "Bebe. I'm dangerous too. We make a good team. But I'm here now O.K? I take over now O.K? We make a plan to fix all dis shit. OK? Payback's a beech. First we start with the punk muthafucka you was just talkin' too."

I nod. No need for anymore tears. I'm feeling just peachy. Thanks to my extra ammo, Susie's got help.

31
Truth be known

Many years ago
In rural Wisconsin

Dr. Michelson shows up at our farm unannounced and outside of his regular visiting hours. He walks right in without knocking. Something he's prone to do because daddy leaves the doors unlocked during the day. When Michelson comes in, he stops short, immediately drawn to the 2 lifeless bodies beneath the stairs. Now, here we all stand. Michelson, me and Delores with our dead parents surrounded in Mr. Luke's blood. Ironically, Michelson doesn't blink when he sees the mess. In fact, from my vantage-point on his right, I see a smirk forming on his face. He doesn't notice me observing. He's too focused on Delores, who's still holding Mr. Luke's shotgun. Michelson walks over to her and takes the gun. Neither of them speak but shared a look I ponder about to this day.

With Michelson's help, we concoct the story me and Delores found our parents dead when we got home from school. Everyone, including the sheriff, knew Mr. Luke was crazy. And thanks to Michelson, they also believed that our mother had severe mental health issues. Because of this, the sheriff concluded the killing was a murder-suicide.

In a small community, news travels fast. Mr. Luke did not allow us to have acquaintances, so when the residents reached out, we were apprehensive. Soon we accepted their generosity. Another farmer down the road offered to purchase our farm. Little did we know Mr. Luke had taken out 3 mortgages. So we got next to nothing. Delores, who just turned 18, married Dr. Michelson, a then 40-year-old wealthy widower. I went to live with them, finished high school and then went off to college to study psychiatry at the urging of Delores. Little did I know her support for my career would lead us down a dark road of no return. You see, Delores had her own plan. It included a life without Dr. Michelson.

2/17/2013
1:00 p.m. Atlanta

I'm sitting next to Delinda's bed in Atlanta General Hospital. When I got here, I had her moved to a nicer room which I paid for. She doesn't have insurance so she was on one of those wards for folks who can't pay.

She's been asleep for a grip. The nurse gave her something to help ease the pain and help her sleep. Earlier, she had a miscarriage and I'm happy as hell. Don't get me wrong, I do feel for her. She's taking it pretty hard, considering she wanted my baby. Having it would've meant staying connected to me for life. But I just can't see Delinda being a mother. Especially to my child. Hey, we both got some growing up to do. Even more, we're both young and should be looking at options. For me, this means a woman who I could possibly spend the rest of my life with. I've been giving this a lot of thought, which leads me to my next move. I plan to break it off with Delinda just as soon as she feels better.

"How you feeling sleepy head?" I ask Delinda once she's awake.

"Um," she says, turning her head towards me.

"Can I get you anything?"

"My baby back," she says, starting to cry. "He's been growing inside me for 4 months. I don't understand."

I'm stunned. Delinda just called the baby we lost "he." She notices my bewildered look and says, "I had 'em tell me the baby's sex. They didn't want to, but I had a right to know."

"Wow," I say. "I was gonna have a son?" All of a sudden I'm feeling hurt. How could I not? A boy? Until now, I never thought of the baby in terms of a real live person. Whether it'd be a boy or girl? Be in perfect health? Have all its fingers and toes? All I've been thinking about is my feelings. Not wanting the baby who wasn't even born yet. Well I guess I got my wish. The good Lord saw fit to also let me know that the precious life we lost was also gonna be my namesake. I grab and kiss Delinda's hand. "I'm sorry we lost our son. We'll get through this together," I find myself saying. She smiles. Damn I'm thinking. There's goes my plans about moving on. Somehow I think this being there for Delinda ain't gonna end anytime soon. If at all.

4:00 p.m.
Miami

I'm still stunned. I barely get out the words "hello." Rae excuses himself from the group and comes over to me. He's grinning but appears nervous. He should be. Loretta Ellis is supposed to be dead. Seeing my look of confusion, he pats me on the back.

"Let's go talk," he says, motioning for me to follow him. On my way out, I nod to the group and wave to Tippy. I'm glad she's still smiling. Perhaps because she doesn't remember much, seeing her mama didn't faze her.

"You're surprised about seeing Loretta," Rae says once we're out in the other room.

"Surprised?" I say. "No disrespect. But I feel like I'm in the twilight zone. I'm guessing this is one of those family secrets that passed me up huh?"

"Loretta didn't die but she almost did. She went into a coma and didn't come out of it until last November," Rae explains. "We kept it under wraps because we didn't know who her killer was. No one knows she's alive outside of her doctors, me and her parents. And you and Tippy of course. My brother doesn't even know."

"I see," I say still in disbelief. I don't know whether to be mad or glad. I've spent the past several years consoling Tippy over her mama being murdered. Now she's alive. How am I supposed to take the news? Don't even know how I should feel about a woman I've never met but only have seen in photos.

"Looks like Tippy's in good spirits Rae," I say. "I guess she took the news well."

"We've been easing up to the part about her witnessing the murder," says Rae. "We brought Loretta in 'cause Tippy's been asking me a lot of questions. She's only been hearing information from Darius. He's been twisting some of the facts. Even left out the part about Loretta. Why I don't know. At least he's been clear about my brother."

"I don't know dude. But I'm sure he's just as dirty," I respond. I pause for a moment, remembering what Rae said earlier. Then ask, "What did you mean when you said you didn't know who the killer was? Does Loretta know?"

Rae leans his head up to peer over my shoulder, making sure we're alone. "We can't do nothin' about who right now. Un-da-stand?"

I guess so, I'm thinkin' and nod.

"Look Jeremy," says Rae. "I appreciate what you're doing. You've been good for my daughter. You're familiar and she feels safe."

"I love Tippy sir. I'd do anything for her. Me breaking things off between us wasn't my doing."

"It ain't necessary to explain. Trust me. I'm aware of my brother's doings. Don't forget, I'm a casualty of his war too. For now." Rae moves a little closer to me then says, "I also know about your baby mama. I won't allow Tippy to be hurt behind y'all's family business. Keep that in mind."

"Yes sir," I say.

"Glad we got an un-da-standing Jeremy." Rae slaps me on the back a little harder this time, making sure I feel a sting.

2/17/2013
Already tomorrow in Atlanta

Today at 4:00, Darius wants me to meet up with him over at a place called the Jaba Café in downtown ATL. Jaba is a hole-in the wall nestled inside the Premier Bank Building, where they serve good Jamaican food. I don't know why he chose to meet there. They stay crowded. People go to eat – get in and get out. The Jamaicans, who own it, turnover tables as fast as they can to avoid long delays. Lunch and evenings ain't no joke. Which is why they also have takeout as an option. Works best for the downtown workers.

Hmm. What does Darius expect? We're gonna break-bread and he threatens me for information about my BFF? Huh. He's in for a big surprise. LMAO (laughing my ass off).

Si. He looks familiar. Ahhh. Si. Si. Dat's who ran up on me outside the liquor store in LA. I was hanging wit' a couple of my crew. I spit on the ground right when he walked by. I guess he thought it was meant for him. He lucky I let him live wit' his punk ass. Tryin' to be hard in front of his crazy crew. Dey wasn't shit. All dey did mostly was some petty theft. Couldn't hang wit' the big boys. He lucky most of 'em got snuffed out, which dey deserved. Dey wanted him dead 'cause he didn't participate in some gang rape. So he disappears. Don't mean he still ain't a wanted man.

When I enter, it don't take but a minute to peep where homes is at. I walk up on 'im texting.

"Hey esse. Don't I know you?" I say to the yella punk sittin' at a table in the back of the café. He looks up and don't say nothin'.

"Ain't dat right esse. We know each other right?"

Yeah I know dis fuckin' Mexican. What kinda game is dis yo? He askin'. I ain't answerin'.

"OK esse, you don't have to answer," I say, sliding into the seat across from 'im. "All you gotta do is listen. OK?" I lean over so the little punk can hear me good. But we interrupted by the waiter. He don't say nothin'. Don't even smile. Got his pen and pad ready doe.

"Give me a minute," I say. He nods and leaves. I take a quick snapshot of the place. Ain't too many people in here yet. The waiter need to be cool if he want a tip.

"Get dis. Don't call my girl no more. Stay away from her. OK? What you got going on wit' yours ain't her business no more. OK?" Then I lean up preparing to leave. "Oh and one more thing," I say. "You can forget about what you think you got on my girl. Like I can forget about who wanna know where you hiding dese days. We clear esse?" I get up and stand next to the table, reach into my wallet and pull out a 50. I throw the bill on the table, giving homes one last look. I bet he don't think he so bad now. Hijo de puta!

32
Unexpecting reality

March 1, 2013
Atlanta

Guess who I run into out shopping? Minding my own business. Luanne. I heard the bitch pulled a fast one. Signed Tippy over to Darius. Wonder what she's getting out of the deal? Robert Ellis is already paying her big money Tippy said.

"Looks like we gots da same idea," she says, walking her boney ass over to where I'm standing. Like we long lost friends. Nosey bitch.

"I doubt it," I say, barely making eye contact. I keep my attention on the rack of infant clothes I'm looking through.

Miss Nosey refuses to take a hint and instead asks, "Someone pregnan'?"

"Maybe," I say, looking at her from the corner of my left eye. "You pregnant?"

"Girl please," she says. "I done havin' kids." She pauses, glancing down into my shopping cart and comments, "You got a lot goo' stuff."

What she's looking at is my assortment of boy's and girl's clothing. Not sure which ones I'll need. I'm hopin' for a girl though. Choosing one last item, I'm done with this rack and now this store since Luanne's ass came in interrupting my flow. I place the two-piece jumper in the cart and look towards the front of the store. Spotting a free cashier I make my move. "Let me pay for this and get outta here," I say, even though I wanna read Luanne's ass, but I'ma play dumb. Gotta be cool for Tippy's sake.

"Yeah OK," she says, chuckling. "Nice talkin' to someone I know doe. Mama and Uncle Joshua both gone, leavin' me all alone."

Paleeze. Who's she kidding? She thinks I'ma react. I could give a rat's ass about what she may know thanks to Darius Broussard's punk ass. Instead I throw up my hand, giving her a phony wave and say, "Have a nice day." No more giving the broad my attention. Today is the beginning of a whole new life for me. With Virgil's help, I'ma be a mother real soon.

Watchin' TiAnna walk off I shake my head. "Oomph. Well I'll say den." Got me real curious. Shoppin' for babies clothes. Hmmm. Whatup?

My phone rings. I click in. "Dis Luanne."

"Hello Luanne. Got some good news. I believe we found the person you're looking for."

Over in Norcross

Me and crazy ass Patrice got into it again. Lately he's been finding more things to go off on me about. This time it was over me asking about a conversation I overheard. He was on the phone with his friend in Miami, the one he's been talking to a lot lately. I could've sworn I heard him say TiAnna's name.

Amanishakhete

As a matter of fact, we've been arguing and throwing blows a lot more since TiAnna's been gone. Not to say we wasn't fighting before. But not quite like this. Patrice is unleashing a side of her I ain't seen.

TiAnna left out of here last month without saying good-bye. She didn't even leave me a note. I was at school but Patrice was here. All he said was TiAnna's daddy showed up and made her leave. I found that hard to believe. Since what went down with Miss T, she's grown up and is pretty independent. I finally got a hold of her a week later. She said she needed to be with her family. I've known T forever and know when she's lying. I suspected something went down between her and Patrice and she didn't wanna tell me. I confront Patrice about it. He hauls off and slaps me in my pretty face.

"No you didn't," I yell at him. Then slap his ass back. Right across his face, which may have helped his looks 'cause he ain't all that. Patrice stumbles, recoups and comes back on me like a bitch. He older than me so he got more strength. But his age can also be his downfall, so I let him wear his self out. I stay bent over, shielding myself from as many blows as possible. Don't want any bruising on my face. I need that in case I got to find someone else to hold up with. Right when he steps back to take a break, I jump up and tap dat ass.

"Now holla-me-bad muthafucka!" I scream at Patrice. I'm spatting, kicking and throwing blow after blow with my arms stretched in eloquent formation like a champion swimmer. Spat, kick, throw. Spat, kick, throw. All in rhythm to the beat of Tommy Crumb's. When I come up for air, I pick up a lamp and one time some book ends and throw 'em at him. Patrice really gets mad then. He don't like folks fucking wit' her stuff. Always bragging about how much she paid. Paleeze. It ain't all that. Don't get me wrong. Patrice got some nice things. But it don't come from places like Jacob Maroni in New York where Tippy gets a lot of her stuff. Yep. I'm learning to hold my own. Got to otherwise I'll end up all fucked up. Tryin' to hide my bruises from the kids at school.

We're done fighting and I threaten to leave. Patrice comes back with how sorry he is and gets to boohooing like some damn baby. I haven't yet, but I'm on the verge of getting the hell outta Dodge. She better lighten up. I'm too damn pretty, too damn intelligent and too damn sweet to take this shit!

"Look Miss Thang," I say to Patrice. "Some shit goin' on. Whatever it is better not involve my friends. I don't give a fuck who you is!"

"It ain't 'bout yo friends," says Patrice, all smug. "You always being suspicious."

"Annd," I say, putting my hands on my hips, leaning back on my left leg, Tommy Crumbs style. "Your faggot ass is mean."

"I ain't yo faggot," Patrice says rotating her neck and head around in a circle.

"Then stop acting like one," I say. "You old as hell. Acting like a damn fool."

"Huh. You don't think I'm so old when I'm fuckin' yo skinny ass," says Patrice.

I drop my head, lift my brows, looking at Patrice. "Hmm. There are days," I say. "Make me long for a young man. Like me."

"You can just get yo sorry ass out den," Patrice yells. He ain't no longer leaning on his back leg. Girlfriend lifts up on his toes, takes two steps forward and drops back down on his feet, making me step back a few pasos. Need some space in case we go to blows again. Shit. Talking about pasos makes me think about T. She's back with Latin Mandingo. I hope she can be happy. Haaah. I miss her and Tippy.

"Shall I go pack my things?" I ask Patrice.

He looks at me with his mouth turned up to one side. "Oomph. You can wait 'till tomorrow." Then he walks off.

Yeah that's what I thought. Old ass queen can't get enough of Tommy Crumbs.

Up in Portland

I'm pondering a decision. My phone rings, calling from a private number. I answer in case it's my daughter whose been missing in action since New Year's.

"Hello."

It's quiet on the other end until the caller laughs. "He, he, he." Then says softly, "I saw you Robert Ellis."

"Who is this? Tippy?"

"Noooo. But close. Real close." The caller hangs up.

"What the hell's going on? My brother's gotta be behind this shit!"

I lay my cell back on the desk. Pushing myself up from my chair, I step away and walk over to my office window. It's sunny so I can clearly see the entire city from all angles. Gets me thinking about that phone call. I'ma put an end to this shit once and for all.

33
Ease on down

March 2, 2013
Saturday in Miami

"You're really leaving?" I ask.

"Yeah," she says, giving me a hug. "Ahhh. Why look so sad Basset Hound?"

"Because I'm feelin' sad," I say, tearing up. Suddenly her smile turns upside down. My fault. I shouldn't be acting this way. They may know what's best. But who's to say she'll be safe? Hollup. Who am I kidding? She's got the best security ever.

"You can come too," Tippy says to me with pleading eyes. "I like your company. You make me laugh."

"I wish I could," I say, breaking a slight smile. I'm remembering how she always tells me to smile. Telling me I always look sad whether I was or not. Now is different. I just got her back and she's going again. A part of me wonders if this is her uncle's doing? He did promise he wouldn't allow my issues to hurt Tippy in anyway. I wasn't going to allow it neither.

"Well you gotta," I say. It's for the best. "I'll stop in to see you soon."

"Will you call me too? Like every day?"

My smile gets a little bigger. "Of course beautiful. I won't miss a beat."

This is the first time I'm close to being my old self around my girl. She didn't get upset when I called her beautiful. In fact, she's grinning. Reaching her lips up next to my left cheek she kisses me. Yeah. This is a sure sign. Deep down she knows.

I'm back at my apartment where I haven't spent more than a minute in the past month. The last time I came through, I tossed out some old garbage. The place smelled funky as hell. Opening up the fridge, I forgot I left it pretty bare. Despite the couple of energy drinks and pitcher of ice water, I'd gotten rid of the expired milk and wilted produce. One thing I'm gonna miss is the chef's cooking. Lots of healthy food, keeping a brother regular. I'm also gonna miss the housekeeping. Since Stephanie ain't been here, the place is the bachelor pad it once was. I went through a bunch of clothes trying to find clean ones. They still all over the bed and on the floor where I left 'em – dirty draws, sweatshirts. I had every intention of taking my dirty laundry over to where I'd been staying. But I was too much in a hurry. I stay too long, Stephanie would show. She did that often when I was around. I couldn't get her to call before she came. She had already gotten comfortable.

Ah shit! Spoke to soon. Better not be Stephanie knocking at my door. I walk over to the door and look out the peep hole. Sure enough, it's her. She's stalking me alright. This shit's got to stop. I don't give a damn about her being pregnant.

I open the door. Stephanie's standing there in a long brown coat. With her hands in her pocket, she pulls back her open coat, showing me her stomach. She's wearing a tight dark red sweater I gave her for Christmas. It's creeping up her belly. She eyeballed it in a boutique we passed, walking along the strip in South Beach last November. Stephanie's around 4 months so she says. Personally, I can't say how she's supposed to look.

I don't say hi or nothing. Instead I ask, "How'd you know I'd be here?"

"A feelin' I got," she answers.

I step aside so she can come in.

"Are you OK?" she asks once inside.

"I should be asking you," I say. "You feelin' OK?"

"Mmm," she pauses. "I've been better."

"Meaning?" I ask.

"Me and my baby are missing his daddy," she says.

"Hm," all I can think to say. In her eyes I see tears forming. I hear pregnant women get all sensitive and cry a lot. But I can't deal with her boohooing right now. 'Cause I feel like crying and it ain't 'cause of her. I turn away, staring across the room where I got clothes thrown across the couch too. I walk over, bend down and begin picking them up.

"I was tryin' to clean the place up," I say with my back to Stephanie, who's right behind me. She places her hand on my back, rubbing me up and down. I lean up and turn around facing her, making her hands drop.

"I'm guessing someone else has your mind occupied," she says, wiping away a couple of dropping tears.

"What makes you ask that?" I say, eyeing her suspiciously.

"You're the one with secrets," she says.

Wow. She can't be serious. She's the queen of secrecy and lies. Rather than feed into this inquisition, I say, "You know Stephanie, this ain't a good day."

"Well why?" she asks again.

"You ask too many questions that ain't your business," I finally say, annoyed. She refuses to let up though. I can tell by the look in her face. No more teary eyes and pitiful puckered lips. Both hands back in her pockets, she's scrunching her forehead, tightening her lips.

Then she opens her damn mouth and says, "Would it have anything to do with who lives behind the gates at Oceanside?"

I do my best not to react. Has the bitch been following me? What does she know? How much does she know?

"Bitch," I say, using a word I don't use. Disrespecting women wasn't a part of my home training. But she got me on fire. The thought of her knowing about Tippy makes me wanna reach out and – "You better not be following me!"

"Well I guess I got my answer!" Stephanie screams.

"You know what," I say, grabbing her arm. "You gonna have to leave. Now!" I pull her over to the door and open it. Letting loose of her arm I say, "Having a baby, which may or may not be mine, doesn't give you the right to run me. I never promised you a rose garden." Reaching my right hand out towards the open door, I motion for her to go. Stephanie hesitates, looking at me like I'm gonna change my mind. Ain't happening. Keeping my hand out, I'm thinking she'd better make a move real quick. She finally steps through the doorway, turns and faces me once she lands on the deck. With her face softening, she opens her mouth to say something, but I cut her off. "No need to come back here. I'll have my attorney contact you." I slam the door.

"Hey you asshole!" she says, yelling and banging on the door. "I ain't the one to fuck with."

I don't say nothing, but let her keep banging for a minute. Then I yank the door open.

"Look. Cut this shit out or I'm calling the police."

Stephanie's eyes get big. She knows I'm serious. Yeah y'all. The heartbroken Jeremy she took advantage of is gone.

34
Time's up

April 16, 2013
In Georgia

I flew in to visit my patient at a private psychiatric facility only me and Delores know about. When I get there, the nurse says to me, "Hasn't been a good day for Mr. Davidson I'm afraid."

"What's going on?" I ask afraid to hear the truth.

"He's been saying the strangest things for the past couple of days," the nurse says. "He's claiming he's a Dr. Michelson and he's here against his will."

"A Dr. Michelson?" I feedback to the nurse maintaining my doctor's look of concern. "Have you been giving him his meds?"

"Yes doctor."

"I see," I say, pondering briefly. "It appears he's experiencing a delusional disorder as a symptom of his schizophrenia. We'll need to deal with his psychosis with aggressive shock therapy and meds." I write out specific instructions, asking the nurse to start the treatment immediately. Stepping away from the nurses' station, I find a private room to make a phone call.

"Hi Delores. It's me."

"Yes Dr. Ryan I know your voice. We grew up together remember?" says Delores, laughing. "How's our patient?"

"I had to change his treatment plan. He's been telling the nurses he's Dr. Michelson."

"Hmmm. Not a nice thing to do. Changing a treatment plan isn't what we should be planning."

"Look Delores. I, I can't."

"Maybe I should pay him a visit. A concerned wife would be the appropriate move for both of us. One less thing to worry about."

Haaaa, I sigh. Since Delores has been with scumbag Robert Ellis, she's wanted to move on "D Day". Not to say I would feel any loss for Michelson. Especially after what he helped our father do to our mother all those years. This is simply payback. But to do what Delores wants would mean we would be accountable for not only kidnapping and fraud, but murder. I can't support my sister on this one. What am I going to do?

At Tommy's
In Norcross

I'm glad Patrice is out of the house. I can have a private conversation. I dial up TiAnna to see how she's doing.

"What's up Miss Tommy?"

"Girl, I wish I could say nada," I answer.

"Uh-oh. Have you finally come to your senses and left Ms. Holla me bad?"

LOL. "TiAnna girl you crazy. You know I can say the same about you and Latin Mandingo."

"Yeah you can. But me and Virgil will have more to celebrate soon."

"Ooo and what's that Miss T?"

"Can't tell you just yet Tommy. But I promise I'll tell you soon. What's up with you?"

"Girl. Patrice's girlfriend in Miami coming to stay with us until her baby is born. I guess Mr. Jeremy kicked her to the curb."

"Ooo whaaat? When she coming Tommy?"

"Girl tomorrow. Patrice is picking her up at the Delta terminal around 9:00 tomorrow night. I ain't feeling too happy about it neither."

TiAnna pauses momentarily, looking over at Virgil with a big grin on her face. "Well you never know Tommy. Miss Thang may change her mind."

"I'd be a happy queen T. Everytime she calls here she sobs about Jeremy. To have her shit up front and personal, well. No doubt she'll have all Patrice's attention, leaving me with jilt."

"Ahhh now Tommy. You ain't jealous? Come on. Maybe you'll have a chance to spring free for a few nights. Catch some younger booty."

"Huh, haaaa. Girl you rotten. I'ma leave that alone in case walls have ears."

"Tommy, you can always come hang wit' us."

"I'll keep your offer in mind," I say. "I'ma get at you later. Let you Latin Mandingo get back to what yall was doing hmm."

"Ok Mr. Tommy Crumbs. Or should I say holla you bad?"

"Yes you can say that. I'm the one bad around here these days. Gotta keep Patrice in line so she won't go off."

"Ahhh, whaat? What do you mean Tommy."

"Girl nothing. Patrice be acting like an ol' ass queen sometime."

"She better not be putting her hands on you Tommy."

"Now girl you know her hands be all over me."

"You know what I mean Tommy."

"Yes Miss T. There's nothing for you to worry about. I got her handled."

"Ok. But just the same, I got my eye on Ms. Patrice."

"A second set of eyes ain't gonna hurt. Thanks for looking out girl."

"Ain't nothing. You one of my girls. Get at you later," I say and hang up. I look over at Virgil who's looking at me with questioning eyes.

"Change of plans," Says TiAnna.

"Ok Bebè. Ready to rock and roll," says the strong voice of my Latin Mandingo.

8:00p.m.
In Atlanta

I've been keeping Luanne company for some time. Staying away from Portland is my best bet for now yo. I also know where they hiding my girl. Come to find out, she's back in Druid Hills at her mama's estate. I'm wondering how they managed to get Tippy to buy off on Loretta's hiding out for 9 years. Rae pulled a fast one. I bet he's also trying to figure out how to dissolve me and Tippy's marriage. To do so, he'd have to expose her. Then Robert Ellis would have every right to come drag her off to the looney farm.

"Ya cain't just go over dere bustin' in Darius."

"I know dat yo," I say to Luanne. We both laying naked in her king bed. She's laying front first on top of me keepin' me warm from my chest to my balls to my legs, feet and toes. Y'all probably ready to call cheaters on me. Hell. My wife ain't here doin' her wifely duties. Yeah. Yeah. She don't remember past 6. But damn yo. After our honeymoon night, I knew she'd remember my mouth and dick inside her pussy. I guess she got spooked. Huh. She can spook on den for now. Until we get dis shit straight and her mama and Rae out da way.

"I'mo chill for a minute. Keep an eye out. The time to make a move will present itself soon."

"In da meantyne Darius?"

"In da meantime, we keep doin' what we doin' yo." I grab Luanne underneath her arms, pulling her up to my readied lips. "C'mon here girl. Quench my thirst."

35
Out Done

April 17, 2013
8:30p.m. in Portland

"I need you to keep monitoring the Druid Hills estate," I say to a friend back in Atlanta. "Rae's in and out of there for some reason. It got to be where he's stashing my daughter. I can't figure out why though, so there's got to be more. Like those strange phone calls I've been getting." I shiver a little thinking about them. Making the strangest thoughts run through my mind. These thoughts make no sense. Loretta's dead. That's what Rae told me.

In looking back on the night at the hospital, they wouldn't even let me see her. To say good-bye and good riddens. When the funeral came and went, they sent my baby girl home crying. Those assholes wouldn't let her see Loretta. Her casket was closed during the funeral and burial. Frankly, the story never made sense. I saw Loretta before they took her away to the hospital. There was nothing I could see, which would prevent them from having her casket open. Her wounds didn't meet her neck or face. They could have easily stitched her cuts up around the lower part of her body and dressed her in one of her fancy expensive dresses. No one would have known. They only leave the casket half open anyway.

"I need you to do something else for me man," I say. "I need you to do some digging about the night Loretta died. I'll provide you with anything you need to get people to talk. Someone knows more than what they've been saying. I wanna know which funeral home did the embalming and what they know and her doctors and nurses at the time. Also find one of our boys in blue who, for the right price, will sing sweet Jesus. Got me?"

"I'm on it sir."

"And say, I want a weekly, if not daily report. Got me?"

"Yes sir. Uhhh. How about this Darius character?"

"Right. Keep an eye on him and my ex too. I wanna know what they up too besides screwing."

Speaking of my ex, she thinks she's pulled a fast one by signing the marriage certificate. Probably feels she's gotta hand she can play 'cause she certainly wasn't too worried about signing. Knowing that goes against my plans. I don't know how much Mr. Broussard knows, but I can bet Luanne is screwing and singing me praises at the same time. Ha. Ha. Ha. At least I know he was the punk she was sleeping with in L.A. Sending my money to him. Punk may already know about Tippy's trust. May even have a plan to get it back. Ignorant fool. Playing with the big boys will get you hurt.

8:40 p.m.
Clocks a ticking

And this fool got the nerve to be standin' here at my door. "What the fuck do you want! I gots to be someplace!"

"We need to talk," I say standing my ground on Patrice's front porch. Tommy answered the door. He was surprised to see me. His eyes got big when I asked for Patrice. He didn't know we knew each other. Why am I here? TiAnna wanted me to come by and pick up something she left. Said she felt uncomfortable coming back over here and didn't want Virgil to come 'cause she's afraid of what he may do. Anyhoo, this gives me a chance to confront Patrice. Let her know she can tell Miss Chelsea the jig is up. I'm telling Jeremy everything. But I'm hesitant about speaking my mind in front of Tommy. I don't wanna start nothing, but his drag queen ain't shit. Can't be trusted. She's a con like Chelsea."

"Patrice maybe me and you should talk out here. Alone," I say, eyeing Tommy, who's looking sideways at Patrice with his mouth open. He's leaning back with his arms crossed doing his Tommy stance. I laugh to myself.

"What's going on y'all," he says, looking at me then back at Patrice.

"First off Tommy, TiAnna thought she left her black pumps here. She wanted me to stop by. Did she call you?"

"Nooo," says Tommy. "She didn't leave nothing behind. Anyway," he says, turning his head towards me, looking down and back up with his head halfcocked. "What the hell black pumps gotta do wit' y'all wanting to talk privately. You got something you've been hiding?" he says, sliding his eyes down to my trunk then back up.

"What Mr. Damon wanna talk about I'm guessing was before you darlin'," says Patrice grinning, looking over at Tommy.

Wow. I can't help but take in how ass ugly Patrice is. She's got her coat crossed over her arm, drag queening it with her blonde wig, thick ass make-up and an orange tight fitting dress. This damn queen knows she's too black to be wearing orange. Looking like a terd.

"Ohhhh," says Tommy.

"Look Patrice," I say, my face burning with embarrassment. "I want to talk about Stephanie. You know she supposed to be having my man's baby."

Patrice leans her neck back. Slightly dropping her head she bats her eyes looking at me. "You wanna talk now? Look honey, you're gonna have to wait on that one." Patrice looks at her watch. "Shit. It's 8:45. Move the hell out the way boy. I'm late." She pushes past me runs to her car, jumps in and speeds off.

"Uhhhh, Stephanie?" says Tommy. "You know that's who Patrice is picking up from the airport. Apparently, she had a falling out wit' your boy. She'll be staying here until after her baby is born."

"For real? Good," I say. "Maybe I won't have to say anything."

"Oh uh-uh," says Tommy, shaking his head. "You gonna bring your fine black ass in here and tell Tommy what the fuck is up."

I drop my head, thinking, then back up at Tommy. "You right. It's time you know the real Patrice and her friend Stephanie. For starters, Stephanie's real name is Chelsea."

"Chelsea!" Tommy says, disbelievingly.

"Yep. The one who had our girl, TiAnna, kidnapped and turned-out by Don Juan. Your Patrice knows all."

9:25p.m.
At Hartford Airport

"Can you page her again," I ask the customer service agent. "They say she was on the plane."

"I've paged her twice ma'am. Like the Delta agent said, Miss Stephanie Miller and the other passengers departed the plane at 9:05p.m. Luggage began to ride the carousel around 9:10p.m., which means she would have picked up her luggage between then and now. Given we have only 2 pieces of unclaimed luggage, it appears she's already come and gone. Maybe she's already left for her destination. Perhaps you should try giving her a call."

"Oh hell," I say, stomping off. "I wasn't that damn late. Glad I wore comfortable shoes. I hate airports." I try calling Stephanie again, but no answer. Her phone goes straight to voicemail. Next I dial Tommy. No answer at home either. "Damn. What the hell is goin' on. Where's everybody."

36
Disappearing acts

April 19, 2013
In Atlanta at TiAnna's

I'm glad I don't have to deal with Patrice. It feels good waking up alone after staying up half the night studying for a human anatomy exam. I knew taking an interest in the medical field would require a scientific course of study. But daaaamn. This anatomy ain't no joke. I grab my robe, slide on out of my room, down the hall passing Virgil and TiAnna's closed-door, on into the kitchen. I'm hoping for some hot brewed coffee before I get in the shower. Like yesterday, Miss T had made some and breakfast for this girl. Got me all perked up and ready for school. I do miss TiAnna and Tippy over at Stone Mountain. T's choosing to stay the course online. Says it makes more sense for her. I hear Tippy's doing the same thing. Good for my girls. I can't see them 2 doing nothing but great things. Especially Tippy the valedictorian.

"Ah shuckums. No coffee." I grab the pot, rinse it out and fill it with water. Throwing in a coffee filter at the top, I fill it in with the dark roast that was sitting on the counter and make a little extra for T if she's up soon. Virgil don't drink coffee. He prefers hot chocolate with extra whip cream. Yesterday, he was grinning at T squirting some on top of his coco. He reached down with his tongue, took a big lick and winked. Mm Nasty I was thinking. Me and Patrice prefer chocolate syrup.

Coffee's done. I grab a cup and add milk and a teaspoon of sugar. I can't help but drool over the glazed donuts on the far side of the counter. I reach over, grab a couple and walk back to my room. I pass Virgil and T's room again. It's still quiet in there. I think they still in there sleeping? I heard the 2 of 'em leave outta here late last night. I did tell her please don't change y'all schedules on my account. I appreciate being able to crash here for the time being. Figure out what I'ma do now since I've finally left Patrice. After Damon told me what went down, I called T and she validated his story. I read her good. I told her she should have said something.

"I didn't wanna mess with your thing wit' Patrice," she said.

"Ah wow. You know I ain't one to tolerate folks messing with my friends. Miss Chelsea made your life a living hell. She deserves what she gets!"

Patrice has been calling since Tuesday evening. She claims Chelsea disappeared after she got off the plane. Personally, I don't give a damn. Anyhoo, I believe Patrice is making the shit up to get me to talk to her. I ain't fallin' for it though. Nada. No way. When I'm back in my room, I hear my phone vibrating. Yeah. It's probably Patrice. I grab the phone to see who's calling. TiAnna's texting me. Says she and Virgil will be gone for a few days and not to worry. Make myself comfortable. You know, what they been up to peaks my interest. But hey, it ain't none of my bizness. Glancing at the clock on my phone I say, "Dang where does the time go?" I toss my phone on the bed. "Let me get my funky behind in the shower. I gotta test to take."

This uppity ass Negro ain't shit

And he's pissing me off. Why Stephanie wastes her time wit' his punk ass, is beyond me. Girl coulda had anybody. Especially since she has the means to start over. The judge got her a new MO and everything. Making her look like an upscale young lady.

"Look Mr. Jeremy Simms, I'm sick of your attitude. My friend is missing. You know the one carrying your unborn child. All you doing is acting like you don't give a damn."

"Like I said Patricia, I haven't heard from Stephanie today nor over the past few days. She knows I was getting ready to send news through my attorney, so she upped and left. She just didn't tell you where she was really going. Looks like she's playin' us both."

"My name ain't no damn Patricia. It's Patrice. P A T R I C E, Paaa trreese. If Patrice had time, she'd read yo ass. But right now, I'm worried about my friend. Chelsea ain't playin' neither one of us. You wrong for saying that. You wrong!"

"Uhhhh. Who's Chelsea?" I ask Miss P A T R I C E!

Why won't you answer?

"Who the hell are you? Did Jeremy tell you to do this?"

All I hear is silence. No one has spoken. All I've gotten are typed notes. They shove them through a chest-high crevice in the one door leading out of this dimly lit room, which feels vaguely familiar. No natural light in here. They've boarded the one window from the outside. Surprisingly, I gotta small bathroom, also dimly lit with the same dark ugly walls. The window in here is also boarded. In this room there's a stash of clothes, a recliner, small TV, bedding and blankets. When they feed me, a tray is shoved through the same opening where they send my notes. If I want more food I am instructed to push the tray back through the hole with the plate turned upside down. They recently gave me a note pad with a marker for me to write down additional requests.

This is how it's been for me since being taken from the airport after flying in from Miami. Rather, I was lured by the limo driver I thought Patrice sent. The driver who was standing near the exit, leaving the arrival gate. He had a sign with my name on it. Told me this was all courtesy of Patrice. A surprise. She wanted me to be escorted in style. The gentleman also said he'd take care of gathering my luggage. I pulled out my cellphone to let Patrice know I was on my way. He stopped. Said she was in the limo waiting. I thought nothing of it. The guy looked legit. He was dressed like a driver. I think he was Latino. He had a slight accent. An older gentleman with a full beard but nicely trimmed. He also appeared a little heavyset. But a gentleman all the same. So I followed him. Like he said, the stretch limo was out front down the way just past the shuttles. You know I should have thought something was up then. When a limo comes for you, it meets you right at the front door. But I had a big smile on my face. I was starting to feel much better.

After what went down in Miami with Jeremy I was truly beside myself. Didn't know what my next move would be. I stayed huddled in my place for a few days crying my eyes out. Patrice called everyday begging me to come stay with her until after the baby was born. She said we'd work through this together. We'd make sure Jeremy paid. Did what he was supposed to do. So I came.

The driver led me to the back door of the limo. Before I knew what was happening, he grabs my purse with my cell and quickly shoves me inside. The doors locked and I couldn't get out. I screamed knowing it was a waste of time. Limos are soundproof. So I stopped screaming and instead settled into a panic. I don't know how long I was back there, worried, frantic and crying all at the same time. My hormones have gotten the best of me because of being pregnant.

But the horror of this experience has made things worse. Finally, I pulled myself together and vowed to fight when I got to our destination. Keeping in mind I have to protect my baby. This made me quite afraid. Fighting for my life could also mean losing my baby in the battle.

The limo slows to a crawl and I think I hear a garage door open and shut. Then silence. I wait but no one comes. No one opens my door. I bang on the windows until my fists are sore. Then suddenly, the doors unlock. My heart starts racing, fearing the unknown. I knew at some point I would have to venture outside these limo doors on my own or they'd end up coming to drag my ass out of here. I reach over and slowly open my right door. Oh wow. It's dark as hell. No lights. Rather than move, I yell out, "What the hell do you want? I ain't got no money," knowing I'm lying. "Hey do you hear me? What the fuck is going on?" Still no response. I slide over to the door, put one foot out. Then I say, "Please don't hurt me, I'm pregnant." Out goes my other foot. Planting both feet on the ground, I stand up with my left hand holding the edge of the limo window. I'm trying to adjust to the darkness when someone grabs my right wrist. I scream and try to jerk free and the person grabs my left one. I keep my hand clamped to the door and kick. He manages to pry my hand loose and pulls me towards him until my belly touches his. He's a strong man. No doubt the phony limo driver. Then I hear "Sshhhhh. Don't want to wake the baby," I hear him whisper. The reminder of my child makes me stop. I don't know what's coming next, but I'm hoping and praying it won't be something god awful like death. I can take most anything else, including rape, even a beating for my child. I've been to hell and back many times.

He pulls me along, stumbling through the darkness. I almost trip a few times, but he has a strong hold on me making sure I don't. We head up a couple of stairs and through a door. I'm assuming we left the garage. It's dark in here too. We walk and walk until we end up here. Here is where I am now. In this room all alone. No one really cares except for Patrice. No one will look for me except for Patrice. Patrice also knows who I really am. Which means no one will come looking for me. Not even Patrice.

37

Truth will set you free

May 20, 2013
In Druid Hills

My room is the same, pretty and fuchsia with my collection of antique dolls. My grandparents bought them for me. They picked up one from each country they visited overseas.

But I'm not a little girl and Dr. Anderson is helping me to remember who I am. She's here with me in my room and wants to discuss the parlor downstairs. She asks me to go with her there.

Once we get to the bottom of the stairs, I see the 2 open French parlor doors leaning back against the wall on each side of the entrance. When we arrived from Miami, those doors were closed. I remember shivering when I walked by. Like right now, my stomach is queasy, my heart is beating so fast it hurts and my legs might buckle. I stop about a foot from the door leaning closest to me.

"You OK, LaTonya?" Dr. Anderson asks. "I'm here with you. You're not alone."

I wanna say I get I'm not here alone Dr. Dummy. But no matter what, I can't shake this awful feeling. What happened in there was really bad and I don't want to remember. So rather than continue, I turn around and run back upstairs to my room.

Dr. Anderson follows me. She says it's time I start to deal with what's holding me back. So far, I've remembered bits and pieces. Even some things from my adulthood with me and mama. Dr. Anderson did say I was getting some of the details mixed up and insists we have to work on straightening things out, which all goes back to the room. We end our conversation with Dr. Anderson saying, "We'll work on this another day."

What helps between my visit with Dr. Anderson is Jeremy's calls. I really like him. There's a reason for this too. Then there's Mr. Green eyes. I don't tell anyone this, but I've been missing him too. I was even tempted to call him. I was rude for leaving him like I did. He's gotta be worried. My Unc Rae-Rae keeps saying to leave Darius alone. At some point we will make my marriage to him disappear. I did say I didn't wanna go there right now. When the time comes, I want to at least face him. My Unc Rae-Rae doesn't seem pleased about this.

Then there's TiAnna. I'm feeling we've been close. Thinking about her makes me sad. Something's off about her. Like me, she's had bad things happen. Even right now, what I'm sensing is danger. For T, there may be no turning back. Somehow, I gotta be there when she lands. Like I was once before? Then all this happened. Keeping me locked inside myself.

Like my gramma told me, the truth will set you free. Haaaaahhhhh. My Gramma Oliver. She doesn't look well. She's really sick and no one will say anything. This is all my fault, being treated like the child I appear to be. OK. Time to make a move.

5/20/2013
In Atlanta

Gross is calling me. Whatever he gotta say betta be good yo. "Whassup."

"Mr. Broussard. Good things are happening. You've got angels looking out for you for sure."

"Uh, ok. What's this about?"

"Geeish. I'm so full of good news I don't know where to start."

"Ok yo. Let's hear it."

"Weeelll, Ok," Gross says, laughing. "Me and my partner Dillan McCloud have been working on you and your wife's cases. First off, we petitioned the court for a new hearing. We succeeded and won. Due to the circumstances surrounding the handling of her trust by Robert Ellis, the judge has granted her emancipation papers. She's free and clear. Ha!"

"No shit yo?"

"No shit yo," Gross says, trying to mimic me. "You know what this means don't you?"

"I'm sure you gonna tell me quick."

"Weelll, ok. Ha." There he goes laughing again. He's bringing me good news, but he sure can get stupid sometimes. "All this stuff about your wife's commitment has been transferred to you. You are now her legal guardian. So it will be up to you how you wish to proceed or not. Which means we, rather Mr. McCloud, can have the court ordered commitment cancelled based on you and a new doctor's orders. Or you can leave them in place. Something to think about. You can let me know later."

Oh hell yeah yo. I'm grinning from ear-to-ear. Can't out fuck da master. "What else you got for me yo?"

"2 more things," says Gross. "First, we will be able to pursue civil charges against Robert Ellis regarding Mrs. Broussard's trust. Between him receiving her emancipation papers and now this, he'll be begging this Dr. Ryan to have him committed. Another issue entirely. As we pursue civil charges, I have asked the DA to pursue criminal charges. Meaning, Ellis is shit outta luck because he won't be able to hire the best - yours truly – to defend him. It would be a conflict of interest ya know."

"Yes I do know, yo."

"And now, the last thing," Gross says, hesitantly. "Good news but perhaps sad news too. Your mother confessed to having Darryl murdered."

I get quiet. Hardly breathing.

"Uhhh, Darius. Are you still there?"

"Yeeeahhh yo," I say, breaking the hold on my tongue. "I'm cool on dat right now. Keep me posted on the other. Thank you sir. Like you said, looking forward to paying the bill." I hang up the phone. I drop my head, closing my eyes close thinking *what you doing mama. You think you doing dis fo' me, but you can't yo. I won't let you.*

Right then Luanne comes into the room where I've been crashin' since this morning. Damn girl kept me up all night. "Not now Luanne," I say without looking up.

"Hmph. Wha' got you sour? Anyway, dis came fo' you," she says handing me a letter. I grab it. Looking at it, I see the return address is from the women's correctional facility in Oregon.

5/21/2013
In Druid Hills

Today I'm sad and fighting the urge to call Darius. I don't know why I wanna talk to him when I can just call Jeremy. He watched over me while I was in Miami and told me to call him anytime. But last night, I had a dream about Darius. He was crying. Calling out to me. Asking me why I ran away. He watched over me too and tried to help me with my memory. That's one thing Jeremy hasn't done. He's been holding back because he was told too. Darius though seems to answer to his own drum. He'll tell me what I need to know.

Picking up the phone, I dial the familiar number tucked away in my contacts. He picks up on the first ring. "Hello beautiful, I was hoping you'd call yo," he says, using that silly word. "I've been worried sick. How you feelin'?"

"Are you mad at me?" I ask.

"Mad? Naw yo. I was going crazy worrying. I tried to find you. I hoped you was wit' your uncle. Iiiisss everything ok wit' you?" I ask again.

"Ummm, weelll." I say, hesitating.

"What's wrong yo? Ain't nobody hurtin' you is they. 'Cause I'll come deal wit' 'em," Darius says, amped up.

"No. It's just, everybody is pretending. They're saying things and not saying things. Like the Basset Hound."

"The Basset Hound? You gotta a dog?" Darius says, thinking Tippy is talking to imaginary dogs now.

"No silly. I mean Jeremy. Don't you know Jeremy? His eyes look like a Basset Hound."

"Uhhh no. I've never had the pleasure. But I wouldn't mind meeting 'im. He hurt you really bad. You can bet beautiful, I'mo let 'im know how I feel about it when I see him."

What Darius says makes me feel icky. My head aches a little, meaning I feel something went down with Jeremy. Not good.

"See," I say. "Everybody's pretending. Are you pretending to yo?"

"Ha. Dair you go. You crack me up when you do dat. But I like it yo. Makes me miss us." Darius pauses then answers her question, "But no. I ain't pretending. My love for you is real. By no means shawty am I perfect doe. I've made some mistakes and wit' regrets. You make me wanna be better."

"Ummmm," I say. "I think I remember you calling me showtee."

"Yeah shawty," says Darius.

"Ummm," I'm at my mama's house. She's here with me. I don't think she's supposed to be. And there's this room downstairs. The door was always locked until the other day. Dr. Anderson came over and wanted me to visit the room. I screamed and ran away. Annnd haven't left my room since then. 2 days now. I'm really nutso right?"

"Ah wow," says Darius fighting back tears. He's thinking Tippy is the only other person besides his brother Jerome who can make me tear up. "Stay away from dat room until you feel ready. Don't let them damn, haaaa," Darius stops and takes a breath to ease his urge to whoop ass! What kinda game do dey think dis is? "You know beautiful, I wanna come take you outta dair. But I don't wanna do nothing until you say so. You should know your daddy and no one else can hurt you no more. I'll tell you why later. Right now doe, tell me what you want me to do."

"Ummm, weelll. I don't want to go back to that Portland place. But I did like our cottage on the lake. It was quiet and peaceful."

"Uh-huh." I say. "Yeah it was. It's still dair. You wanna go dair?"

"Ummm? Yes."

"OK den. Here's what we'll do. Let me set things in motion. Can you hold tight until tomorrow? If not, I'll come over - "

"No. I can wait until then. I'll just stay up here."

"OK cool. Keep dis between us. You can call me anytime between now and tomorrow. Don't matter what time. Uhhhh, I'll tell you what," Darius says, looking down at his watch. "It's noon time. I'll call you later this evening. Keep your phone close in case you need me before den yo."

"OK yo," I say back to him laughingly.

"OK yo. I love you girl and only you. Un-da-stand?"

"Yeah. Me too. See you tomorrow," I say then hang up.

"Huh, wow. Almost got me believin' dair is a God," says Darius. He's so excited he jumps up and does the Dougy dance and sings, "Heeeyyy. My wife is coming back to me oh my. We ain't gotta hide. Jeremy's going bye, bye, bye. Robert Ellis is going down, down, down. Rae-Rae and mommy dearest getting dair's too. Things are gonna be alright."

"I am Darius Winston Broussard signing out."

38
What's what

May 24, 2013
Nighttime in the ATL

No Patrice around making excuses to fight. TiAnna and Virgil coming and going all hours of the day and night; the house feels like mine. I'm acing my tests at school and holding my own, feeling my cheerios honey. Mr. Tommy Crumbs, getting in the streets tonight. Haven't used my special ID in a while.

"Hmmm. What shall I wear?" My pretty clothes about to bust through this little ass closet. Got to admit Patrice did buy me some nice things. Haaaaaa. Miss Patrice. I do miss her a little. Hims did take care of me good in all sorts of ways. LOL. Luckily I got some change in the bank. Patrice called herself throwing a $1,000 up in there the other day. Thaaaank you. I still ain't going back. She gots ta come clean about that Stephanie, Chelsea, Chili shit! Anyhoo. Musta been a good payday at the club where she gives head in the back room. Like I didn't know. Oh well. She brought home the bacon and the extra change was nice, since I had cut back my hours at the Rec. School be kicking my ass. I think I already told y'all. Anyhooo, back to it's all about me time. Hmmm? This would be cute. Tommy ain't wore red in a grip. Naw. Too forward. Don't wanna look like a trasamp but I do plan to get me some. I'ma head straight to dick hall honey. All them fine Negroes hangin around the deck. Pressing their asses against the rail, sipping Cosmopolitans, Kamikazes and Courvoisier or core-va-sir like they say in the Netherlands.

At least that's what Miss Patrice says. She's Black, part Dutch once lived in Amsterdam. She was born as Patrick to a white woman who got caught up with a black army brother passing through. Her mom tended bar in one of the top hotels there where she met Mr. Military ho. He romanced her for the weekend. Promised to stay in touch and never did. At least she had his name and pertinent information. Come to find out he was married. Surprise. Had a family guess where? Yep. Right here in the ATL.

Patrick lived in Amsterdam until she was 22 and lived openly gay starting at age 16. He changed his name to Patrice at 18 and worked the red light district so she could save enough money to come here. What she really wanted was to find her daddy. I don't know what she thought she'd say when she found him. Hi I'm Patrice, your transgender son. How y'all doing? Or whatever they say in Dutch, which she rarely speaks.

Patrice actually knows 6 different languages outside of her own. Spanish, Portuguese, Chinese, French, English and Hebrew. Ha! Yep. Patrice says back home it was mandatory for the kids to learn several languages. Given they were part of the international trade zone and hot tourist destination, the country wanted its citizens to easily communicate with the rest of the world. Smart huh? We arrogant asses over here could take a few lessons from them. Rather than thinking we all that, we should at least make it mandatory to learn some foreign languages. And I don't mean just Spanish. Hmph. Pick 2. Your choice.

Oh. I bet you wondering did Patrice ever find her father? Yes. Was it a happy reunion? Paleeze. Her daddy and his family are Southern Baptist. And you know how a lotta black folks, especially hardcore Christians feel about Homosexuality. Me and Patrice both know what it feels like to be ousted by our parents. Poor Patrice got it twice. Being left behind as a half-breed of a black army man, which is tough enough. Then to be scorned because she chose to be gay. She actually found out where her so-called daddy worked. He's a regional VP for a liquor distributor. One day she waited for him outside his job. Musta been like 10 years ago when she was in her 20s. Fucker acted like he didn't know her mama. Patrice kept pushing. Finally, a few weeks later he asked her to meet him. Patrice thought everything was going to be hunky-dory. Nada. Instead, the damn man asked how much would it take for her to stay buried. You may think he hurt Patrice's feelings, but she's a tough queen. She made him pay her enough money to where she don't have to play down at the club. That's why he got that bad ass house in Norcross. Whooo. I'm glad I got something on her ass. Start some shit here. Now holla-me-bad damnit!

"Ah hell. Who's at the door?" Patrice don't know I'm here. Dressed but with only my socks on, I run out to the front room. Outside the peephole I see a gray-haired old man. Oh. It's TiAnna's daddy.

I open the door. Speaking through the screen door I say, "Hello sir. TiAnna's not here."

Randall nods, looking at me with a slight frown. He remembers me being with Patrice.

Turning to the side like he's getting ready to leave he says, "How long will she be gone?"

"I don't know sir," I say shrugging my shoulders. "I haven't seen much of her over the past few weeks."

"Hmm," says Randall. "She won't return my calls. I don't know why she's avoiding me."

"I don't know about that sir. Buuutttt," I start to say, stopping myself. I'm trying to stay out my girl's bizness, except I am a little worried. I hope she ain't into that drug stuff again. Randall's looking at me from the side of his right eye. See what I done started. "Sir. It may not be my place, but I am concerned."

"What do you mean?" he asks.

"I really don't know. I just feel something's up with her and her friend. When I do see them which is rarely, they be acting nervous. T's gotten really quiet. You know that's unusual 'cause she loves to talk," I say, chuckling.

"Hmm," he says rubbing his chin. "Thank you for telling me." He turns, takes a step forward and stops. Looking back over his right shoulder at me he says, "You still got my number?"

"Yes sir."

"Call me if you need too?"

"I will sir. I will."

Then he heads down the stairs and out to his car sitting in front of the house. I stare at him until he pulls off. Closing the door, I'm thinking about how he must be feeling. He looked so sad. So much shit has happened to that nice man thanks to that damn Chili. I hope she gets hers.

In what has become my cell

I'm still not clear on what's happening. I've been fed, given fresh clothes, bedding and toiletries. A short, stout woman, who dresses like a nurse and claiming she is, comes into see me regularly. She even wears one of those outdated nurses hats with her graying black hair tucked underneath. Her face is partially covered with a surgical mask around her nose and mouth. From what I can see, she has caramel skin with thick dark brows, matching her large brown eyes. I think she's Latino too. She's got an accent like the fake limo driver, who comes in with her to stand guard. He stands in the shadows, in the corner nearest the door. Considering he's always wearing a jacket, I get the feeling he's carrying a gun. I may be pregnant, but I believe he'd use it on me if I try to escape.

The nurse always brings a medical bag. The man places a small lamp at the head of my bed and sets up a partition around us for privacy. I guess I should be grateful. At first, I wouldn't allow the woman to touch me. Eventually, I give in for my baby's sake. And every visit I ask, "I wanna know why you're doing this?"

She never answers my question. Only thing she talks to me about is my baby. Asking me how I'm feeling. Wanting to make sure I eat all my food, which is actually a highlight of my long days here. The food is really good, well-balanced with lots of fruits and vegetables. I also receive prenatal vitamins. Recently, I was given a music player that pumps out soft music. Paleeze! I'm pregnant, not old and ready to die. Also they gave me a treadmill for exercise and a TV with limited channels. I've been watching lots of reality shows. Sometimes I turn on the news. Why I don't know. I certainly don't expect to hear anything about me being missing.

Ooo ouch. Pains me to say the word. I hope dying isn't in my destiny. If this is the case, then why am I being cared for? Must have to do with the baby. Owe. The baby's kicking again. She kicks more when I worry. Yeah. He is really a she. I've known this since informing Jeremy and the judge it was a boy. I was hoping maybe the test results were wrong. The baby's sex would change magically. I even admitted this to the woman.

Today I'm quite emotional. Tearing up during her visit I ask, "Will my baby be OK?"

Looking into my eyes, she nods her head, patting my hand reassuringly. For a moment I sense her compassion. Catching herself, she drops her eyes.

"You doing real well," she says. Bringing her eyes back to mine, she says sternly, "Please keep doing so for both your sakes. Está bien?"

Ha! So she is Latina. Good to know. 'Cause I do plan to survive this. Me and my baby. And when we do, I'm coming for you and yours. "Está bien," I say to her. Yes. Things are ok.

39
Lights on

May 25, 2013
Morning in the ATL

Damn what a night and I'm glad to be heading home. I was hoping I'd get laid and I did. Didn't think though I'd be wit' somebody like him. I want my man slender and toned like me. Dang the Negro was 'bout 300 pounds of pure fat. Trying to sound cool wit' his high pitched voice. Remind me of how this one rapper sounds. He does do combos wit' big names. Hmmm. Can't remember his name. Think it's pharaoh or something like that. Anyhoo, the dude I was wit' can suck dick.

I pull up in the driveway next to T and Virgil's Cadillac. I wonder how long they plan to be around. Glad I got sense enough not to bring strangers home. I don't care who "Messiah" is wit' his funny talking ass. He be expanding his words and adding extra one's into a sentence like, "Heeeyyy ara Tommy ara you wooonnaa harg a wit'da best ara I'm yo boy." I wanted to tell Negro paleeze, Tommy Crumbs ara the best. But I left it alone. Negro's got some big ass hands. I'd have to taze' his ass if he got out of line. I'm threw wit' beatdowns.

Once I'm inside TiAnna's

I holla, "Hey girl."

"Back at you," T says, jumping up from the couch. She gives me a hug. "How you be?"

"Better than ever," I say grinning.

"Ooo you nasty," she says. "You gotchu some didn't you?"

"This queen never kisses and tells," I say, jokingly.

Right then Virgil walks in from the back room with no shirt on, hugging a towel around his neck and cheeks. Mmm. Latin Mandingo got a nice hairy chest. I'm tryin' not to stare. I make this macho man uneasy since I like real men.

"You all right baby," TiAnna says looking over at Virgil.

"I'm gettin' a rash," he says pulling the towel away from his cheeks.

Ooo ouch I'm thinking without reacting. I can see it from over here.

TiAnna walks over to him and puts her hand under his chin. "Yeah, no shit. We're gonna have to figure this out. Let's put some cream on it for now." Miss T turns back to me and hollers, "Excuse us k? Gotta take care of my boo boo." She's smiling but looking a little nervous. And so is Mandingo. I wonder does it have something to do wit' the rash. Hmm. Maybe I should be callin' them nasty. Or worse.

I got my memory back

Late last night, I forced myself to go down to the parlor. I stood inside shaking, trying to remember. I even prayed and asked God for help. After about an hour, my memories came back about the night mama died and everything else up until the day I lost my memory back in Portland. It was surreal. I saw me. A scared little girl walking in on mama being stabbed. But his time, I was a spectator, feeling like

I was in charge and could control my outcome. So at that moment, I chose not to let what happened that night take over my life anymore. I had to face up to what happened and mama's role in it.

When I got back to my room I broke into tears. I wanted to call Darius, but decided to hold on until he came to get me this morning. Then I can get the hell away from these people. Mama and Unc Rae-Rae or should I say daddy.

Speaking of Mrs. Loretta Ellis, she's knocking at my room door. I don't answer. Instead, I pull the blankets over my head in case she comes in. The door opens. I hear her footsteps. Reaching me, she sits down next to me on the edge of the bed and brushes her hand over the top of my blanket from the top of my shoulder to the tip of my fingers.

"My puddin's still sleeping," she says. Then she starts humming our song. The one she hummed to me when I was a little girl. *"Go to sleep, go to sleep my baby child. One little horsey, 2 little sheep. Go to sleep my baby child."*

So damn silly. I'm not a little kid so stop calling me puddin' I wanna yell! Shit. I wish she'd stop touching me. How could she. How could he.

Another knock at my door and in walks that man. Loretta turns toward him and whispers, "She's sleeping."

"Oh," I hear him say only he's not whispering. I hear his footsteps. When he reaches my bed he says, "Well she can wake up. Her company's arrived."

Ooo. He sounds pissed. Darius must be here already? Holla. I'm not making a move yet. Gotta quickly think this through. I don't want them to try and keep me here. Suddenly, I hear more footsteps. Several in fact. Uh-oh. In walks Darius who says, "I don't trust y'all yo. I've got my friends in blue right outside this room. I'm only here to collect my wife and her things."

Holla. My cue. I throw back the blankets to Loretta's surprise. I Jump up, scramble across the bed and onto the floor, heading straight for Darius. I hug him really tight without looking back at those 2 lying assholes.

He says, "You alright yo?"

I let him loose and nod. You know, I ain't even crying no more. Right now, I'm filled with anger and I plan to unleash it at the 2 people I loved more than life. I turn around and face them – Rae and Loretta.

"I remember everything and I ain't wacked no more. In fact, I feel stronger than ever and I have the 2 of you to thank for it, including that asshole Robert Ellis." *Hmm. Look at them staring. Even trying to look hurt. There goes Loretta dropping fake ass tears.*

"Oh stop the fucking crying!" I yell at her.

"LaTonya!" says that man sternly, taking a couple of steps towards me.

"Oh paleeze. Now you sound like my other daddy. He calls me LaTonya when he wants to be bad ass. You know the one who treated me like shit since you've been gone Loretta?" Her mouth drops wide open when I call her by her name. Daddy Rae stops. He claps his hands together, tightening his mouth. He wants to say something, but he's holding back. Funny. You can tell he and Robert are family.

"The 2 of you make me sick," I say. Then I read 'em. "All because of you I had to suffer. From the time I was 7 when I watched Lydia stab you over and over. Oh paleeze. Don't look at me like y'all surprised. Like I said. I remember everything. I was standing outside the parlor and heard you 2 arguing about him," I say pointing to Rae. "You were sleeping around with him and he was married to my BFF's mama and you were still married to Robert. She even knew I was his real kid," I say, pointing at that man again. "And you," I say, pointing to Loretta. "You laughed. Told her she was nothing.

Couldn't have him 'cause he was yours. He'd always be yours. You told her she was classless and a second-hand tramp from the projects. Uh-huh. Those words came outta your mouth." I put my hands on my hips, leaning like my girl TiAnna. I even do the sister-girl neck role. I'm feeling it now damnit! "Braggin' about how you had it all to give. Could have any man you wanted. And now you got 2 of 'em fawning over your ass like little babies. You're such a sucker," I say looking at Rae. "A wimp like my other daddy. Tell y'all what. You don't have to worry about me no more. As a matter of fact, I dare you to start anything with me or my husband. Do I make myself clear?"

Neither one of them say anything. Ooo snap. I think Loretta's getting a little angry. Look at her. She gets up, walks over and stands next to Rae. 2 against 2. I bet you me and mine will win. Besides we got 2 policemen outside my door. The men in blue Darius referred to and who I winked at when I was holding Darius. One of 'im is black and fine.

"Please get the fuck outta my room. Oh excuse me. Your room Loretta. I'll have my things and out of here before you can say, "What the fuck happened to our little girrrlll ha! See ya. Wouldn't wanna be ya."

Loretta grabs Rae's hand who hesitates. The Rae I know doesn't like to admit defeat. So, I just stare at him, meaning stand down. He'd better get the fuck out. Finally, he takes a hint and leaves with his woman. Once they're out the door, I say, "Please give us a moment," to the police and then shut the door.

Turning to Darius I say, "Let's get the hell outta here yo. We got things to discuss like getting every bit of our $100 million. Then we can deal with Robert, Rae and Loretta."

I'm LaTonya Ellis-Broussard and I approve this message.

40

Changes

May 26, 2013
Back to Tahoe

It's a beautiful Sunday morning. I got up early and made a nice breakfast of sausage, pancakes, eggs and potatoes. And garnish it wit' fresh strawberries on the side. I even picked a rose from the garden, brushed off the bugs and laid it on the tray. I'm in a pretty good mood considering.

Last night

My wife didn't say much when we left Druid Hills yesterday. We went straight to the airport and hopped a flight back to Tahoe.

Before going to get Tippy, I called Uncle Dan to tell 'im we'd be heading back in. He was glad to hear we was OK. He said he'd ask the Jacobs, who have an extra key to the cottage and live a couple of miles down, to have groceries waiting there for us – if we didn't mind. I told my uncle we'd appreciate the gesture. It's been a long haul for the both of us. He don't know me and Tippy got married.

He does know she's got her memory back and is emancipated. He won't have to worry about anyone harassing him and his wife. He covered for us both times. And I am grateful yo. I plan to take Tippy and go pay him a visit really soon. Now dat my mama done copped to another murder, we need to stay in close touch.

We got here early evening around 7:00. Like Uncle Dan promised we had a fridge full of food, including already cooked fried chicken, mash potatoes and gravy and white folk's potato salad – the store bought kind dat ain't got no flavor. Made up of mostly mayo. At least we didn't have to deal with no mess or anything. When we was here before, I did keep the place up. The yard's been done too. Uncle Dan keeps a landscaper on payroll. I'm glad for small favors. I don't like yard work. He made me help him wit' dat when I was staying in Oxnard. I hated dat shit.

We ate dinner in front of the TV. I know Tippy was thinking how wrong the potato salad was – I know I was. But neither of us complained. We just enjoyed the peace and quiet. No loud city noises. No wacked parents. Only da sound of nature – birds, crickets and frogs. We watched the Johnson's Family Vacation and fell asleep on Welcome Back Roscoe Jenkins. Earlier this morning, I picked my girl up, carried her into the bedroom and put her down. She didn't budge and inch. She's was as comfortable as she was before we left this place the last time. Yeah. Between me and the call of the wild, girl can't help but feel good yo.

Back to breakfast in Tahoe

"Breakfast is ready," I say walking into the room. My beautiful wife is lounging in bed watching TV. She sits up when I enter. Looks like she's already gotten up, taken a shower and washed her hair. She braided it into one thick braid and wrapped it around the crown of her head. She's the only black girl I know who don't do weaves. I ain't saying there ain't others. I'm saying the ones I've been around wear mostly weaves.

"You ready for dis," I say setting the tray stand of food across her lap.

She giggles, picking up the rose and smelling it. "Very sweet," she says. "Who's gonna eat all this?"

"Me," I say kicking my slides off. I crawl across the bottom of the bed and sit on the other side of her. "What you watchin'?" I ask once I'm snuggled up next to her. I grab a piece of link sausage and toss it in my mouth. "These things is small ain't dey? We need some hotlinks, polish sausage or somethin'."

"Ick. Hotlinks," Tippy says, turning up her nose. "Too spicy."

"Oh dat's right. I keep forgettin' you got white in you."

"First of all Darius you're the one with white in you Mr. Green eyes. And second, not liking hotlinks doesn't have anything to do with white folks. They like hot shit too."

"Uh-ha, ha." I glance at the TV. My girl's watching Oprah who's talking to a guy about spiritual awakening. "Missing church?" I ask.

"No Darius. I'm not missing church. I happen to like Oprah's Super Soul Sunday programs. Lots of diversity."

"Hmm. Ok. Whatever makes you feel better," I say. She lowers her head.

"You OK shawty?"

Tippy looks up meeting Darius's eyes. "I saw my daddy the night Lydia stabbed Loretta," Tippy says still referring to her mama by her first name.

"What do you mean yo?"

"I saw him. He was watching from the door on the other side of the parlor. The door which leads to the back part of the house." Tippy pauses, dropping her eyes back to her plate.

"Are you saying he was there the whole time yo?"

"Yep. He saw the whole thing. Like me. But I couldn't move. I wanted to yell at him to stop Lydia from hurting Loretta. But he didn't. So I forced myself to scream and ran into the room. I ran over to Lydia, punched her and yelled stop hurting my – mama!" Tippy breathes deeply then continues, "Lydia yelled 'you little bitch' and pushed me and fell on top of Loretta. She was laying on the couch bleeding. Next thing I remember is being held by my – Robert Ellis. There," she says. "I got it all out. Finally. Now I feel at peace except my stomach is nauseous. It's been like this most of the week."

"What can I do yo, besides hold you until you tell me to stop? Even then I may not."

"Forgive me Darius. I think I'm gonna up chug his…" Tippy throws up all over the tray and blanket.

"Let it all go," I say, moving the tray to the bottom of the bed. I pull back the blankets from under her and toss them to the floor along with her soiled robe, then wrap her up in a clean one. Grabbing a napkin, I reach over and wipe her mouth.

"Here drink this," I say handing her a glass of water. "All this shit you been carrying. Gotta get it off you."

"Yeah," Tippy says, leaning back against the bed. "You should know there's one thing I can't shake at least for a few months."

"What's that beautiful?" He says, rubbing the side of my right cheek with the back of his left hand.

"I'm pregnant!" she blurts out.

Darius eyes get really big. "Pregnant?"

She nods and says, "Sorry."

My mouth drops open and we stare at each other for a few. Then I can't help it. Here I go tearing up while staring into my girl's beautiful eyes. "I'm not yo. I'm not." I lean over and give her a big kiss, right in her mouth through the throw up an all, which don't taste so bad right now. Then I say, "I was wonderin'… uh…" then stop abruptly.

"What were you wonderin'?" Tippy asks.

"Weeellll," I say slowly. "I was noticing you was pickin' up a few pounds. Ain't no big thing but now I know why."

"Yeeeahh," Tippy says slowly. "Musta happened when we got married. I haven't seen a period since then."

"Hmmm," I say briefly looking up at the ceiling then back at Tippy. "So we gotta be around 4 ½ months huh?

"Yeeeahh," she says. "We'll have to find out for sure so we can be ready."

"No need to worry yo. I'll get us in to see someone around here for now. Then we can discuss where we go from here. Meanwhile it's time to celebrate. Darius and LaTonya Broussard fixin-ta have a baby!"

41
Mama fo' sho

June 8, 2013
In Atlanta

Over at Atlanta Station, I'm hanging wit' my boy Damon. He's down about his baby mama losing the kid he didn't want from jump. Me. I got baby mama and ex-girlfriend drama. They both missing. One of 'em nobody knows where to or why. The other 'cause she wants to be.

Today is June 8. I can't blame Tippy for wanting to hide. I just wish I could be wit' her. This is the day her mama supposed to had died 9 years ago. Now she's alive. Earlier I tried to reach her but kept getting voicemail. Rae didn't have much to say on the subject. Only that she's away. Dr. Anderson says she hasn't heard from her but couldn't go into details because of confidentiality. Damon called TiAnna for me. She said Tippy did text her a few days ago. Says she's all better. Remembers it all. But needs space. This is good news, but I'm still worried.

I tell Damon in confidence about Loretta. He's shocked as hell. "Wow! This is some freaky shit. TiAnna must not know because she didn't mention it."

"Probably not. They're still keeping it hush, hush until they find a way to tell the world Loretta ain't really dead. They do know who the person is that attacked her. Maybe they waiting until they get this person in custody."

"Phew. And I think I got problems," says Damon.

"How's Delinda?"

"Man she's still playin' the wounded warrior. I was hoping to pull back on our relationship. Except I told her I'd stick by her through this. I think she knows I want out, so she's playing me like a fiddle."

"Sheeish. Women. I believe Stephanie doing the same thing. She disappeared shortly after I told her we can communicate through my attorney. Her friend Patrice think I'ma believe something else is up like she's in trouble or something. Huh."

"Hmm," Damon says, scrunching his forehead balling up the corner of his left lip.

He's doing it I'm thinking. "Don't you think it's about time you tell me what's up between you and Stephanie? Y'all former lovers or something?"

Damon turns away to avoid looking at me when he says, "I wouldn't call it dat."

"Then what would you call it then," I say getting irritated. "Stop bullshitting Damon!"

"Alright, alright," Damon says. Turning back toward me, he pierces my eyes with a look so serious I thought for sure he was gonna say Stephanie was really an alien or killer or somethin'. What could be worse? "It's time I tell you the truth about Stephanie."

"The truth," I say looking at Damon. "Would it have anything to do with the fact her real name is Chelsea?"

Damon's mouth drops open. "Uhh, you know?"

"No I didn't know. But you just confirmed it. Patrice accidentally called her that when she spoke to me. Then she tried to play it off. I tell you Damon this shit's been eating at me. Please tell me it ain't the same Chelsea who pulled that shit on TiAnna."

Damon shakes his head. "I wish I could man. But I can't keep this from you anymore."

"Huh-haaa! So you knew it when you came to visit me in Miami and you didn't tell me? Damon man, you s'pose to be my boy. You knew all along this Chelsea bitch was playin' me?"

"Jeremy. I, I've wanted to tell you. I had good reason though."

"Good reason! Oh hell no! Ain't no reason in the world would keep me from telling my best man the truth about a $2.00 ho. A wanted criminal. You should have told me Damon. I wouldn't be in this mess. Now I find out my future son or daughter's mama is a ho!"

"Jeremy let me explain."

"Fuck you Damon!" I haul off and sock him dead in his mouth. Falling back, Damon holds his jaw with one hand, holding up the other, using it as a white flag. We're starting to attract attention from people passing by, but I don't care. Look at his chump-ass. He ain't gonna fight. I use to whoop his ass when we were kids before we became bros. I should whoop his ass again in memory. Instead I say, "Stay the fuck away from me man! We threw!" I turn and quarterback sprint my number 1 ass outta there, leaving number 2 in the dust. Next time he won't be so lucky.

Back at my parent's house

I've been hanging here since the beginning of summer break. Today, mama plans to cook up some of my favorites – collard greens, smothered chicken, mac and cheese, biscuits and peach cobbler.

When I get there, I head straight for the kitchen. The hot food is simmering on the top of the stove, so I grab me a plate from the cupboard over by the sink. Looking out the window into the backyard, I see mama lounging with her book under our big tree, which sets out a ways near the back fence. My daddy built me a treehouse up there when I was 6 years old and it's still there after all these years. I still go up in there every now and then.

With my plate in hand and strawberry soda, I join her under the tree, giving her a kiss on the cheek first before sitting in the other chair that pops usually sits in.

"Hi baby," she says. "What's wrong?"

She can see I'm angry. I'm still reeling from what happened between me and Damon earlier. I take a few more bites of my food before telling her what went down. Of course she's as shocked as me and disappointed in my boy for not saying something.

"Don't worry Jeremy. I'll talk with your daddy about this. We'll get this straightened out."

"Thanks mama," I say. I finish eating without saying anything else and mama leaves me be. When I'm done I excuse myself, telling her I plan to take a hot shower and clear my head. I give her a hug.

"It'll be OK," she says, trying to reassure me. Deep down though I have a feeling ain't none of this gonna work out good.

I wait until my son's inside the house before I make a call. He still hasn't forgiven his uncle, but he's my best bet for now. As for Jeremy's stepfather, I'll share this with him at some point. Over the years, I've gotten better at not trying to handle things myself. At times though, I find myself falling back into my old ways. For the first 4 years of Jeremy's life, it was just me and him. As a single-mom, you run the show – have to be both mom and dad.

"Hello Judge," I say when my brother answers.

"Hey girl. How's my favorite sis?"

"Your favorite and only sis is OK. But I need your help."

"Oh. What can I do?"

"I need you to help me find a missing person. Jeremy's acquaintance, Stephanie."

The Judge pauses, shivering a little at the mention of Stephanie's name. "She's missing?"

"Yes I'm afraid so. Can you help?"

"I'll be right over."

The Judge hangs up the phone before I tell him meeting me here may not be a good idea. Oh well. Lord knows, I've wanted my brother and son to reconcile. Maybe this situation with this Stephanie or Chelsea girl, whatever her name is, will bring them closer together.

I've been having pain

The nurse says no need to worry. My baby isn't due until the middle of next month. All I'm having is Braxton Hicks. To keep me calm, she stays close, keeping a closer watch over me. Making sure I take extra care.

"Stay calm little one," I say, rubbing my stomach. Hopefully this will help minimize the stress I may be causing my little girl. I don't want her to feel my fear. Not knowing what's going to happen is getting me down. I'm praying that once this is over, it was for good reason. Maybe Jeremy's the one behind this 'cause he doesn't trust me to take care of myself. I wish this were true except he's been treating me like shit because of what he's been up to lately. This could only mean one thing. Tippy. She's gotta be somewhere close. She's the only one who makes him crazy.

I look over at the nurse, who's sitting their quietly like always. She's staring at me through her dark eyes. The more time we spend together the more she feels what I'm feeling – fear – except, unlike me, she knows what's coming. I lower my eyes and for the first time let the tears roll. The day will come when I have to say good-bye.

Time to fess up

"Girl what you been hiding?" Tommy asks TiAnna when she comes into the kitchen. Before that I was in here having a good ol' time, chomping down on some greasy fried chicken I picked up from the Rec. "You want some," He asks handing her the box. "You look like you've been eating plenty."

Tommy's looking down at my stomach. He thinks I'm gaining weight. Good.

"Whassup Miss Thang?"

Walking over to the counter where Tommy's sitting, I grab the chicken box and search through it until I find my favorite piece, a breast. Setting the box back on the counter, I pull out the barstool and sit next to Tommy. Before I say anything, I pull off a piece of the breast, put it in my mouth and chew. "Mm, Mm, Mm. This is good eating," I say closing my eyes savoring the moment. Then I blurt out, "Me and Virgil kinda been keeping this under wraps. We wanted to make sure I was OK."

"And?" says Tommy.

"And. I'm pregnant. Me and Virgil's having a girl."

I'm sitting with my mama

In the area of my parents' bedroom we call mama's boudoir. We're huddled side-by-side on her beautiful Victorian couch backlit with weeping willow lamps. We have the deck curtains drawn, letting in the midafternoon sun. Mama's wearing her beautiful red Japanese silk bathrobe over her frail looking body. We hoped mama would pick up some weight since she's done with her chemo. But she hasn't gained a lick 'cause she's had no appetite.

Mama's in good spirits though. Even put on a tad-bit of makeup. Says daddy is arranging a surprise for her later down in the parlor. She thinks it's one of daddy's romantic dinners he's famous for. My daddy enjoys serenading mama. When he arranges dinner in, he turns the parlor into a themed regal diner. I wonder what theme he has planned? So far he's had designers create moods from the Orient, Tahiti, Reo, Kenya, Nepal and Barcelona. He makes sure they spare nothing, which is why they've been able to make magic happen. Like for the Kenya theme. Much to mama's surprise, daddy had caged exotic animals brought in. Mama wasn't overly excited. Daddy got a kick out of mama squirming every time the Lion roared and cheetah's rattled their cages. She said thank God there were no snakes.

So I'm trying not to sing the blues because mama's got enough to deal with. Besides, I want her to be in the best of spirits for her private party. God knows she deserves one after being bedridden most days. Also, this is our special time together. A day when she no longer has to pretend I'm gone.

"How's my granddaughter?" she asks.

Well there goes my plan for trying to not sing the blues. I'm trying to hide my disappointment, but the expression I feel on my face won't let me. What happened between me and Tippy hurts me to my core. Rae's really hurt by her actions too. And Darius? Rae swears he's going to do everything in his power to get our daughter away from him.

"Not good mama. She won't answer my calls or Rae's."

"Give her time," mama says. "She'll come around. You know she's like you." Mama giggles.

"Yeah well," I say with a smile. "One things for sure we both like the bad boys."

"Now, now. Rae doesn't like this Darius because he probably reminds him of himself at that age. He needs to let him be. Let Tippy find out things for herself. She's not a little girl anymore and she has all of her memories. Believe me her toughness will rise to the top. Remember she had to contend with Robert Ellis and damn trifling Luanne all these years," says mama, squinting her nose and lips, like she's smelling a foul order.

I laugh. Mama rarely curses. She and I both feel contempt for Luanne. "Why don't we change the subject," I say. We don't want to ruin our celebration today.

"Yes ma'am," says mama. "A celebration this is. But -" she starts to say and hesitates. But then says, "You don't want to talk about this Loretta, but it's time we tell the truth?"

What mama's referring to is not something I care to discuss. "Mama this is not the time. Anyway it would just make things worse. Please. Let's leave things as they are." I grab mama's hand and look at her, pleadingly. "Tippy has enough to deal with. All Robert would need is to have another excuse. No mama. I won't do it. And neither will you. You promised."

"Alright. I'll leave this be for now," says mama patting my hand. "But before I meet my maker I want to set things right."

"Mama what are you saying? I say almost in tears. I can't lose my mama now. I need her more than ever. "You're not going to die no time soon hear me?"

Joselyn Oliver nods at Loretta but keeps quiet about how she's really feeling. *I'm thinking the last thing I want is for Loretta and my husband to worry. But I do know Lord, you will call me home soon. This June 8 will be my last one. So despite Loretta's pleading, I'm going to set things right in your name. When I do, the truth shall set us all free.*

42

Loving you for real yo

June 9, 2013
In Tahoe

Darius is paddling us in a rowboat along the lake. I'm stretched out in my shorts, t-shirt and bare-feet wearing sunglasses to shield my eyes from the striking sun. Yep. I'm getting my tan on, the slight breeze cooling my skin. Above me the chattering birds are making a beautiful racket. I bet you they're singing to me. It's my 18th birthday y'all. I'm legal and have made it to adulthood. Holla! *Happy Birthday to me, happy birthday to me, happy birthday dear fine, gorgeous, hot, sexy, wonderful girlishcious meeeee, happy birthday to me.*

This is the first time I've spent my birthday in peace. The last birthday turned into a sham thanks to Robert Ellis setting up all my friends and Rae. Any reminder of him now only pisses me off! As far as I'm concerned it's my turn to say all bets are off. Period point blank!

My BFF and Tommy phoned me this morning. We spoke 3-way. This was the first time I'd spoken to Tommy in a grip and as usual he had me rollin'. T didn't have much to say when I told her I was back with Darius and I didn't have much to say about her and Virgil. I guess neither one of us like the others choices. But they're our choices. The call ended with T telling me she had a surprise of her own and would tell me later. Tommy says he expects all of us to get together soon. Maybe down at Stone Rec for a nasty burger and fries. The party is on him. We all agreed we'd be in touch.

Then there's Jeremy. I let his happy birthday message go to my voicemail. He has a new life now. A baby on the way and I have no time for baby mama drama.

My grandparents called too. I did speak with them only because gramma's health is failing. I wouldn't want anything to happen to her without me saying, "I love you." I did promise to come see her next weekend. I'm feeling she doesn't have much time.

Loretta and Rae left me a voicemail 'cause I still refuse to take their call.

As for Robert Ellis, he didn't call and I didn't expect him too after Darius informed me about my emancipation papers.

A few folks pass us by in their rowboats and motor ones. Most of the loud boating action is way at the other end of the lake. So, when the loud ones do come by I yell out, "Damnit! Messing up my zone." Darius laughs, yelling at 'em "You're messing up my wife's zone yo!" Ha. Like they can hear over the loud noise. Funny. This one couple in a rowboat yelled the same thing. I could tell they were white because of how they said yo. Then again they could've been like Shonny. Except we rarely see black folks up in these parts. I'm grinning when I think of Miss girl-on-girl Shonny. Darius says she called to invite us over on New Year's Day but we were on our way to California. Anyhoo, I'm glad she's with her friend Lucinda and they're well. I plan to call and say hey soon.

I love it here. Feels to me like no one can touch us. Or they don't dare try. I have a feeling it wouldn't go over well. Darius is usually on the phone checking in with someone he calls his boys. Tells me, he keeps 'em close by. He also told me about this guy Jodeci and his girl staying at the Prescott house.

I lift my head every now and then to peek at Darius. He smiles when I do. I hope he's watching where he's going because his eyes are focused on me. He's bearing his muscles and tattooed arms never missing a beat and rarely stopping to take a rest.

Darius has some tight tattoos. On his left arm is a bald eagle. He says for him it represents unlimited freedom. On his right arm, he added the Andikra African symbol for humility and strength – a sort of cross with a small open circle in the middle; the top and bottom stems split left and right into what resembles coil looped wires; and the center stems extend out on both sides with arrow shaped tips. Darius says he got his tattoos shortly after leaving the streets of LA. He says those dangerous days taught him a lot. How to move forward with his life with absolute freedom and determination, never allowing anything or anyone to stop his flow. But mostly he's working on being humble like Jerome tried to teach him. He says he's been failing at this miserably but because he has me in his life, he knows he can master the heart.

Like Jerome, Loretta tried to teach me humility. So Darius and me have this in common and I choose to hang with him even after some of the stuff he's pulled. Like telling me Luanne and I were close so I'd be OK to marry him. I get Darius is imperfect. He's never pretended otherwise. It's the people in my life who acted all saintly. They turned out to be the real devils.

The other day Darius admitted that at first he was interested in my money. But that has changed and he loves me more than he loves himself. 'And that is a hella lot yo.' He then said we can drop our case against Robert Ellis because he has his own money rolling in. Darius sold a few more songs. Another to Fella Jiles and the other to Anuff who plans to use it on a future album. He just released his album Evolution of Anuff, which is climbing the charts. Darius says

Anuff approached him about doing a music video on his hit "Dem Jeans" and asked me did I want to appear in the video wearing the only fuchsia jeans wit' my fine ass yo. Of course it would have to be soon. We're going ahead with our family. I must say, I am excited more than I thought I'd be. I hope we have a boy so Darius can be the daddy he wanted his daddy to be. We can have a girl too. Except Darius already says she'd be spoiled just like me.

Me? Spoiled? I don't know why Darius thinks I'm spoiled 'cause since being wit' Robert Ellis I ain't had much. Shit. He put a stop to my credit card the day I left the Portland house on New Year's. He couldn't take my car 'cause he paid cash for it and put it in my name. Darius says my car is safe and the GPS disarmed. Good thinking Mr. Green-eyes.

Luckily, I have money in my personal account Ellis don't know about. The one where I stashed all of my paychecks from RJ Builders (after I cashed 'em) and money draws I took from credit cards. It wouldn't matter. Robert Ellis could start his bullshit 'cause I had a nest egg to fall back on. Actually, he was the one who told me all women should have their own private account. Always remain independent and keep money hidden in case your man starts some shit he would say. Hell, he should know. He's the biggest shit-starter there is. Anyway, I checked on my account the other day. All is intact. I have close to $35,000. Not much since I spent a lot, like when I maxed out my $5,000 a month credit card limit, after pulling cash. Darius don't even know about my account. Unless of course, he went through my wallet, which he probably did. He did have my diary which he recently returned. Anyhoo, he doesn't ask me for anything. Although I do offer. He said he is the man and he plans to take care of his wife.

So there you have it y'all. I'd take the green-eyed boy with a horrible past – which wasn't all his doing – and who deep down has a heart like his brother Jerome. When Darius smiles, Mr. Pretty White teeth comes shining through. I believe Jerome keeps a watch over his brother, kicking him back to reality when he starts slipping. So, I do have help. Good looking out Jerome.

Mostly, I've been getting my head together. Yesterday was a little tough to deal with since I no longer have to mourn mama's death. I sure didn't celebrate her rebirth. It may not have been her fault for me not knowing, but I'm angry just the same. Someone should have told me. Maybe not when I was still young, but at least when I was able to keep a secret. As much as I use to sneak up on folks and hear some of everything, I haven't told any secrets yet. I've kept them buried. Like the time when I was 6, I heard my grandparents in their room doing-the-do. Shucks. I didn't mean to go in there, but the door was open. I stopped when I got near their room door. They was loud as hell. Ick. Old folks screwing. Well hey, if I'm wit' Darius that long, no doubt we'd be doing-the-do too. He's damn horny. I don't think he'd ever stop.

Darius stops peddling, once we've moved up the lake a ways and docks near a clump of beautiful trees atop the beachfront. I sit up and first look at the island across the lake. Panning left, the crowd of boats and spectators have disappeared. And to my right, more of the same. I smile, grateful my man loves me. Great place to commit a murder and dump the body. Me and Darius don't have a pre-nup. He'd be set for life.

"What you smiling about," he says poking me with the end of the paddle.

Oops back to reality. I'm looking at Darius grinning. "I'll keep my thoughts to myself. Don't want you to get any ideas."

Darius's scrunches his forehead, pulling up the left side of his lip. I can see his eyes squinting at me through his dark glasses.

"I hope you wasn't thinking nothing silly yo," he says.

"Silly? What do you mean yo?" I say teasingly.

He smiles and says, "I didn't like the movie you insisted we watch last night."

My turn to scrunch my forehead, but I keep smiling. Darius hates when I do this. Act shady.

"You know what movie I'm talking 'bout yo. The one where the husband offs his wife. Then she comes back and haunts him. You said that's what you'd do to me if I got stupid." Darius straightens out his face, looking at me like he did last night when I made the comment.

"I was just playing," I say.

"Were you? I mean, do you think I'd do something like that? Like I said before we can go get a prenup anytime. I want you to know I'm over the money thing. A $100 million would make ya do crazy shit doe.

"OK crazy shit," I say, reaching out my right leg, tickling his stomach with my toes.

"Girl stop," he says, giggling and grabbing my foot. "You know I'm ticklish as hell." To stop me from doing it again, Darius begins rubbing my foot, pulling it up until my toes reach the tip of his nose. "Hmmm. Still fresh," he says giggling. Lowering my foot to his mouth, he draws in my big toe, wraps his salivating mouth around it, sliding down to the bottom and back up gently sucking along the way. He reaches the top of my toe, kisses the tip, then moves onto my next toe, the next and the next, finishing up with my baby toe. Then he wipes my toes dry with the bottom of this T-shirt, staring at me like a puppy, begging for a snack. Except this puppy can't wag his tail. He would if he could. Naw. I don't have to worry about Darius. I got him hooked. Besides, I'm all that and a bag of expensive ass chips.

"I love you too," I say. "But I ain't sucking your crusty toes."

Darius laughs. "I wouldn't want you too," he says. "And my toes ain't crusty. Besides, I ain't one of dem gay wads."

I curl up the left side of my lip. Tilting my head down, I pull down my glasses to the middle of my eyes to peek at Darius. I don't like those kinda remarks but Darius says he means no harm. I have gay friends and what they do don't bother me.

"Oops. Sorry baby. Slip up yo."

Pushing my glasses back up, I smile and nod.

Darius then asks, "Ready for an adventure?" He nods his head up looking to his right.

I turn my attention in the direction. A flash of light makes me squint. Hmm. "Sure," I say, "I'm feeling adventurous. Maybe we'll find a pot of gold."

"You see a rainbow?" says Darius, laughing.

"Yeah. Don't you see? Right there," I say pointing off into the distance.

"Uh-huh, I see," he says grinning. "You got x-ray vision. Come on." He jumps out the boat, motioning for me to stay put until he secures the rope to the post on the landing, then he helps me out. I grab our backpack with snacks and Darius grabs a blanket. As we ascend the small hill directly off the landing, I see what the flash of light was. Not too far from where we're standing, a birthday lunch is set atop a red and green checkered blanket. Off to the side is a small table with a portable strobe, methodically turning and flashing to the sound of soft jazz.

"When did you do this?" I asked.

"You know," he says, pausing. "It's nice to have help when you need it."

"Well thank you," I say kissing his left cheek. "And thank your boys or whoever helped." I grab Darius by the hand, running and pulling him over to our table for 2. Yep. He loves me yo.

43
Luck down

June 13, 2013
Portland

"This is bullshit! Ain't no way in hell!"

"Look lover. You gotta calm down before you have a stroke."

"Calm down my ass! Your sister was s'pose to make sure this didn't happen! She screwed me! And she'll screw you! I bet money!"

"The last person I'm worried about is my sister. I go down, so does she. My concern is for you lover. I have faith you'll work your way out this like you always do."

Sitting on my lady's couch, I drop my head into my hands. I flew right here after shit crashed. Did 80 all the way, taking those damn coastal curbs like a racecar champ. Didn't think twice about the possible hazards, like passing those slow ass trucks. I was too damn angry.

Earlier in Portland

I rise as usual in the morning at 4:30. I shower, take in a hearty cup of coffee and fix me up a real American breakfast. Got rid of the chef. No need. I cook for myself and my girl cooks for me too when I visit her. Plus, I sent the kids to be with their mother in Atlanta for the summer. Hell yeah. No kids. But, I do miss they're little chubby asses. No continental bullshit either, pastries and granola like Luanne feasts on. Curious how she stays so damn boney, eating so much sugar. One time I asked her did she have that "throw-up disease." She denied it. Says it's all in her genes. How would she know? She doesn't even know her real people. Her fake mama is voluptuous and always has been since I can remember. During the old days, I don't want to remember. Anyhow, I had to put my foot down when feeding my kids. They ate what I did. Jayden resisted most times. He wanted what his mama had who he's more like in a lot of ways. He doesn't like to hang around me and do manly things. He's more feminine than any little boy should be at 9, which he and his sister turned on May 25. We had a nice time on their day before they left. Brittany asked about Tippy, which is quite unlike her. Neither one of them were close with her. Even if they wanted to be, Tippy wouldn't let them. My oldest child never forgave me for my affair with Luanne, which she holds against the twins. Her mama was also far from perfect, but I think she'd forgive Loretta for her indiscretions.

As for Jayden, him being gay wouldn't surprise me. Brittany on the other hand tries to appease me by taking his place. She watches sports with me, which I think she enjoys. Especially basketball. I see how she stares at certain players. Loves to tell me, "He's cute daddy. I wanna meet him." I respond like any other loving father, "Over my dead body." At least she's straight.

Last year, Brittany accompanied me on a fishing excursion with my friend Larry Hughes. I had a ball. I've wanted to go fishing since I was a kid. Living in flat, waterless Atlanta doesn't afford those luxuries. My father promised to take me fishing in Alabama where he says there are fishing holes where you can catch some great sea bass. He broke his promise by running off with another woman.

Morning time is when my mind's most clear, which is why I get to the office around 6:00. I'm sitting behind my desk, getting ready to call and check in with my partner. It's 9:00 a.m. in Atlanta. This time he calls me first which is rare. I pick up the phone. He's frantic, saying the Atlanta office employees' paychecks bounced, including the contractors he paid yesterday.

I told him to calm down. No doubt there was a mistake. "Let me contact the bank and call you back," I say to James.

"Yeah, yeah man," he says. "Betta not be any problems. We're on project crunch time around here."

"Man I hear you. We're picking up on this end. No doubt, our priority is to keep our top of the line staff happy. So no worries man. Cool?"

"Good to hear Ellis. You know I wasn't too keen on our Portland expansion. At least not for another 3 to 5 years."

"No you weren't James. But like I told you before, I plan to prove you wrong."

"For all of our sakes let's hope Robert. You indebted us by $90 million to your silent investor."

"That's what my friend prefers," I say. "He's one of those socially responsible billionaires who's doesn't expect a return on investment anytime soon."

"Good," James says. "In the meantime, please go handle this bank mess so we can get back to work. I promised the staff this check situation will be handled by lunchtime. And because of the screw-up, the boss is buying."

"Yeah I'm on it then. I don't wanna have to do the same thing on this end. You'd make me look bad."

"Yeah alright stingy," says James. "I'm gone."

He hangs up before I can respond to him calling me stingy. Hell I give bonuses once a year for good work. But come on now. We can't be setting precedence over a simple misunderstanding. By noon they can buy their own lunch.

No sooner after I hang up from James, I get a call from the security guard downstairs. As part of the move, we purchased this 12,000 square foot commercial space near Montgomery Park in northwest downtown. Our new office has 55 employees to the Atlanta office of 125 people. In both locations we employ administrative support staff, project managers, architects, interior designers, engineers, environmentalists, IT and Web coordinators. We keep a scientist or 2 on contract and go out to bid for construction crews. The RJ company has definitely helped the economy.

My long-term vision is to create a global eco-friendly community where humans can co-habitat within a healthy, safe and energy efficient space, infused with green spaces for community gardening, operating entirely on renewable energy. This system will reenergize the environment and put an end to global warming. It will also accelerate the growth of green jobs. I developed a business prospectus and submitted it to the Obama Administration right before we moved here. I heard from the President's people in February. They want to hear more about my vision and will arrange for me to sit down with the President and the energy secretary the first part of next year. Right now they are focused on rolling out Obamacare.

My man, the President. I admire him and his family for having the stamina and dignity to carry the brunt of racism since they've been in office. Frankly, I think there ought to be a law against disrespecting and bashing the President publicly. Things have gotten out of hand because rednecks hate the black man in office. The highest office in the land deserves our respect regardless. I despised W and his daddy, but I would have never done to them what these racists are doing to this black man and his black family. We are an embarrassment around the world and morally wrong. I did my best to honor my mother's training and that was to respect authority, respect the position. Otherwise I would've flattened my daddy the day I ran into him when I was 16. Despite of what he did, mama never talked bad about the man to me or Rae.

"Yes Orval," I say to the middle-aged, black security guard.

"Good morning Mr. Ellis," he says. "I hate to bother you so early but there's a young lady, a gentleman and 2 police officers, asking for you."

I lift my eyebrows, a smirk formulating on my face. My first thought is they got my daughter. Probably pulled her from the Druid Hills estate I've had under surveillance for some time. According to my spy, the only occurrence out of the ordinary was the cops that showed up there a few days ago. I didn't call them in, but I did inform the authorities here where I thought she may be. I did all but threaten them to do their jobs. Perhaps they moved forward with bringing her back here. That's why they're downstairs.

I jump out of my chair, jog over to the closet and pull my suit coat out and put it on. Something tells me to grab my briefcase and laptop. I do, in case this is the news I've been waiting for. Maybe I'll be celebrating early. Head up to see my girl at the coast rather than wait until tomorrow. Thank goodness today's date lucky 13 falls on a Thursday.

Once I come off the elevator, I see Orval standing in front of the security desk across from the officers who are standing behind a white young lady. She's blonde probably early 30's. I have to say, she's fine and curvy with big tits and legs. The man has his back to me but turns to greet me when I reach the group. He's familiar. I adjust the back of my coat collar, still smiling. They're not. Having my daughter institutionalized is no laughing matter. Standing in front

238

of the young lady I say, "Hello I'm Mr. Ellis," extending my free right hand, holding my briefcase in my left and laptop strapped across my shoulder. She shakes my hand, introducing herself as Trisha Larson. Extending my hand to the dark-haired white man, he says his name is Dillan McCloud.

"Mr. Ellis," says Trisha Larson, "I'm from the Multnomah County District Attorney's Office."

And the white man says, "I'm Mr. McCloud from the law offices of Gross, McCloud and Shreve's."

I scrunch my brows, feeling my smile slowly fade. I keep quiet cautioning against being too hasty. Standing in front of me is the DA's office and Tippy's criminal attorney's partner who got her off when she beat the shit out of that Uriella who was murdered recently. Certainly hope there's no connection.

McCloud takes the lead, handing me a thick 11 by 14 envelope. I take it. He speaks. "Mr. Ellis, I am here to inform you of 2 things. 1. Guardianship of your daughter has been revoked. She has been legally emancipated. This means you have no authority over her, including discussions and decisions about her mental health which have been transferred to her husband Mr. Darius Broussard."

I still don't say anything. I recently heard about this sham of a marriage and set in motion to have it annulled. Despite the fact I did give Luanne partial guardianship, she had no right. I'd planned to deal with her later.

"2. We have set in motion a civil action against you regarding Mrs. Broussard's $100 million trust fund. We have gathered evidence you perpetrated a fraud, illegally using Mrs. Broussard's trust to infuse RJ Builders and Designs with capital."

"Which is where the DA's office comes in sir," says Trisha, handing me a piece of paper. "This is your subpoena to appear before the grand jury on Tuesday next week. The DA is considering pursuing criminal charges. You should know we've been in contact with the DA's office in Atlanta who is handling things on that end. They've already frozen your assets, files and equipment and we've done the same here. As of right now, RJ Builders is off limits to you and your partner and ATL employees will be asked to leave for now. We'll notify employees here also." Trisha pauses and continues, "Sir, you will no longer be allowed to enter this building as of right now. Mr. James Wilson is being informed as we speak. He's also being informed of his rights and depending on the outcome of this investigation, he may also be under indictment."

Frankly I'm pretty calm considering. My biggest concern is about how this news will affect the company, our assets, cash and human capital. Finally I say, "We have lives at stake – workers and clients. The company will default with no one at the helm."

"We've considered this Mr. Ellis," says McCloud. "We have a temporary solution. For now, the Judge has transferred temporary control of the company to Mr. and Mrs. Broussard. They already have a plan in place. Hopefully, we will be able to reopen on Monday and handle financial affairs accordingly. We'll be working with the trustee on how to handle this to minimize any damages. We will ask employees to hold tight until then. Oh and we did manage to approve paychecks for this month. And right before lunch," says McCloud, snickering.

"Mr. Ellis we will need you to hand over your briefcase, laptop and any business keys you may have," says Trisha.

"Oh hell no!" I say, feeling indignant. You ain't getting my personal belongings." The officers behind the 2 shuffle a little, reminding me of why they are here.

"Personal or not Mr. Ellis, these things are part of the investigation. In the interim we cannot risk sabotage. Speaking of which, there are officers waiting for you at your house. They have been ordered to remove all equipment and files from your home office."

Now my anger is rising. My home office includes personal information which has little to do with RJ Designs. I'm hoping they don't know about my safe. I keep a stash of money and special documents I can use on rainy days, including information on what's owed to me from associates I've helped along the way.

Reluctantly, I hand over my laptop and briefcase and pull my keycard and associated keys out of my left pant pocket. My cellphone is tucked away inside my jacket pocket on silent. I'll be damned if they get it.

"Is this everything?" she asks.

"What do you mean is this everything? You want my draws too?" I say vividly angry. I don't give a damn.

"Good," she says snidely. "You can follow these gentlemen. They'll make sure you leave safely and without incident." She smiles and steps aside for me to pass.

I'm so caught up in what is going on I forget all about Orval, standing off to the side. I finally catch him looking at me shaking his head like I don't notice. He stops abruptly when I look him in the eyes. This proud black man will not lose. I'm only on temporary luck-down. Robert Ellis will be back. Y'all can rest assured those who think they're screwing me, will pay.

44
Déjà vu

June 13, 2013
8:30 p.m. Atlanta

Tonight, I plan to find out what my darling daughter TiAnna's been up too. So far she's hidden from me her miraculous pregnancy. I saw her go into the house an hour ago with her stomach sticking straight out. Pulled up in that damn Mexican's Cadillac.

I look down at my watch. The clock's a ticking. Something tells me she'll be heading back out soon. This seems to be her normal pattern Tommy told me when I stopped by the other day. When I called earlier he said, "She came in for an hour, changed and left again. Even grabs clothes for Virgil on occasion."

Thinking about this turn of events has me worried. How did she get pregnant considering her circumstances? She has HIV and she's sterile so I thought. If she's not, the question then is who's the father? Virgil's been locked up and she was only in Portland for a hot minute. Tommy Crumbs is gay.

"Here she comes with a suitcase." I put my sunglasses on to shut out the peak time Atlanta sun in front of me. She shouldn't recognize me in this rental with tinted windows. I plan to stay way back so I won't spook her. Being jumped by Don Juan's people the night she went missing still weighs heavily on her mind. I can tell. TiAnna jumps into the Cadillac, pulls out from the driveway and drives off like she's in a hurry. Damn. I hope she's not driving herself to the hospital. Where is her damn Mexican?

TiAnna's heading in the opposite direction so I have to turn around. I'm down the block with 2 houses between us. We're heading out of Stone Mountain down a highway where you rarely see cars especially at night. The few street lamps need replacing. As for houses, there are a few set back from the street and on large lots. A chill goes up my spine as we head further down the road. This is familiar ground we're traveling. I don't know for the life of me why my daughter appears to be heading in the direction of Don Juan and Chelsea's old house.

About 30 minutes out, TiAnna's up ahead driving over a street bump. She makes a quick left, which confirms my suspicions. Rather than go any further I pull off to the left side of the road, pulling in behind a group of 5 cars nestled under a couple of cozy trees. I believe they belong to the house way at the other end of the gravel road off to the left and in front of us.

The last time I drove through here was a few days after we rescued TiAnna from the clutches of these 2 maniacs. I wanted to see where they held my daughter. What she had to endure. The yellow tape was still up but I went in anyway, like the uninvited guest. I walk around the place and sat in the room TiAnna was locked in. I swear for God y'all I felt my daughter's pain, her anger and could hear her voice. The day I finally found out through Chelsea's letter where she was, her energy got stronger. I heard her call to me. I answered and I told her I'd find her. When I did, I told her no one would ever hurt her again. I repaid a debt. And that is what I did the night I shot and killed Don Juan.

45
Returning the favor

June 13, 2013
Lake Tahoe

I'm still reeling from my birthday. The day ended up with me and my husband doing-the-do in the middle of our picnic. Darius was being so damn careful I wanted to scream. "You're not going to hurt the baby," I told him. "And besides, I heard the more the merrier. Then when comes time to deliver, the baby will slide on out." Darius laughed. He said he didn't know much about delivering babies but somehow that didn't sound quite right. "I know huh," I said. "I heard my gramma Ellis say that to my mama once. Mama and daddy had so much sex when she was pregnant with me, I slid on out."

I don't know why I've been thinking about gramma Ellis lately. We weren't close and she died 4 years ago. Deep down maybe I'm feeling sorry for Robert Ellis. He's got nobody now. Not me and not even his twin brats. I hear Luanne is going for full custody now that he's under investigation. Sheeish. He just got served.

"Hey baby you feel like talking?" Darius says, coming into the bedroom, holding out my cellphone. He's been monitoring my calls, at my request y'all. Don't get it twisted. "Larry Hughes is on the phone."

Larry Hughes is an acquaintance of my father who lives in Portland with his wife, daughter Debra and son Terrence who's home for the summer. Terrence attends Howard University Law School in D.C. The family relocated to Portland from Pennsylvania a couple of years ago after Mr. Hughes purchased a successful business consulting firm from an acquaintance he met at Wharton School of Business where they both attended graduate school. My daddy told me Mr. Hughes knows his stuff. He's headed start-ups, turnarounds, mergers and acquisitions for a variety of financial, telecom, software engineering and IT companies. Five years ago, he sold a successful start-up for $300 million. He's the only man daddy says could give him a run for his money.

"Yeah sure. Put him on speaker," I say to Darius.

Darius comes over and sits on the bed next to me. He hits speaker phone and lays it between us.

"Hey, Mr. Hughes. Everything OK?"

"Yes boss," he says, chuckling. "Please call me Larry."

Darius whose head is lowered listening intently looks up at me and winks.

"Ok. Larry it is. I take it you've met with Mr. Gross and Mr. McCloud?"

"Yes," Larry says, grinning. "Such formalities."

"That's how I was raised. Respecting my elders usually doesn't come with calling them by their first names." *Unless of course they lose my respect I'm thinking,* cringing at the thought of Robert and Loretta.

They were the ones who taught me to give respect to those who blow out more candles than me.

"Nothing wrong with that," says Hughes. "Uhh," he says, pausing before he continues, "You don't need me to tell you this, but we are a reputable firm. What's going on between you and your father won't have any bearing on our partnership."

"No worries. I chose you to handle RJ Builders and Designs for a reason. When will you be meeting with staff?"

"First thing Monday morning - tomorrow. I've sent one of my trusted soldiers to the Atlanta branch to manage things there. We plan to hold a virtual staff meeting at 7:00 in the morning Portland time, leaving Atlanta in the dark until 10. We've already released key managers, leaving in place human resources and public relations. We'll see how that goes. As you know, we can't take any chances. Your father and his partner had loyal staff around them. Usually Ops and Finance are the most sensitive. We're also prepared to handle the media frenzy which is beginning to surface. I will be the spokesperson. The PR Director will field the calls and prepare my statements. I will copy you and the law firm on everything we do. You'll definitely be in the light."

"Like I suspected, you have everything under control. You'll also provide me with new log-in information and remote access?"

"Yes. As a matter of fact my IT guy is handling that as we speak. Everyone, those employees we plan to keep, will be issued new access cards and passwords. Before that, we plan to reiterate policies around confidentiality, no media access and discussions with anyone outside the organization especially Mr. Ellis and Mr. Wilson!" He laughs. "See what you got me doing?"

I giggle. "I'm a positive influence. At least that is my intention."

"Yes you are," says Hughes getting back to being the serious businessman. One thing Robert did right was introduce me to him.

"How's Mrs. Hughes and Debra?"

"Very well," he says. "They're out spending my money."

"Tell them hello for me," I say.

"I will. Debra's wanted to call you. But doesn't know when it's the right time."

"Please tell her she can call me anytime. She may get my husband on the phone, but I will let him know she's somebody I will take a call from."

"I'll do that. And congratulations. I didn't know you had gotten married."

I look over at Darius. "Yes. We had a quiet ceremony. We're both still getting use to the fact we are husband and wife. Say hey Darius." I say, love tapping the front of Darius's left knee with my right foot.

"Ahem. Hello Larry," says Darius, grinning. It tickles Larry Hughes.

I tap Darius's knee again this time a little harder. "Darius. You know better."

"I approve," says Hughes. "Man-to-man. And the bosses husband."

"Yes that he is," I say, smiling at Darius. "Please feel free to discuss any information with my husband if I'm indisposed."

"Will do LaTonya. We'll talk again tomorrow." Hughes hangs up.

Darius clicks us off and says, "Yo boss lady. I still say you would make a great executive."

"Thank you sweetie," I say getting up on my knees to lean over and give him a kiss. "We both know I'm not ready. I've yet to finish high school and besides I have other things to worry about."

"Is —"he starts to say but I cut him off.

"The baby is fine. Please don't worry."

"Ok. I will try not to worry less. As for you," he says, "You're extremely smart so all you gotta do is take the high school completion exam. I bet you don't even have to study Miss High IQ."

"Yeah I guess I could," I say. "I'll look into it."

"No worries yo. I got all the information for you. So whenever you're ready."

"Of course. I should've known," I say smiling.

He leans over kisses me on the cheek and says, "We still planning a trip to ATL to see your granny?"

"Yes Darius. I think we should head out there this week. Gramma isn't well. I'm afraid —"

"Now, now beautiful. No stressing. Your grandfather is handling her well no doubt. You are my responsibility." Darius leans up. Putting his hands on my shoulders, he gently lays me down. Time to give baby and mama a full body massage."

"With strawberries?" I ask Darius.

"I think I can manage that. Hold your thoughts. Be right back."

Darius leaves the room. I clasp my hands behind my head and cross my legs, thinking *I made you a promise last year Mr. Robert Ellis. You've been served. Now my turn to show you what pain feels like.*

46
Reborn

June 20, 2013
In Druid Hills

Gramma Ellis called me this morning. She spoke in a soft voice and sounded very weak. "Please come see me baby like you promised. Can you come today? I'll have grandpa arrange y'all flight. Darius is welcome here anytime."

The Oliver mansion

I get nauseous when we pull up to gramma's gate. I almost ask Darius to turn around, but we forge ahead when the guard lets us in.

Once inside, I feel sadness sizzling beneath my cold heart, which gets colder when I see Loretta. She greets us along with my grandparents' house manager Ms. Jacob, who also serves as gramma's assistant, helping with menial administrative duties. Ms. Jacob has been a part of this household for years and was the one who referred Chester and Eloise to Loretta and Robert.

"Mama's been asking for you. Glad you could come," says Loretta reaching for my hand. Instead of taking hers, I step back thankful Darius is standing behind me in case I fall. My Darius is being a perfect gentleman although he's still mad as hell for what they put me through. I turn my eyes from Loretta's to avoid showing my almost tears. Blinking them back I turn to Darius. "I'm gonna go up and see gramma. Can you take our things upstairs?"

"I'll show you where things go," Loretta offers, assuming Ms. Jacob's role.

Right then Granddaddy Oliver walks into the foyer. "Hey pudding," he says, reaching out his arms for a hug. I take a step towards him allowing him to do most of the work for our embrace. It's the least he can do. He gives me a warm hug and a kiss on the forehead. "You alright?" he asks dropping his head to meet my slightly lowered eyes. I look up at him and nod. He smiles, knowing not to push too hard. He lets me go and walks over to Darius extending his right hand. My polite husband returns the gesture. "How about I show y'all where you gone be?" He says to Darius then looks over at me for approval. I motion to Darius to follow granddaddy. I'd prefer him having polite conversation with granddaddy over Loretta any day. She's good at getting information from you, you don't want shared. Granddaddy will be a gentleman because he has a gentle soul. He believed keeping the situation with Loretta from me was more for my benefit. If Robert Ellis had been the perpetrator, it would have been dangerous for me to know her real status. There's no way I could've kept quiet. I'd be in mourning daily after seeing her. I can only imagine how everyone must've felt seeing her comatose for all these years.

Still what Loretta did doesn't excuse what happened. My anger is mostly about her secret affair with Rae. The man who always treated me like a daughter. Now I know why. Remembering the arguments, he and daddy had, I should've known all along. Rae calling Robert on his bullshit, telling him all bets would be off. Then there were our phone conversations. He'd say good-bye with, "Remember your daddy loves you." Huh. All this time I thought he was trying to convince me Robert really did love me. What a joke.

Speaking of the devil here comes Rae. Good thing Darius has already started up the stairs behind granddaddy followed by Ms. Jacob. He looks over the banister and stops when he sees Rae enter through the doors. Rae looks up meeting Darius's eyes. Darius smiles and nods. Certainly not the reaction I was expecting, but he's instigating. Darius probably really wants to jump over the bannister like Spiderman, wrap Rae up in his web and beat the shit outta of him. Hell, he may get the chance. I notice Loretta nudging Rae in his left side with her right elbow. Rae takes the cue and offers Darius half a nod. Then he turns his attention to me giving me one of his lady killing smiles. Hell I'm your daughter fool! He does that on purpose because I always tell him how fine he is. Damn. My own daddy. How disgusting. Saying stuff like that was OK when I thought he was my uncle. I give Rae a half smile. I can't help but love my real daddy. He did what he could, given the circumstances, including going to jail to save me from Robert's misery.

Rae doesn't move from his position beside Loretta but says, "I've been hearing about RJ Builders and Designs in the news. You got game girl. Your daddy taught you well. This daddy," he says pointing to himself. I half nod, acknowledging his guidance along the way. He did help me to come into my own. But I'm no longer their little girl and he knows it.

One thing I do know for certain is that I couldn't have done this without Darius. I bet Rae knows too but won't admit it. I'm not naïve as y'all think. I can handle Mr. Darius Broussard. I know what buttons to push and those not to push. I also know Jeremy wouldn't have been up for the challenge. He would have insisted I let all this go. Looks like things worked out like they were s'pose to. We all got ours in the end. But the story ain't over yet.

47

Is it time yet?

June 28, 2013
Outside of Stone Mountain

Following TiAnna has led me here. I've been waiting 2 days for her to come out of the house she went into. Living through my funk. My goal is to venture through once TiAnna and her friends are gone. One time I did see a limo pull out and come back a short time later. She has company.

In case I had to stay here for longer than a few hours, I loaded the trunk with a survival kit – 2-gallon bottles of water, snacks, protein bars and my special drink in the glove compartment. The bottle stays untouched until I pull over and do it in. Then I toss the bottle for good measure.

Except now, I'm hungry for some real food. I'm a real man with a hearty appetite and who's not interested in going on a diet. I hope the waiting ends soon so my stomach will stop growling. For now, I make due and hold my piss, going mostly during the night unless I have to. Lord knows I was hoping no one saw me from the house up the road.

I soon realize the house is empty. There's no comings and goings. When I decide to take time to really look at the cars on both sides of me, they are old and rusty and haven't been driven. No wonder this area is a perfect hideaway. No other people around for miles.

8:00p.m.
The house empties

First the Cadillac. TiAnna was driving and on the passenger side was an older Latina looking woman. A few hours later, out comes the limo. I figured that was the last of the crew. But I waited an extra hour just in case.

I grab my flashlight in case I need it and hurry on over. I walk rather than drive the mile.

I get to the door and feel Mr. Chill heading up my spine again. Wondering what might meet me on the other side, I cautiously open the door. You know, the last time I was here I sat until it turned dark. I laughed thinking the ghost of Don Juan might show up and I'd whoop his ass. I was toasted by that time, like I am now. Seeing a haint wouldn't bother me none. Especially not him. Sorry ass nigga. The only man I'd ever call a word I'm not fond of.

I get fully inside the house without incident. The lights are out; the switches don't work, so I flick on my flashlight. I stand there getting my bearings, figuring on which way to go first when I hear a sound. I stretch my ears, hearing a whimper coming from the back room. I follow the sound, leading me to the room where TiAnna was held. Huh. I just may run into something paranormal. Let me get my ass ready to run in case it's someone else besides Don Juan. I ain't no damn ghost buster.

I get to the room. The door is open. Leaning my head around until it's inside the entry, my eyes, which have already become accustomed to the dark, go immediately over to a bed in the far right corner. I shine the light on a blonde-haired woman lying there. She's no longer making a sound, so I can't tell whether she's dead or alive, but I'ma find out. I tiptoe slowly over to her, hoping to avoid any more possible surprises. With each step, *I'm thinking I'ma have a decision to make. Depending on who this person is, will dictate my next move.*

At the same time
Over in Norcross

I finally convince Patrice to meet with me. She's leery about anyone connected to the criminal justice system, despite the fact this Judge is on the out. Apparently, Chelsea did tell her about me, my name and everything. One thing about getting to close to a ho, you end up telling them things you shouldn't. Which is why she knew so much about Jeremy, Rae and all the shit I helped Robert Ellis pull. Robert's getting his shit back like me. I guess what they say about "reaping what you sow" is the God's honest truth.

"Why do you need to know where her old house is?" asks Patrice, who's scrunching her forehead. I bet she's thinking why she didn't think maybe Chelsea is hiding out there.

"It's a feeling I got," I tell her. "Please tell me. She could be in trouble."

"Patrice leans back on her right foot with her left arm folded underneath her other elbow, tapping her forefinger against her lip. "How about I take you there?" Patrice offers. "OK let's do this," I say sounding like I'm giving orders. But I can't help myself. Chelsea is in trouble. Patrice grabs her purse and keys and off we go to rescue my girl.

Knowing Chili like I do

Chelsea would've called me by now despite me pretending I mind hearing from her. I like her determination, which drew me to her the night we first met. We were both at a bar downtown at a hotel, which was hosting a conference for those of us in the law profession. The management didn't play when it came to hookers and johns. Good for business perhaps, but it would mean lowering the standards from that of a 5 star hotel. Lucky for me, Mrs. Simms opted to stay home. We started having troubles in our marriage long ago, but we could put on a good front. Being with Chelsea wasn't the first time I had cheated and my wife knew it. Me and Robert Ellis were cheating buddies along with being partners in crime. There's something about power. It can move you to greatness or it can be your waterloo. Well y'all know what happened to me. And my wife warned me to slow down. But no sirree. You couldn't tell this judge anything. Now he's singing the blues and no one's listening now that I need them.

Remembering Chelsea the night I met her, she was dressed in a bright red business suit with her blonde hair thrown behind her back. I first noticed her fine legs, which she had crossed inside black laced nylons. She spotted me too. Peering at me sipping from her Cosmopolitan, I knew she hoped I'd be the one she'd end up with. Hell. I'm a fine middle-aged brotha. And I look like I got bank. Chelsea turned out to be a lot of fun, besides a good lay. I soon found out I could talk to her about things I couldn't tell Mrs. Simms. She'd listen and kept things to herself. Besides she would take me up on my offer one day. And it would've paid off long-term if she didn't insist on having my nephew. She wanted to be a lady of leisure, be spotted in the limelight and couldn't have that with me. But Jeremy? He's my sister's son so he has my respect. But I am not a fan. He's a spoiled ass mama's boy and frankly Ellis's daughter didn't need to be with him. Two spoiled brats wouldn't work. Can you imagine their offspring?

9:15p.m.
On the road

Patrice is driving as fast as she can without getting stopped. We pass through Stone Mountain heading down a back highway. Only one car passes us, heading in the opposite direction and driving like a bat out of hell. Strange I'm thinking. I quickly let the thought go when what happened this morning re-enters my mind. My wife Elsa's attorney served me with divorce papers. She moved back to her hometown Savannah last week, staying with her sister until we clear up our divorce mess. She told me to keep the house. Wanted no parts of it.

Our house is as majestic as they come but lonely. Elsa and me never had kids because we never made the time. My career was going gangbusters and Elsa enjoyed being the wife of a judge. We got invited to all the big parties and even attended a function at the Whitehouse. Robert Ellis wanted me to run against Senator Rutherford. He wanted someone inside the big house to push things his way. I opted out. I've done enough for Robert Ellis over the years. This thing with his daughter's trust could put a nail in my coffin. I knew when I signed the trust over to him based on his daughter's signature she gave under duress would come back to haunt me. But I did it anyway. Old Judge Simms is always there as long as I get mine. I did make $10 million off the deal. With my bank connections, we made sure the payout was untraceable.

Ellis got his payback. I tried to tell him his daughter wasn't as naïve as he thought. I often wondered whether she was crazy as she let on. Did she really lose her memory? Or was she playing a game to keep Ellis off of her? I do know her condition kept him on edge. He regularly showed concern and told me. I'd sympathize, but warned him Miss LaTonya would probably end up turning the tables on him one day. And look what happened.

9:30p.m.
We pull up into the driveway

We get out of car and race inside the dark house Chelsea once owned with Don Juan. Patrice turns on the little flashlight hooked to the end of her key chain. I follow her around until we reach a room.

Shining the flashlight inside Patrice yells, "You were right!" We run over to Chelsea. Patrice leans over and grabs her wrist. "She don't have no pulse," she says, sounding panicked. Here's where I take over. I'm much calmer, so I do CPR.

"Come on Chelsea," I say pumping her chest alternating with pinching her nose and blowing into her mouth.

"Don't you die on me," says Patrice who's kneeling beside me, praying. I imagine a Transgender can love God too.

"Come on baby. Wake up. I don't intend to lose you now."

Chelsea begins sputtering. When she's fully awake I grab her to my chest and hold her. "You're alright now. The judge has you."

10:30p.m.
At the Simms's home

Since Elsa opted to leave me the house, I had the locks changed and told her I'd send her things wherever she wanted. Or she could arrange to have them picked up. So at MY house is where I stash Chelsea although Patrice wanted her to go back to Norcross with her. I explain to Patrice I may be down on my luck but Chelsea's safest with me.

Right now I don't feel right about sharing my soon-to-be ex-wife's bed with Chelsea, so I lay her on the king bed in the largest guest room. On the way here, I did call a doctor friend who will be over shortly to do a workup. He knows to keep things on the DL, so I hope we don't have to take her into a hospital. Legally she's known as Stephanie Matthews, but having recently delivered a baby and no baby to show, would raise unnecessary suspicion. Baby snatching is a crime, but we're not talking about just any baby snatching. We're talking about the baby of a woman who's wanted for kidnapping.

I leave Chelsea's side for a moment and walk over to the green leather recliner in the left corner of the room next to the fireplace. I take off my jacket and throw it across the arm of the chair. Reaching over to the wall, I turn the air conditioning on low and the gas fireplace on for ambiance. Then I head back over to Chelsea's bedside. Looking from side-to-side, I admire the Italian art I recently purchased through a broker. This guy can find you just about anything. Once, I sent him in search of a rare ruby. I had planned to give it to Elsa on our wedding anniversary 4 years ago. But we got into a heated argument so I ended up keeping it. It's still in my safe. Who knows, there may be another woman out there more deserving.

This room is my man cave and the biggest guest room in the Simms's mansion. I had it remodeled 3 years ago and finished in dark redwood, dark green leather furniture, gold and black accent colors, to reflect a space fit for a king – ME. Elsa would put me out of our bed so often, I needed a place I could call my own – home away from home inside my own house. My bookshelf has numerous novels. No law books though. I remand them to my law library at the east end of the house. In here, I do read fiction by some of my favorite authors like Walter Mosley. I also keep many magazines full of naked women. Besides Chelsea, the only other person I let stay in here was my Kuwaiti friend the Shah. Man's worth about $700 million. I helped him link of his illegal oil holdings here in the states. I've been thinking about giving the Shah a call. He's one favor I've yet to call in. And one I only vowed to call in an emergency. I'd say what's happening to me is definitely worth a call.

I sit on the edge of the bed and watch Chelsea sleep. So far she appears peaceful stretched out against my burgundy silk sheets. Pulling the bed spread up around her, I stroke the sides of her cheeks. All I can think about is how to keep her safe if I happen to go away. Until then I plan to turn over every damn brick, dig up every inch of red dirt until I find our son.

48
Gone on in

June 30, 2013
In Druid Hills

Me and gramma Oliver talk and sing silly songs. We also sing a couple of her favorite gospel songs by Cece Wynon. This is really nice with only just the 2 of us. Gramma let me share my feelings about Rae, Loretta and Robert and she didn't judge. She also let me know Darius was part of the Oliver family despite how others may feel.

"You know baby," says gramma, "I've had my share of demons too. I may have done things for my own sake at times, but the Lord has forgiven me. So, before I leave this earth, I plan to make everything right. I hope you can forgive me one day."

I grab gramma's hands and hold them against my heart. "I already have," I say.

She smiles and says, "Remember this when the time comes and forgive your mother too. Otherwise, you won't be able to fully love yourself or anyone."

I kiss gramma's hands then lean down and kiss both cheeks. Sitting back up, I smile and think *oh boy, another secret is about to implode. And you know, I think I know what's gonna happen. Once y'all find out, I'll tell you if what I was thinking was right.*

She's gone on in

Last evening gramma passed away. I left the room right before she died but granddaddy and Loretta were there with her. Honestly, I'm glad I wasn't there for the finale. Seeing Loretta breakdown after losing her mama would have torn at my heart. Make me forget how angry I am at her. Gramma Oliver wants me to make amends with Loretta and Rae like I've already done with her and granddaddy. I told her I would do my best to fulfill her final wish.

Downstairs
In the Oliver parlor

Planning for gramma's funeral turns into an event. Ms. Jacob, gramma's 2 sisters, her baby brother, granddaddy's eldest and only sister, along with Rae and Loretta are handling the arrangements. The elders plan to read some of gramma Oliver's favorite bible verses during the service. The elders include gramma's parents – Papa Joe and great grandma Delilah – who will be coming in from Montgomery, Alabama tomorrow. I can only imagine how they must feel about outliving their daughter.

Granddaddy's parents – Franklin T. Oliver IV and Coretta Oliver – will fly in from Barcelona where their retirement villa is located. Franklin IV is the son of Tangee, the African slave boy, who was fathered by the white slave master Franklin T. Oliver II. Tomorrow, a lot of history will be under one roof. A nice distraction from the rest of the crazy bullshit. Me, I decide to stay out of the planning, but

Darius offers to help. Loretta welcomes him. Hmm. I'm not impressed.

Gramma's funeral will be held a week from today. This will give them enough time to announce Loretta's miraculous return. I'm calling this the fireworks before the big storm gramma righted before she passed. I wonder how Loretta plans to inform Robert Ellis she's alive and well? She's probably planned a grand entrance. That'd be my style.

Leaving the parlor, I check my cellphone messages. The news of my gramma's passing is big news given how prominent she was. So far, I've received calls from Shonny, Julie, Ms. T my Portland Hairstylist, Tommy, my BFF, Jeremy, Damon and AJ aka DaMenace. Grinning, I think of what I could've had with this white boy. Some of the callers relay condolences from other distant acquaintances. I figure I give most of 'em a call back.

First I'm gonna check in on my granddaddy. Of course, he's taking this really hard, but tries to hide his feelings. So he's disappeared from the fold.

This year marks my grandparents' silver 40th anniversary. They were seen as the happiest couple around. My granddaddy was a good husband. I'd be surprised if he ever cheated. He worshiped the ground Jocelyn Oliver walked.

"Granddaddy," I call to him, knocking on their bedroom door. At first I don't hear anything so I'm thinking he's asleep. As I get ready to turn and leave, I hear my granddaddy. "Come on in puddin'," he says.

I open the door and go in. Granddaddy is standing over by the entry to the back deck. He motions for me to come over and join him. I follow him outside and we sit in the cushy chairs, me to his left. He sits, crosses his ankles and folds his hands into his lap. Staring straight ahead, granddaddy's avoiding eye contact not wanting me to see how much he's been crying. Sadly, the extra puffiness engulfs his once happy looking Gizmo eyes.

"This spot is where me and mama shared many nights talking. She'd listen to everything I had to say," he says, chuckling. "I talked so much about business I'm surprised she stood it. She was a great woman your grandmother. She was one of a kind. But stubborn as hell," he says, shaking his head. "When she made up her mind about something, there was no arguing. And I let her win. I loved her. She could do no wrong in my eyes." Granddaddy turns his head slightly, glancing at me from the side of his left eye and says, "You know that darn woman had the nerve to tell me it was OK to open my heart to another woman after she was gone, as long as she ain't a white woman or her nemesis Kathleen Turner." Granddaddy shakes his head grinning.

Kathleen Turner is an aristocrat and also a member of the Links and Jack and Jill. Since I can remember, gramma Oliver and Mrs. Turner did their best to one-up each other. Whether it be fundraising for a charity or decorating their homes on Christmas, Mrs. Jocelyn Oliver refused to be outdone. Which is why she was the one who ended up marrying my granddaddy. Gramma told me in college, granddaddy had his eye on both her and Mrs. Turner, but gramma made sure he paid attention to only her. She said at first her reason for going after granddaddy was to piss off Mrs. Turner, but it didn't take long for her to fall in love with granddaddy's sweet self.

Apparently Mrs. Turner is a widow too. Lost her husband as recently as last year. She's sophisticated and shapely like gramma. But gramma has her beat on elegance and style. Also gramma's uppityness appears natural and part of her practiced M.O. As for Mrs. Turner, she tries too hard. I meeean. She sticks her nose way up, holding her cheeks and mouth really tight, making 'em look like she had a bad facelift. She's got nice naturally light brown hair though, which she wears in a blunt cut.

Kathleen Turner is Republican but her family isn't wealthy. Her late husband made all the money as VP of Telecom Brinks for 25 years. Must've been all those stock options he had 'cause Mrs. Turner is doing quite well.

Sheeish. All these people dying so young. My grandparents are only in their mid-60s. I hope my genes push beyond 80 at least. And my granddaddy? I hope he hangs out for many more years. I've heard of really close spouses, following the dead one soon after.

"Everything OK puddin'?" granddaddy asks, grabbing my right hand and bringing it to his lap.

"Yes. I'm worried about you though."

"No need. Only thing is this big ol' house. Don't know what I'ma do now," says granddaddy. Setting his bended right arm and elbow on the chair arm, he lays the side of his head in the palm of his hand. Closing his eyes he says, "What are you and Darius planning?"

"We're planning to head back to Tahoe. I told Darius I'm through with Portland, Oregon."

"He, heee!" granddaddy laughs. "I can't say I blame you." He remains quiet for a moment. Lifting his head, he turns to face me. "If you and Darius want to make this your home, I'll stay out of your way. This place is sho big enough. Don't worry about Loretta and Rae. I'll make sure they respect your boundaries."

I don't respond right away. When I do I say, "I'll talk it over with Darius. If he doesn't, I'll stay for a while."

Granddaddy smiles and says, "I'd like your company. You can help me sort out my next move. Like maybe selling this house?" He pauses then says, "You know, I have a feeling that boy will do anything you want him too. He promises to do right."

I smile and ask, "And you know this because?"

Still smiling granddaddy winks.

Uh-huh I'm thinking. My granddaddy may be a mild mannered man, but when it comes to his granddaughter, he don't play. In his own way, he made sure

Darius knew what time it was. Huh. The least of Darius's worries is Rae. The man to watch out for is Franklin T. Oliver V.

49

Pieces of a Dream

4ᵗʰ of July 2013
In Portland

What better way to start the fireworks than to face Robert T. in person. We've finalized mama's funeral arrangements and plan to hold her service at the Druid Hills Sanctuary on the hill overlooking the gravesite where she'll be buried. Church on the Way will have no involvement. Mama stopped associating her good name with them when the Bradley's got arrested. Since the incident, the church has been struggling to make a comeback. They've installed the deputy pastor as head of the congregation. But the public isn't naïve. No doubt, the deputy knew all along what was going on despite his denial.

I told Rae I needed some time alone. He looked a little put off but I assured him I'd only need a couple of days. He says call him. He'd be at his house where he rarely stays now that I'm well. But he's not comfortable with giving up his place and moving into my estate. He says he feels like he'd be living off his woman. Funny. Rae has never asked me for a dime. If I offered, he wouldn't take it. He's definitely not like Robert T. in that respect. Rae's got his own money, which I've never questioned him about. I ignore the stories and he assures me the past is the past.

I didn't tell Rae about today. He would have intervened or at least insisted he come with me. This day is between me and Robert T. The man who wished me dead.

Tomorrow we will make my reappearance known to the public. We've decided to keep Lydia's name out of the press for the sake of TiAnna and Randall – for now. Our PR people plan to keep this low key to not overshadow mama's upcoming day on July 7.

I've been tracking Robert T whose been spending his days hiding on the Oregon coast. With one of his cheap whores I suspect. Today he's in Portland speaking with his attorney. I hope they advise him to plea. Either way he's going to lose. The grand jury plans to move forward, which means Robert T. should be arrested soon. When they do, they should keep him locked up. He's a flight risk. Robert T. has connections everywhere, including a Kuwaiti Shah.

For the past week, I've been pondering about how Robert T. and I would meet. Calling ahead wasn't an option. What I've come up with was to expose myself to Robert T. in a public setting. If he passes out from shock, there will be folks around to revive him. I chose to wait for him in the bank building downtown where his attorney resides. I can't miss him where I'm standing. Near the elevators I also have a clear view of the exits.

My eyes drift to the far end elevator. I watch the light start from the 22nd floor where Robert T.'s attorney is. The light drops to 18. Stops. Starts again, picking up speed, dropping rapidly down to the 6th floor. Stop.

My heart is beating so loud it's winning over the patter of feet, spilling out around me.

6, 5, 4, 3, 2, 1. The elevator doors open and out poor a handful of people down to the last one. No Robert T. The doors close and back up it goes. Breathing deeply, I relax. My jumpy nerves. This waiting in anticipation is more than I was expecting. I hope I'm able to follow through. Robert may have to hear the news the way everyone else will.

I watch the elevators come and go for about another 10 minutes. Giving up, I turn and –

"I was wondering when you would show," he says.

Startled by the person standing behind me, I drop back a step, catching myself so I won't be the one who needs reviving. One thing we've always been able to do is look at each other in the eyes. His stocky short ass makes us near the same height when I'm wearing flats like today.

"Well, well. Robert T. How long have you been standing there?"

"Long enough to get a good look," he says, smiling. A chill runs through me, knowing the intent behind his answer.

"You're looking well put together. Definitely an improvement over how you once dressed," I say snidely. He's wearing a beige Steve Harvey suit, canary yellow shirt and burgundy tie. My eyes drop quickly to his feet. He's wearing Magnanni's.

"And you as well, Loretta. You always manage to look good in anything you put on."

I'm pondering Robert T.'s reaction to seeing me after believing I was dead for 9 years. He's pretty calm and doesn't seem surprised at all.

"Sounds like you were expecting me, Robert T."

Robert Ellis still smiling never moves his eyes from mine says, "Loretta, I've known all along you were still alive."

I scrunch my eyebrows slightly. "You've known all along?"

"Let's say I suspected," he says. "The night Rae came to me with the announcement of your so-called passing, he was too damn calm. As much as he loves you Loretta he should've been torn up. His behavior said it all." Robert T. pauses and says "I recently had one of my boys do some checking and found out what your family had been up too. The closed casket scenario. I should've known."

All I can do right now is turn up the side of my lip and cross my arms in disgust. You can't get anything past Robert T., who always finds someone willing to talk, for the right price.

"Yep," he says. "Then your parents offered to buy our house back. How's our lovely home anyway?"

Rather than respond, I tighten my folded arms to refrain from slapping the shit out of him.

"Then there were the times Rae would come by the house. I caught him copying the pages of Tippy's diary. To read at your beside no doubt. How thoughtful," Robert T. shakes his head. "You know Loretta, because of your parents' quest to blame me for your attack they sacrificed our own daughter's happiness. Mm, mm, mm. How are you and our daughter getting along these days?" Robert T. says, laughing.

My anger is showing. Bringing up Tippy and knowing how she feels about me, hurts me deeply. Although I had no control over my own life for 9 years, my daughter blames me for my absence. Robert T. is right about one thing, my parents wanted him to be the one convicted and put away for life. Having witnessed the whole thing he's just as guilty.

"You got a lot of nerve Robert T. You were there and you chose to do nothing."

"Oh you're wrong my darling wife," says Robert T, holding up his right forefinger, shaking it back and forth. "Hey you know. We're still husband and wife. How about that?" Robert T. drops his smile straightens his face, looking concerned. "Uh, anyway I did call the paramedics and the police. I couldn't let that crazy woman do something to our daughter. Our daughter. The one I raised!" Robert T says, pounding his right fist on his chest. "Not you! Not Rae. You know what? You can say what you want about Robert Thomas Ellis. But know this. When you look into to our daughter's eyes, staring back at you with contempt, remember those are my eyes, staring back at you," he emphasizes, "With contempt. I made her into who she is. And I taught her well. Rae didn't do shit!" Robert T. breathes, calming himself down. "I think we're done here, Mrs. Ellis." He prepares to leave. "Oh, just so you know. My marriage to Luanne wasn't legal. Not because you were still alive, but because I set it up to make it look real to keep her quiet. Everything was fake from the minister to the marriage certificate. There's no way I would've committed bigamy. So far now, you're still my wife. As for a divorce, we can negotiate. But right now, your presence is making me itch."

"You'll get yours Robert T," I finally say, shaking a little and holding back my angry tears.

"Well bring it on," he says. "Don't forget I've already gone up against the devil himself and lived to tell about it. Ha!" Robert T. turns and walks away. Without turning back, he throws up his hand and says, "Tell my brother hello for me."

I stand there without moving, tears rolling down my face. I must look distraught because periodically people would stop and offer their help. I wipe my tears away. I'm Loretta Ellis and stronger than this. I won't let Robert T. get the best of me. I leave the bank building and cross the street to where my driver is waiting. He nods when I approach and opens my rear door. I slide in without looking. My brain is doing flips from my meeting with Robert. Suddenly a voice startles me, interrupting my thoughts.

"I hope you got what you came here for."

Seated on my left is Rae. Damn these Ellis boys. My eyes are red from crying but I'm done feeling sorry. "Robert T.'s known about me all along," I say.

Rae lifts his eyebrows, tilts his head to the right, shrugs and asks, "So are we done here?"

Nodding I say, "Yes. We're done here."

50
Out with it

July 5th
In Norcross

"And why should I believe you?" Patrice asks.

"Cows I ain't got nothin to gain thru line. I dun been lied to too much in my life. It's hard to trus. Believes me. I knows how ya feel."

I lean back on my sofa, kicking my feet up on my coffee table. Staring at this bold heifer sitting across from me. You know, she could just be plain stupid and I could be too. I took a chance by agreeing to meet wit' Miss bad hair day. Lord have mercy on this po' black white child. It's bad enough she can't speak worth a damn. Ain't got no education. Just trash is all. Trash trying to be all sadiddy. And to think she was married to Robert Ellis. I don't know the man personally, but I do know he's a multi-millionaire with a billion-dollar nameplate.

You're wondering why she's in my house ain't you? You should already know. Yesterday, I got a visit from a detective wanting to find Chelsea. Says he has information about her real mama and it ain't

Lydia Johnson. Of course, I was skeptical as hell. First, Chelsea turns up missing. Next someone steals her baby right from her womb. Now I'm being told this game Chelsea ran on Lydia and the family was all for not. Which means Miss Thang ain't really her sister. Damn shame.

I called the judge to check on Chelsea who's hanging in but depressed about her baby being gone. The doctor he has watching over her keeps her sedated. The judge suggested I get all the information I can from this Luanne Ellis broad. Then we'd determine the truth later.

"I tell you what," I say to Luanne, pointing and tilting my right forefinger up and down. "Let me take this information to Chelsea and put her in touch with you. Having another mama and an inheritance may intrigue her. Huh. I ain't gonna lie. I'd be more interested in the money myself. Ha, ha, ha, holla-me-bad."

"Ok," says Luanne, smiling. "Fine by me."

"It's gonna have to be suga," I say, standing up. "I don't want to appear like I'm rushing you, but I am honey. I got things ta do, people ta see. Hear me?"

"No prob," says Luanne.

"Come on girl, let me show your Ebonics talkin' ass outta here," I say to Luanne as I step around my table. Oops y'all. She ain't laughing. "I'm just playin' wit' you girl," I say touching her on the arm, walking her to the door.

"Naw dat's ok," Luanne says. "Dis yo house. I jus appreshate you lettin' me come by."

"We'll be in touch," I say, letting her out the front door. "Be safe."

Once she's left my porch, I close the door. Nothing but drama. Damn. What next besides me planning to whoop Tommy Crumb's ass. You don't walk out on Patrice. I'll show you what time it is.

Amanishakhete

In Atlanta
The news is spreading

And I've wanted to call you. "Girl, how you holding up?"

"You know T, I feel stronger than ever. I made a determination to never let lying ass people and their bullshit get me down ever again. I have to say I'm like Robert Ellis in that respect. Once you feel the burn, you'll never allow yourself to be hurt again."

"Good for you Tip," says TiAnna, pausing. When she does I could swear I hear a baby crying in the background. But whose baby could it be? Probably belongs to Virgil's kin."

"Do I hear a baby crying?" I ask.

"Um yeah," says TiAnna. She's hesitating. But why?

"Hmm," I say, shrugging my shoulders looking over at Darius, sprawled across the bed.

We ran in here about an hour ago to take a break from the downstairs family traffic. Some of the out of town guests are staying here. The last 2 of the 10 guest bedrooms got filled with my gramma's favorite niece Antoinette and her family who flew in from Las Vegas. Antoinette is gramma's brother's oldest daughter. She's half black and half Japanese. Uncle James married a Japanese woman he met when he was serving in the Air Force. I think gramma liked Antoinette 'cause she's a Republican. The rest of her nieces and nephews no what time it is. They support President Obama thank you. Ugh. Speaking of Republicans, Senator Stanley Rutherford will be one of the distinguished guests and volunteered to be a pallbearer. I heard this just happened and we know why. Loretta is back in town. I may get up the nerve to say to him "Don't you know by now she doesn't want you fool." But then again maybe she does. Who knows, she may have been doing him too. Maybe the big secret gramma plans to right is Rae's not my biological dad either but it's actually Stanley Rutherford? Wow. Wouldn't that be the shits?

"Her name's LaKenya. She was just born," says TiAnna, taking in a deep breath. "She's mine and Virgil's."

My mouth drops open so far, Darius may have to pick it up. "You have a baby?"

"Yep. I gave birth to her on June 28 and she's definitely my miracle Tip," TiAnna says, sniffling. "I never thought the day would come when someone would call me mommy."

No sir like I said

"I've never seen this girl," I say. Shit I'm lying like hell. Glad we're on the phone.

"Very well Mr. Justice or AJ or is that DaMenace? Anyway, we wanted you to be aware of our recent findings. We plan to circulate this through the news media see what we come up with," says the LAPD.

"Thank you for working hard on this sir," I say, ignoring his sarcasm on what to call me. "Apprehending my wife's killer is my priority."

I hang up after the officer does. Oh wow. I'm staring at a fax they sent me. The girls who found my wife's body say they remembered something else about the girl they saw. The sketch I'm holding is what the artist came up with based on their description. Damn. The hair, the dress, the height resembles TiAnna. The face is way off but getting close and personal like I did, you'd know it was her. What am I gonna do with this shit? Just be my luck they thank I planned the shit to be wit' her. Ah hell naw. I gotta make sure ain't nothing left but dust between me and crazy.

At Darius's house on Prescott

I gotta find them damn keys. Where the fuck would dat nigga hide somethin' like dat? I done turned up every inch of this place. Done everything except for ask 'im straight out about it, chancing he may know nothin'. But my daddy thinks he do. Shit dere go my phone. It's my boy Darius. Time to play nice.

"My man. Wassup?"

"Checkin' in yo. Y'all got things cool dere right Jodeci? Last time I came through you had the place in a mess," Darius chuckles.

"Sorry 'bout dat man. Naw we cool here."

"Good den yo. Not sure when I'll be back dat way. My girl ain't touching down in dat place no time soon yo. So I'll be sending for her car in the next couple of days."

"Oh? Wassup?" I ask Darius.

"You know man. A whole lotta shit yo. Too much to brew on now. I'll get back wit' at you doe. Say send my mail if I got any. Most stuff is already headed dis way. Moms knows where to send my shit already."

"Oh yeah. She been touchin' down huh?" I ask trying to play it cool.

"Yeah yo. She sent me a letter I ain't opened."

"Well den Darius. I hope she OK considerin'."

"Yeah yo. Be in touch." Darius hangs up.

I was downstairs when Darius called. Now that we through talkin' I can breathe. I drop my ass down on his sofa and kick my feet up on the coffee table with my slides on. I gotta big smile on my face. Yep. I believe we've made progress. What better place to stash a key then with her son indeed.

51
Just wacked

July 6, 2013
10:00p.m.

I'm on the phone scolding Tommy. "Tommy why did you go over there? You've been through this before. You know she's wacked. Where you at anyway?"

"I'm at a friend's house," I say sniffling while my friend puts sav on my bruises. "TiAnna, you gotta new baby. No need of me bringing you my drama."

"Tommy, you know you're welcome here anytime and as long as you need to be. Virgil is in charge here and won't let nothing happen to anyone of us. And I'm damn sho not scared of that bitch. Ooo. Don't let me see her. I'm glad you got out of there when you did."

"Barely," says Tommy. "She caught me off guard. She was claiming she was getting us some cocktails. Then all of a sudden the dick bitch is all on top of me, beating me with a stick and shit. Crazy ass bitch! Standing up I could've at least given her a run for her money. Owe." My big ass Messiah got some rough hands. "Be more careful boo," I say to him.

"Ooo Tommy you over at that rapper's house ain't you? I can't believe he likes boys. Ya never know."

"Uh-uh. Ya don't," I say to T. "Girl I'ma let you go OK. Gotta take me a pill or somethin' to make this shit stop aching."

"Tommy maybe you should see a doctor?"

"Nada." They ask too many questions.

"Well maybe it's time you turn Patrice in. Let 'er rot in jail."

"Naw. I'll deal wit' it in my own time. Hey hug Tippy for me when you see her. I doubt I'll feel like going to her gramma's funeral tomorrow. Oh and kiss Miss LaKenya for me too. Just so you know the ol' coon got jealous when I told her about your baby girl. Given her friend ran off, I guess she thought she was gonna be an auntie."

Shit. Tommy told Patrice about my baby. "Well OK boo. You get some rest hear?"

"Yes darlin'. You too," he says then hangs up.

Before I can tell Virgil what Tommy said, someone knocks at the door. I run over and look out the peep hole. Virgil who was sitting across from me watching the game looks up and asks, "Who dere?"

"Patrice," I say, whispering.

Virgil throws up his hands and says, "Well whatchu waiting for? Let 'im in?"

About the same time over in Druid Hills

"I can't believe you Darius. You know she don't look nothing like my BFF."

"I'm just sayin' yo. She's wearing your friend's signature hairstyle. And I seen her wit' dat dress on. Ain't it one of doze originals?"

"T don't wear a lot of designer originals. The stuff she has I bought for her or she got from our designer friend. He doesn't do a lot of freebies. Why you hatin' Darius?" I say love smacking the back of his head and stretched out at the foot of the bed. I'm laying on my right side, my head on my left arm. Darius is right next to me lying on his stomach. His chin plopped on top of his clasped hands. We're upstairs watching the news. Earlier we had a big feast with the family where we all had a chance to laugh, talk and cry remembering gramma.

Gramma's funeral starts at 11:30 in the morning. Afterwards, we'll head down to the cemetery for her burial, then back here for a celebration of her life. The limos will be out front to pick us up around 10:15, so we can get to the sanctuary and settle in before the spectators. Like I said, this will be a big deal. I heard Colin Powell and his wife will be attending and that awful Supreme Court Justice and his wacked white wife will be too. I still can't get over her saying Anita Hill should apologize for what happened years ago. She knows her man wanted a black woman who didn't want his fugly ass. Racist! In that vein, the Romney's sent their condolences but won't be coming. Hallelujah!

"What's wrong with you and T all of sudden? Y'all use to be cool."

"Hm," Darius says.

"What do you mean? Stop playin'."

"I ain't playin' yo," Darius picks up the remote and turns it to some hip hop channel.

"Ooo snap. Please turn the sound down. You know I don't like hip hop much."

Darius clicks off the TV. Turning over on his back, he tosses the remote to the other end of the bed, re-clasping his hands in back of his head.

I scoot over next to him, stretch my arm across his chest. "What's wrong?"

"I gotta tell you somethin' yo."

"What yo."

"Naw for real shawty. Dis is serious. I shoulda tol' you 'bout dis long ago. But there was never a good time. Now this done happened. Your girl may have been the one to off Uriella."

"Well tell me somethin'," I say calmly.

After contemplating on pause for a moment, Darius finally comes clean. He tells me everything about the night TiAnna killed Joshua. Then about what DaMenace said to him when he ran into him in Portland. TiAnna had been up to see him.

"I'm sorry beautiful but dat ain't no coincidence."

After Darius finishes I shut down for a moment making him wonder what I'm thinking. He's probably wondering if we'll end up in divorce court over this. Huh. How would the judge respond? "Mrs. Broussard your reason for wanting this divorce is?" And I would answer? "Because Mr. Darius neglected to tell me my BFF is a serial killer who murdered 2 people and he helped get rid of the first body." And the judge would say, "What would you have preferred he had done?" And I would say, "Call the police on the bitch. Best friend or not, wacked is wacked!"

Rather than get angry I ask, "How far is the first one buried?"

"Deeper than a rainy day," he says. "Won't be any problem."

"You'd better be right. My BFF better not go to prison for neither one of those foul asses. They didn't deserve to live." I breathe deeply then say, "As for Uri, you may want to make sure. Un-da-stand?"

"Yep," he says.

I'm so exhausted from all this shit I decide to just turn over and go to sleep leaving Darius to wonder who the hell is this new LaTonya Ellis-Broussard.

52
Decisions

July 7, 8:00 a.m.
Portland time

I've decided to visit my sister on the island. We only live a couple of hours apart, but we rarely cross paths. In fact, we've grown apart since we first plotted to have my husband committed to a maximum security psychiatric hospital. Before his presumed demise, Dr. Michelson believed he had it all. The successful practice, trophy-wife half his age and on occasion even my sister. We did anything and everything to keep Michelson happy so he wouldn't carry through on this threat to send us away for our parents' murder.

The day I met Robert Ellis my life changed. I met him at my sister's graduation at Emory University. Michelson was with me. Most everyone who saw us together figured we were father and daughter rather than husband and wife. Ellis, however, knew differently. Catching me outside the ladies room, where he had followed me, he introduced himself and asked "So what's your story?" I responded, "How much time do you have?" He says, "As much as you need."

I talked Michelson into staying over in Atlanta. Given he was much older he often fell asleep early. He'd stop taking Viagra at the warning of his doctor, so staying up to have sex wasn't an option. When we did, it was over in 2 minutes for which I was grateful. Sex with him was so bad, I often found others to bide my time with. Like the paper boy, or postman, young healthy bucks closer to my age. Well I don't have to tell you what happened when Robert and I got together. We had sex and then some. We talked and laughed and I ended up bearing my soul. What I said didn't faze him. Somehow I knew it wouldn't. This man was different than any man I'd known and I'd only known a few. He was strong, very sure of himself and fearless. I could tell he had also been hurt by those around him but refused to let them define who he was.

Over the next several months Robert would arrange for us to be together. I'd visit him under the guise of visiting my sister who decided to stay on and practice in Atlanta. There is where we came up with a plan to get Michelson out of our lives for good. My sister Sheila was in on it from the beginning. The plan was for her to move back to Wisconsin and work at Michelson's practice. My role was to encourage Michelson to let go of the rings and allow my sister to run things so he and I could spend more time together. It didn't take long for Dr. Ryan to get entrenched in Michelson's business. She began seeing his patients and brought in new ones. They loved her.

One day we put the plan in full motion. My sister concocted a dummy patient with serious psychiatrist issues. This patient would soon be Michelson. Robert Ellis's good friend Judge Simms helped us to get Michelson committed to an out of the way facility in Georgia. He's been there for the past 10 years heavily sedated and under my sister's care.

Now after all these years, our plan is being threatened. My sister has been doing her part. But now all of a sudden she's getting a conscious. Apparently, she's being questioned about her role in LaTonya Ellis's commitment. I've been trying to get her to understand agreeing to commit her doesn't mean she was in on a conspiracy. Dr. Ryan is well respected around the country so there should be no question. Nor should she be allowing anyone to question Robert's reasoning. I happen to love Robert Ellis. He may never be mine entirely but what we do have has meant more to me than any other time in my life. My sister, because of her stupidity and sudden enlightenment, will not ruin my life or Robert's.

"Hi sis," I say, giving Sheila a hug once she lets me in. "How's your headache."

Sheila sighs. "Delores I haven't slept in days. When they take this to trial, I am going to be called as a witness for the prosecution."

"Oh really," I say. "I'm puzzled. You've stuck to your story. There's no reason for them to think differently. You have plenty of references coming in."

"Yes I do Delores. But that doesn't stop me from being nervous. My world is crashing down around me."

I pat Sheila on the back and say, "Say, why don't we forget about this for today and talk about maybe taking a vacation. We haven't done so in years. And you got a birthday coming up. Sheeish girl you will be 44. You need a man. Or are you hiding something?"

"Oh stop," says Sheila. "I'm not Lesbian. I just haven't found the right guy."

"Well I think it's time you did," I say.

"And what about you?" Sheila asks.

"Don't start," I say. "You know how I feel on the subject of Robert. He's all the man I want."

"Haaah," Sheila sighs. "Maybe that'll change once we go on vacation."

"Maybe so," I say to appease her. "Why don't you sit down and relax. I brought you some of our favorite coastal tea. I'll brew us a cup. Then we can talk more. Remember I'm your sister and I love you. We are all we have." I grab Sheila and give her a big hug. Sadly she is not all I have. She's my past and my future has already been spoken for.

Virgil's staying behind
with the baby

Me and daddy Randall plan to go to the funeral together. I'm picking him up 'cause he wants to talk. On my way out, I hug Kenya and Virgil, stopping at the door to admire them. My heart softens every time I realize this beautiful new family is all mine.

Last night I thought the jig was up. V handled things and I was definitely proud of him. First, he lambasted Patrice for questioning our Kenya's paternity. She didn't once mention Chelsea but Virgil did manage to bring her up without giving away the goose. He accused Patrice of being a co-conspirator because she probably knows about my kidnapping. She could go to prison like Chelsea and for a long time. Next he laid a big one down. One thing about being in jail, you run into people who talk about shit they have on someone. Virgil knows another transgender who knows Patrice. He told Virgil, Patrice was here illegally; her mama helped her get out of Amsterdam, quick. One of Patrice's johns turned up dead. She was the last to see him alive, so says another red light hooker, who needed to beat theft charges. Virgil ended things with Patrice, warning her stay away from our family, stop spreading lies or face the consequences.

Whether Patrice will or not, I don't plan on finding out. First, I don't appreciate what she did to Tommy. And for her to even open her mouth to try and question me about my baby. I mean. No one, but no one is taking Kenya from me. I'm glad I held on to Tommy's extra set of house keys.

Over at my family's home

It's always good to see my brothers. "Hey y'all," I say to JR and junior, giving them each a hug.

"Man, don't you look fly," says JR, stepping back looking me up and down. "Don't look like you just had a baby."

"You sure don't," says Junior. "And you even changed your hair. Since when do you wear long-haired weaves?"

"I'm a new mommy so I thought this would be a good time for a new me. You like?" I ask turning and posing with my hands on my hips. My brothers nod. Daddy Randall, whose been standing back quietly, smiles but the look on his face makes me know he knows more than I want him too.

"OK boys, your sister and I got something to talk about before we get outta here."

Waving at the boys, I follow daddy who's heading for his TV room. He sits in his recliner, crosses his legs, looking over at me seated to his right on the little sofa.

He says, "First, I want you to know LaKenya is your daughter and my granddaughter, so I will do anything to protect you and her. Get me?"

"Yes sir," I say.

"Next," says Randall, "Before we go to the funeral, you should know the full story behind your mother's suicide and why she did what she did.

53

Tell the Truth Day #1
The funeral

July 6, 2013
10:45 a.m.

As we planned, the immediate family is the first to arrive in limos forming at the top of the sanctuary hill. We won't need them to travel anywhere but back to my grandparent's estate. For now and because the ceremony and burial are all in one location, the family and guests plan to march behind the pallbearers, who will follow the marching band and drill team to the first hill below, which has a pathway leading to the family crypt. We'll all carry a flower to be handed to us on the way out of the sanctuary. We will place the flowers around gramma's casket, which will end up in front of the crypt's entrance on top of a grand stage done up in style like for dignitaries and saints.

Gramma Oliver considered herself royalty, and as the lady of the Franklin T. Oliver V manor she was treated as such. Like I said my granddaddy never spared any expense on her behalf and he didn't today.

Riding up the hill in our limo, I'm recalling spending a day here each year along with Rae Ellis paying our respects to Loretta. We'd be surrounded by mountains of her favorite purple roses everyone would bring. We should all ask her for a refund. To prepare for her day, florists had to special order the roses making the price costly for some folks.

We're ahead of the family pack, Darius and I in the 2nd limo along with Aunt Antoinette, her white husband James; Aunt Jalisa, granddaddy's older brother's daughter who's recently divorced and a diehard Democrat; his son Samuel and wife Mavis both Republicans who campaigned for Barack.

Darius and Samuel's been joined at the hip 'cause he knows and admires Darius's music. Thankfully that's all we talk about on the way over. The past couple of days, the political battles made things intense. Rae made sure his opinion was heard especially during his spat with Antoinette's husband over the economy and how worthless or not the President was. I remember Rae saying "Look damnit, I am an Obama disciple. Don't be dissing my black President." He stopped short of calling James a racist bastered like he normally would've. Darius did chuckle a few times and even agreed on comments Rae made. Often I'd give Darius a look to make sure he hadn't forgotten what ship he's was sailing. He'd wink. I have to admit Darius can play the game better than me most times. I let my anger get the best of me and tell everybody to "go to hell" like I've been doing.

We get out of the limo and fall in line behind the first group – Loretta, Rae, granddaddy Oliver, his parents and gramma's, all 4 in their late 80s with a lot of stamina. Especially Oliver IV. He's got swag big time. With great grandma holding on tight, the ladies can forget about getting close. Loretta is holding onto granddaddy's left arm, leading him up the walk way. Rae is walking behind the elders out of respect I guess. Really doesn't matter where he stands, he's always been accepted as one of the family above and beyond Robert T., who sent me a letter, which arrived yesterday special delivery and I have yet to open. I hope the letter isn't laced with anthrax. I brought it along hoping to get up nerve to open it.

Ironically, today of all days is recognized nationally as "Tell the Truth Day." No one knows the origins of this day but it's considered an annual holiday. Ha. Does anyone really honor this notion? Commit to telling the truth for an entire day? And don't say saints and clergy. Paleeze.

Inside the white and black marbled sanctuary held up by tall Elizabethan style pillars and ceilings with large white chandeliers, fountains and Christian statues cover the floors carpeted in golden lamiae.

The family is being seated on schedule giving us time to rearrange ourselves and get comfortable. I don't think the service will be too long. I heard my granddaddy say to the planning committee don't get too crazy. We don't want to be sitting in there for hours. Have to have compassion for those who have weak bladders. He did laugh, doing his normal bounce, bending at the knees, up and down on his heels. I was glad to see, granddaddy being his jolly ol' self for a moment.

I'm seated in the front row alongside granddaddy who wanted me beside him. Darius of course sat to my left. Also in front is Loretta on granddaddy's right, the grandparents and my grandparent's siblings. Rae sat behind Loretta, putting him close to me. I glanced at him once out of my right eye. Mr. Charmer must've known I was coming 'cause he met me with a wink. I smiled on the right side of my mouth. Hopefully he didn't see me.

Gramma's white casket is displayed on stage with the choir and pastor. Loretta invited a conservative black southern minister to reside over the event. He is from one of the big black churches granddaddy's parents once attended. They love their black churches and could never understand why granddaddy didn't put his foot down when gramma wanted to attend Church on the Way with all those white folks. Especially since she attended all of the large black functions. My guess was she had no competition there. Granddaddy isn't into white women and no chance of him running into any old flings or potential new ones.

Darius is reading through the program, which is designed like the ones you get for a play. Gramma's beautiful photo graces the front cover, introducing articles, poems, hymns and family photos and gramma in action on the inside. My gramma made sure she hired her own paparazzi to appear at every event she attended. They never followed right of next to her. Gramma was much more subtle, but she always had her smile on and poses ready. This is usually how gramma's photos ended up on many society pages or in political news articles.

I open my program to the front page, running my fingers down through the schedule, which includes the typical choirs, grandchildren, nieces and nephews special presentations, prayers and speeches.

12:00p.m.

The ceremony is in full swing after starting on time. Ms. Denorsha spoke and the elder reading was well worth the wait. My grandparents made me proud and gramma would have been proud too.

12:30p.m.

The service ends and the usher let attendees leave row by row right after the family. As planned, we step in behind the pallbearers who follow the New Orleans style parade. Gramma loved the jazz scene there. The band is playing upbeat music, making me wanna do the bebop. Then wouldn't you know it, they play Flat Foot Floochie, me, gramma and Loretta's favorite song we use to dance to when I was little – 2 women and a happy little girl dancing havoc on Luanne's invisible ass. I refrain from doing the hop dance we use to do but Loretta who's in front of me with granddaddy, looks back at me and starts hopping. Shit! I can't help but bust out laughing. Then I quickly cover my mouth eyeing Darius and Rae who's looking at us curiously. Definitely one of those secrets I still keep.

We pay our respects placing flowers alongside her casket on the stage. We had an array of flowers, each meaning something special to gramma like my favorite fuchsia ones to Loretta's purple roses all signifying gramma's love of family.

Gramma will be laid to rest later on, giving us the rest of the day to say goodbye. We've come to the end of the ceremony. Invited guests begin to crowd around the family to give their blessings. Ms. Denorsha gives me a big hug and tells me how proud she is of me. Shit. I haven't seen this woman since I don't know when. I think I was 5 or 6. I introduced her to Darius. She hugs him too telling him how handsome he is. "Take care of our girl," she says. Hmm. If she knew how street he was she would fall over and die right here. We'd have to bury her too.

Waving in the distance is TiAnna. She looks beautiful. She's mouthing, "I'll see you at the repast." I wave looking between her and Randall to see if she brought the baby. I don't see Virgil so she must've left Kenya home. Wearing her hair long for the first time has me curious. Darius eyes catch mine and he puckers his lips, lifts his brows quietly saying, "See. I told you yo."

Me and Darius have yet to tell anyone about me being pregnant, including T. I plan to tell her face-to-face. That day will have to be soon. Me trying to hide my stomach underneath oversized maxi dresses, blouses and sweaters ain't foolin' nobody. Especially Loretta. When we run into each other, her eyes drop straight to my stomach then back up at me with a smile. Rae's already commented on how much food I've been eating, avoiding discussing my weight gain. If he suspects like Loretta that I'm pregnant, he's being cool about it. I'm grateful for that given how much he despises Darius. To know I'm bringing a little Darius into the world, well – they'll just have to accept it. Oh yeah y'all, we're having a boy. We found out the birth of the baby right before we left Tahoe.

Weight gain is the only drawback to this whole pregnancy ordeal. I've already been complaining to Darius who won't allow me to stress over it. He says we'll work my weight off once the baby's born. I mean. We haven't missed a beat yet.

I grab Darius's hand so we can start heading back to the car. Ahead I see granddaddy Oliver, Rae and Loretta talking to a man standing in front of them. For a minute I think I'm seeing things. There's no way Robert Ellis would show his face here. He didn't even like my grandparents.

But then Darius says, "Uh-uh. Dats your daddy yo."

I stop, halting Darius by my side. "Wow. He got nerve," I say. "I wonder what he's up too?"

"Tryin' to intimidate folks yo."

We're quickly interrupted by a familiar voice. To Darius's dismay, Jeremy Simms is in the house. Glancing over at Darius, he gently places his hand on my back. "Hello LaTonya," he says, stepping around to face me. He hugs me ignoring Darius, who's fuming. I can feel him. Jeremy's gesture is out of concern but he's also doing this for show.

"Hi Jeremy," I say, gently pushing him away for Darius's sake. "Thanks."

Darius has had enough and pipes in without any introduction. He tightens his lips, scrunches his nose and says, "Oh you're Jeremy." Then he glances at me. I'm smiling but scrunching my forehead like "Don't start any shit." Letting his face soften Darius says, "You're right. He does look like a dog."

Jeremy wants to respond, but he doesn't thank goodness. The testosterone between the 2 of 'em is already bubbling. I need to put these 2 boys on simmer before they turn it up, so I say, "Thanks for coming Jeremy."

Darius grabs my left hand and says, "Yeah thanks. You may be excused. Me and my wife have to tend to our guests."

OK. Darius is starting to piss me off with this needless attitude of his. I try to give him the look again but he and Jeremy are too busy staring each other down. Yanking on Darius's arm, I squeeze his hand really tight until he flinches. Shit! I ain't playin'. Then wouldn't you know, Robert Ellis is heading this way. Except I welcome his interruption. When he reaches us, he glances at Darius, then Jeremy turning up his nose. Then he turns back to me and says, "I've been worried about you."

I squeeze Darius's hand tightly. I can feel him readying himself to pounce like a panther protecting what's his. By this time, Rae and Loretta have joined us. Granddaddy starts to follow, but his sister grabs his hand and pulls him gently, making him go to the car. With her eyes, she pierces the back of Robert Ellis's head.

Rather than tongue-lash Robert Ellis like he probably expects, I take a page out of Rae's playbook. "I'm fine thank you for asking. And you're looking well considering," I say politely but smirking.

Everyone here knows Robert Ellis so he's beginning to draw a crowd. Even TiAnna and Randall opted to join us with TiAnna squeezing in between me and Jeremy, taking her place beside me like she usually does when she feels we're being threatened. T looks over at Loretta without smiling. T knows. Rae feels this too. He holds out his hands to both of us, then lays 'em on his heart.

Robert looks at Loretta, Rae and back to me again. "Like I was saying to your mother I'm here to pay my respects and make sure our daughter is OK," He says, emphasizing the word "our", but he's not smiling or smirking, giving us the Robert Ellis devilish grin like he normally does. This time he's visibly angry. He says, "You may not have had a chance to look at your belated birthday present. I hadn't heard anything so I figured you probably tore it up, spit on it or whatever and that's OK. But just so you know, I've signed everything over to you and handed you the reigns to our company. I think you hiring Larry Hughes was the best move. You got brains girl. Of course you would because you are my daughter," he says this time emphasizing the word "my". Loretta begins to sway back and forth nervously. She sure ain't grinning and hopping now. "Ain't that right Loretta," he says looking over at her. Now he's got everybody's attention.

OK. Here she comes, I'm thinking. Poor Unc Rae-Rae. His face saddens because he also knows what's coming next ain't good. Me I'm pretty calm. Like I said before, nothing at this point will surprise me, except for the fact he's handed the company over to me without a fight.

Robert Ellis reaches into his side jacket and pulls out an envelope. Holding it up in front of Loretta he says, "This is addressed to me from your mother." Robert tears up, shaking as he takes in a deep breath. Loretta is starting her tear action too. "You hated me that much?" he says with his voice cracking. "You took my daughter from me. I would've preferred you just kill me. But not take my daughter, having me believe all these years she really wasn't my biological daughter. But we know better don't we Loretta."

No one's moving. Shit. I don't think anyone's breathing. Rae definitely looks like he's getting ready to breakdown.

My daddy turns to me, hands me an envelope and says, "Here's clear proof. I'm your biological father. Not Rae."

The final installment of the LaTonya Trilogy coming in 2020

CHAPTER 1

To Tell the Truth Day
Part 2

The Awakening
1:15 p.m.

Robert Ellis morphs into a mummified stance. His face wound so tight like it's going to bust. Slowly he closes in on his once-thought-to-be-dead wife dismissing the watchful eyes of the people surrounding him including those of his brother Raymond Ellis.

Rae is always ready to defend his precious Loretta, but this time he isn't defending. His brain went numb right after hearing his brother's words – that he wasn't the father, but Robert is, and he says he's got proof.

Rae's eyes fill with water while wanting to shout *you a lying motherfucka*. Except the words gurgle up, stop in his throat, quickly fizzle away. First time for Rae given he's quick with his tongue. But all he can do is stare in amazement like the other guests standing close by. All except for Tippy the one he's known as his daughter since birth. The one he's had to threaten his heartless brother over to keep him from doing damage to her, which he's managed to do anyway. Rae's thinking if he had made it known Tippy was his from the beginning despite Loretta's wishes, maybe Tippy wouldn't be married to a hoodrat and having a baby she doesn't think anyone knows about. No matter what my brother says, this doesn't change a thing. *Baby girl is always going to be my daughter. Damn you Loretta! I can't even look at you right now. I may pull a Robert and bust you in your ass.*

I glance at my uncle who's staring at me while his wet eyes spill down his cheeks. No swag no Rae Ellis smile. I've never seen my uncle, I mean daddy, I mean not, cry really. He's good at hiding his feelings. It would go against his Mr. Cool MO. I attempt a smile letting him know I'm right there with him. But then my real daddy breaks in with his loud ass spoiling the moment.

Robert Ellis made his way up to Loretta, stands close enough to spray shouts of spit on her face. He shakes Joselyn Oliver's letter near Loretta's nose, "I feel like slapping the piss outta you, dammit!"

Hmm. I imagine if my gramma Ellis were here now, she'd have a thing or 2 to say about her son's so-called wife like she use to call her when she thought no one was listening.

"Now ain't she shame," she'd say. "So Loretta was da one trippin'. Blamin' you Robert when she had her back up against da wall."

But hell, they both were cheating on each other I'm thinking. Sick, just sick.

Speaking of Mr. Cheater Rae, here he goes. Pulling his shoulders up, he steps in front of Robert facing him with his back to Loretta. She quickly steps back to avoid his force, but still wearing him as her shield. Damn. I wish like hell they'd knock each other the fuck out. They've been wanting to do this for a while and could even throw a few at Loretta. Here you lying winch. Bam! Ooo. Taking me back to the days of the Loretta Ali and Robert Frazier fights.

Except all this craziness is making my baby kick. Reminding me I'm no little girl. I'm a woman now with a husband by her side who leans down and whispers, "We should get you outta here. We can deal with all this later."

The big secret

The day gramma Oliver died she told me she had a secret she planned to divulge before she passed. One she held close all these years for Loretta's sake but had to make right before she met her maker.

I told y'all I might have had an inkling of what the big secret was. Jokingly I said what if Senator Stanley Rutherford turns out to be my real daddy. Not Unc Rae-Rae or Robert Ellis. Huh. Who would've thought Robert Ellis would show and announce he was the daddy and had been all along, putting an end to Loretta and gramma's deception.

My eyes scan the survivors connected to Robert and me. My Darius, my once lover Jeremy, TiAnna, Randall, Unc Rae-Rae and Loretta. I'll leave you to choose which expression goes on whose face from mouths dropped, lips turned up, hands on hips standing with an attitude, tears rolling and pure rage. Unlike them, I am neither shocked, angry, crying or have an attitude. For the first time, I'm feeling sorry for the love triangle – Robert, Rae and Loretta – who for whatever reason chose to use me as a pawn in their twisted game. Knowingly or unknowingly, they fucked up big time.

Standing on my right, TiAnna overhears Darius and puts her 2-cents in. "Yeah Tip this bullshit you don't need right now.

Personally, I want to stay and watch the showdown. But I'm inclined to agree with my husband and BFF. I can deal with all this shit later.

Oh, by the way, y'all should know I had a feeling Robert Ellis was my real daddy. I came to this conclusion the night before gramma Oliver died. I had the strangest dream. Robert Ellis called me to apologize. He said that I was his daughter despite what everyone else had told me. And he was going to make things right between us, if it meant giving up his last breath. My suspicions were confirmed when gramma Oliver said she had a secret she needed to divulge and earlier when Robert Ellis handed me the company without a fight. Hmm. Robert Ellis apologizing? Showing remorse? The devil has died and gone to heaven. Or has he?

From behind me a concerned Jeremy leans in between me and Darius, squeezes my arm. Damn I'm thinking. My husband's got me covered fool. But I still appreciate my ex-boo looking out for me despite Darius looking at him like *I'mo kick yo Basset Hound ass yo.*

"Thanks," I whisper. "I plan to head over to granddaddy's for the repass. Do a quick meet, greet and thanks for coming, then get some rest."

He smiles then glances over at TiAnna and says, "Watch out for our girl." He backs away still without acknowledging Darius.

"Yeah read the evidence," I hear Robert say pulling my attention away from my frowning husband. He slams the document against Rae's chest.

Still hard to believe

Rae played Loretta's fiddle all these years only to find out the strings were about to break. After reading the document, Rae's fiery red eyes burn back at Robert who shoots back with a grin. Rae then turns and faces Loretta who steps back some more probably getting ready to make a quick exit. Crumbling the evidence in one hand, Rae tosses gramma's secret at Loretta.

"We're done here," he says and walks off leaving Loretta to gaze after his fine-ass.

Then remembering her 2 other victims, she first glances back at Robert and says, "You'll pay for this."

"I already have," says Robert. "Now it's your turn."

Rather than respond Loretta turns to me. She opens her mouth to speak but chooses otherwise. Good thing. We're all looking at her like she's a damn fool. She backs away then turns and heads in Rae's direction who's already made his way to the limo. If I were Loretta, I'd look for another ride. Ike Turner could be waiting for her ass.

About Boss Amanishakhete

Inspired by her own life, Atlanta Author Amanishakhete (Uh-ma-nee-sha-keet), named after the ancient Nubian Queen Amanishakheto, conjures up an imagination full of colorful characters that make up the LaTonya trilogy. Readers never know what's coming next when they turn the pages of her amazing new series filled with characters from all walks of life – characters she feels she channels.

"They speak to me," said Amanishakhete. "I definitely hear their voices and let them say and do as they please."

No wonder this fresh new fiction writer captures the attention of readers from 16 to 60.

Along with fiction writing and authorship, Amanishakhete is a Word-Soul artist who writes and performs her own lyrics underscored by original music composed by Portland hip hop artist and producer Anuff. Amanishakhete plays herself in the series. Fans can purchase her music at CD Baby and iTunes.

Born in Osaka, Japan to an Air Force family, but raised in the states, Amanishakhete holds an Associate of Science and Bachelor of Science degrees in Business and Communications supported by Business and International Relations graduate studies in London, England and a Master of Fine Arts in Writing.

Visit Amanishakhete:
Amanishakhete.com
Ashakhete@gmail.com

www.ingramcontent.com/pod-product-compliance
Lightning Source LLC
Chambersburg PA
CBHW031700170626
46808CB00005B/1534